Praise for the Novels of Dixie Cash

Tangy and a little bit dirty-a mystery cooked up in the heart of BBQ country. — *Kirkus Reviews*

Cash neatly mixes woo-woo weirdness and romance with the gosh-darn Texas humor fans expect from this light crime series. — *Publishers Weekly*

Cash's relentlessly feisty heroines attract trouble faster than a skunk in a perfume factory but, delightfully, manage to come out smelling like a rose. — *Carol Haggas*

ALSO BY DIXIE CASH

I Can't Make You Love Me, but I Can Make You Leave

Our Red Hot Romance is Leaving Me Blue

Curing the Blues with a New Pair of Shoes

Don't Make Me Choose Between You and My Shoes

I Gave You My Heart, but You Sold It Online

My Heart May Be Broken, but My Hair Still Looks Great

Since You're Leaving Anyway, Take Out the Trash

You Can Have my Heart, but Don't Touch My Dog

A Domestic Equalizers Novel

※

Dixie Cash

DEDICATION

This book is dedicated to animal rescuers everywhere who work and sacrifice to make a place for abused and unwanted creatures of all kinds. They have a special place in heaven.

It's also dedicated to Sandi Walker, especially, founder and owner of SECOND CHANCE FARM in Granbury, Texas. Sandi is one of those people.

ACKNOWLEDGEMENTS

I want to acknowledge and thank my beta readers—Laura, Carolyn, Mona, Cathy and Tina—for taking the time to read this book and give me comments. But most of all, I thank them for telling me it's funny. I was out on a limb here and I needed to hear someone say it's funny even if they were fibbing to me. Their input was invaluable.

Prologue

HE DIDN'T KNOW how long he had been lost, but judging from the hollow feeling in his stomach and the thin shadows cast by his body, he had been homeless a while.

His best friend had told him a hundred times not to wander off. When he had heard those words in the past, he hadn't been sure what "wander off" meant, but he had a good idea now. Wandering off was what he had done. Wandering off had made him homeless, lost and hungry.

He had found others like himself on the streets, some friendly, some not, all with a hint of fear in their eyes, all prowling for food. He gave a wide berth to the territorial ones. His intent wasn't to challenge or take away another's place. He wanted only to find his way home to his comfortable spot at the foot of the big bed, to where his friend would scratch his head or belly and give him treats at the end of a day's work.

Oh, what he would give for one of those treats right now. He would even welcome a bath. Given the chance, he would dance and prance around and wag his tail. After he had made his friend laugh, he would flash what humans called a "grin," behavior that never failed to garner affection and sometimes an extra treat.

Nighttime. The air had cooled and the number of cars that had zoomed past him all day had dwindled. This was when he missed his friend the most.

Suddenly, an enticing scent diverted him from his thoughts of home. He raised his nose for a better sniff. Food. His keen sense of smell detected the aroma coming from somewhere across the street. Maybe his friend was waiting over there with a delicious treat. His mouth watered at the idea of a bowl of Kibbles 'n Bits and fresh water.

He stepped off the curb and stopped short, allowing a big car filled with young humans to pass. They were laughing and yelling. One tossed a can from the window and hit his hind leg. The blow hurt a little, but he didn't let that stop him. He trotted on across the street, toward the smell.

Chapter 1

DEBBIE SUE OVERSTREET—former PRCA barrel racing champion, co-owner of one of only two beauty salons in Salt Lick, Texas, and founder of a private investigation service—swept the last of yesterday's sand into a neat pile at the Styling Station's back door. Her business partner and best friend, Edwina Perkins-Martin, sprawled in the styling chair at her station reading the *Odessa American* newspaper.

Debbie Sue opened the heavy door and swooshed the sand outside into the already-hot sunlit morning. She slammed the door and returned to the salon. "Damned sand. How can so much of it come in overnight?"

"The wind," Edwina answered without looking away from her reading. "It's in the wind."

And God knew there was wind in West Texas. It blew from the northwest, it blew from the southeast and sometimes it blew two hundred miles an hour in a circle and caused all kinds of grief.

Debbie Sue walked over to the payout desk and perused her schedule for the day. Her first appointment—a perm for Mary Sue Mason—would show up in fifteen minutes. "Hmm. I've got a trim at two o'clock and after that, nothing. It's so hot. I might get out of here early and go home and lay down naked in front of the air conditioner. Or I might fill the bathtub with ice water for a good soak. Or I might do something really crazy and cook something fantastic for Buddy's supper."

"Like what?" Edwina asked absently, still absorbed by the newspaper.

"Oh, I don't know. I might barbecue a Gila monster. Or cut a hunk of meat off one of Rocket Man's hindquarters."

"Sounds good," Edwina said.

Just as Debbie Sue thought. Edwina was paying no attention to her. "What are you reading, Ed?"

"This article on the front page. Remember that story about some brave asshole beating an elderly woman to death in Midland?"

"The home invasion and robbery? Yeah. What a despicable crime."

"The meanest thing I've ever heard. It says here they've arrested somebody named John Wilson. Says he had an alibi. Three of them at last count. None of which panned out."

"I saw the report on TV news this morning. They said the evidence against him is strong. They found a lot of the poor woman's belongings in his car and a witness even saw him leave her house the evening of the murder."

"Did Buddy see that report? Is he going to get involved?"

Debbie Sue's husband, James Russell Overstreet, Jr., had once been the sheriff in Salt Lick. Now, he was a

Texas Ranger captain revered in the whole of West Texas. Even the governor held him in high esteem. Buddy had once acted as his personal bodyguard when the governor had come to Midland, which, as far as Debbie Sue was concerned, just went to prove that all someone had to do to adore Buddy as much as she did was get acquainted with him.

With the Texas Rangers being state cops, Buddy and his colleagues typically took on major crime solving only in rural counties that had limited or inexperienced law enforcement.

"Nah. Midland doesn't need the Texas Rangers," she told Edwina. "They've got their own cops. But it doesn't matter anyway. The guy's already arrested."

"But Buddy must know something about it. What did he say?"

"He looked me in the eye and said, 'Don't even think about it.'"

And that had been the extent of this morning's conversation about John Wilson between Debbie Sue and one of the best cops in the great state of Texas. She loved Buddy from the depths of her soul, but she hated him trying to control her before she even needed controlling. And the question of if she ever truly did need controlling was still being debated between them. She sometimes wondered if the whole thing was a ruse on Buddy's part because they seemed to settle every one of those arguments in bed.

Edwina looked up from the paper and adjusted her new lime-green cat's-eye glasses. For years, she had worn glasses with red frames covered in bling, but the glasses she wore today had a plain retro look. "Hmm. Imagine that. Was he reading your mind again?" She blew a gum bubble the size of a golf ball and popped it.

"I wasn't thinking about getting into it. But hell, Ed, how could we not be curious about it? We're detectives."

"No, we're not, Debbie Sue. We're nosy women who follow cheating spouses and insignificant others and pry into who they're cheating with."

"Ed! How can you say that about us? We're licensed private investigators. We took the test and everything."

"I don't care, girlfriend. We don't chase down cold-blooded murderers."

Edwina had never had the enthusiasm for crime solving that Debbie Sue did. For Edwina, their investigative adventures had been mostly about having fun and being in the know of some of the locals' best kept secrets. Thus, serious crime like murder turned her off.

"If you aren't interested in it, why did you bring it up?"

"I'm interested as a concerned citizen, not as an insane woman who wants to chase after a killer."

In a way, Edwina was right, but Debbie Sue had a hard time admitting it. She released a great sigh. "I know, I know. Buddy's still pissed off over what happened with Roxie Jo Denman's murder. I'm afraid he's going to divorce me for the second time any day now."

Edwina's brow furrowed. "Well, I have to say Vic wasn't crazy about that one, either."

Vic Martin, Edwina's husband, had a more liberal attitude than Buddy about the cases the Domestic Equalizers had taken on. Like Edwina, he had been interested in the fun of it. A retired US Navy SEAL who stood six-foot-five, weighed two-fifty and knew three hundred ways to kill you quietly, he feared neither man nor beast. But even he had worried when the Domestic Equalizers ended up right in the middle of solving the murder of up-and-coming country music singer Roxie Jo Denman.

Edwina wagged her crimson-tipped finger like a pendulum. "Like I told you, girlfriend. Cheating spouses and insignificant others." She returned to her reading.

But Debbie Sue wasn't one to give up, especially when the Domestics Equalizers, which she regarded as "her baby," was under discussion. "I remind you, Ed, since Roxie Jo's murder, the Domestic Equalizers has been idle except for a few cheating husbands and that fiasco where LaDonna McKenzie suspected her silly husband was sneaking up to the top of the water tower with Marilyn Haygood."

Edwina looked up. "And I remind you, Dippity-Do, that it might not have been a fiasco if you hadn't followed Earl up there, then been afraid to come back down. Calling our pitiful little fire department to climb up there and bring you down wasn't your finest hour. You should've remembered you're afraid of heights. Thank God you had your phone with you or you might still be up there."

Debbie Sue hated admitting it, but sometimes curiosity and hardheadedness got the best of her good sense. Half of Cabell County had been gathered around and staring up at the water tower, watching poor Johnny Bolling—who was an auto mechanic most of the time—coax her into letting him carry her down the water tower ladder long after she had failed to find Earl and LaDonna. Being reminded in such a public way that Debbie Sue Overstreet wasn't Wonder Woman had tarnished the Domestic Equalizers' reputation, for sure.

Her mouth automatically twisted into a scowl. She summoned her indignation. "Well it didn't look as scary climbing up as it did going down."

"Hmm. What was worse was finding out later that Earl and Marilyn had really been in a motel in Odessa all that time. They hadn't ever been up there on that water tower. It was all an ugly rumor."

"Oh, hell, Ed. Now you're starting to sound like Buddy."

"That's because I agree with him. I repeat, we're not supposed to investigate murders. My God, Debbie Sue. We could get ourselves killed. And I like my aging hide and body all in one piece."

"But can we get hurt just looking into it a little? What if we were able to discover something important to the investigation? Just think what that would do for the Domestic Equalizers' reputation."

Edwina folded her paper, rose from her chair and began putting her station in order for the day. "Speaking of Midland, remember my niece Sandi? My middle sister's youngest?"

Debbie Sue knew Edwina as well as she knew herself. The hardheaded woman simply didn't want to discuss the murder in Midland, so she changed the subject. Debbie Sue swung her attention to Edwina's family even though keeping up with all of the nieces and nephews was next to impossible. "Let's see. Would that be the one who's a registered foster parent for the animal shelter?"

Debbie Sue couldn't keep up with all of Sandi's animals either, but having three rescue dogs and an aged horse herself, she empathized with anyone who collected unwanted animals.

"Right. Sandi Walker," Edwina replied. "She's got a parakeet that needs a permanent home."

"She rescued a parakeet? From where and what?"

"I think somebody died and left it homeless. Sandi says it knows a bunch of words and talks like a person. I'm gonna adopt it and give it to Vic as a present. He'll love it and they can keep each other company while I'm not home."

Vic Martin had never struck Debbie Sue as being a man who worried about being alone. Even if he did, he wasn't home alone all that much. After retiring from a stellar Navy career, he had bought a big rig and was now a long-haul trucker. He traveled the highways of the whole USA, saying he wanted to see the country and meet the people he had risked his life protecting.

Debbie Sue had to ask, "And who's gonna keep *it* company while Vic's on the road?"

"Maybe I'll bring it here to the shop. I could put a cute little cage right over there." She pointed at the corner by the window. "I could paint it a pastel color to match the bird's feathers and maybe put some flowers around it.

"Cool idea, Ed. It could see the outside and plot its escape. Or if it talks so well, maybe it could look over our shoulders and kibitz when we're doing manicures."

"I was thinking Vic might even take it in the truck with him. For company while he's driving, you know?"

Chapter 2

Midland, Texas

THE LAST THING Sandi Walker wanted on a blistering July day was a trashy alley. As a specialty pet food merchant and the owner of LaBarkery, the only gourmet pet food bakery in Midland, she demanded that the area around her shop's back door be neat and clean. LaBarkery did not need an open invitation to bugs and vermin. Sandi had been known to rent a high-pressure hose and blast the alley. Her neighbors called her the "alley policeman."

The other shop owners up and down the strip mall claimed to feel the same about the alley, including the owners of the mom-and-pop burger joint two doors away. The eatery was the largest contributor to the alley debris. So far, neither its owners nor their teenage employees had contributed much physical effort toward keeping the area clean.

To make matters worse, a few weeks back, the City of Midland had placed a dumpster directly across the alley from LaBarkery's back door.

So after Sandi finished her lunch, she gathered her trash and stepped outside to face the alley.

If a garbage bomb had exploded, the area around the dumpster couldn't have looked worse. Plastic bags that had never made it into the dumpster lay torn open, the contents scattered everywhere. A cloud of flies swarmed it. The stench made her hold her breath.

"Ooh noo," she groaned.

The temperature hovered around a hundred, but what choice did she have but to pick up all of it? She squared her shoulders and marched back inside. She donned a mask, goggles and her heavy-duty rubber gloves, then dragged her own garbage can from beside her back door and began to pick up waste. Most of it had come from the burger joint. No big surprise there.

"I'm going to have another talk with those people," she grumbled as she plopped stinking, sloppy hamburger leavings into the garbage can.

Just as she reached for a sack of discarded French fries, a large scruffy dog came from behind the dumpster and began to wolf down everything in sight. It was so thin its sides were sunken. It had been on the street a long time. She hadn't seen an animal so starved since a weekend trip to Juarez with her friends. Down there, mongrels ran free, but they were timid and scared, slinking around with their tails tucked between their legs.

Common sense told her to give a stray dog a wide berth, but her heart went out to it. She had never been able to ignore an animal in need. For proof, six rescue cats, two large mixed-breed dogs, a barky miniature Schnauzer and a shivery, grumpy Chihuahua lived with her at home. Also two squawking Leghorn hens she called Sophie and Snow White, a Rhode Island Red hen named Anastasia and a dominating one-eyed Rhode Island Red rooster she had named Christian

Grey. Add to that group, a recently acquired black-and-white gerbil and an opinionated African Grey parrot the SPCA had rescued from a biker sports bar after its owner passed on.

As she replaced the lid on the garbage can, she said to the stray, "Hey, sweetheart, are you friendly?"

Tucking its tail, the dog looked up at her with soulful brown eyes, but kept its distance, as if it feared a blow or some other cruel treatment. She felt a stab in her heart. "Aww, don't be afraid, baby. I won't hurt you."

The dog inched toward her. It began to wag its tail and dance around. It was a male, she noticed. He wore a collar, but no tags. He belonged to someone. Had some jerk abandoned him? Left him to get by the best he could?

Sandi related all too well. Been there, done that. Not that long ago, she, too, had belonged to someone then been abandoned. A heaviness filled her chest.

The dog came to her carrying a burger patty in his mouth. He laid it at her feet and looked up, begging for her approval.

Been there and done that, too, she thought with disgust. Or at least, something like it. As if approval from an ass like Kenneth Coffman, her second ex-husband, was important.

"Oh, thank you, sweetie," she said to the stray. "But you shouldn't be eating garbage. It isn't good for you."

Bending over, she scratched behind the dog's ears and she would swear to anyone who asked that he smiled at her. Her heart swelled. She continued to scratch his ears and stroke his face. "What I make for doggies like you isn't just pretty," she told him tenderly. "It has lots of good nutrients for doggies baked inside. Yes, it does. Yes, sweetheart, it does."

His big brown eyes focused on her face as if he understood her every word.

She couldn't just walk away and leave him. The city's dogcatcher prowled the alleys and would surely pick him up. And he would be euthanized like so many other unfortunate animals left to stray. But she couldn't take him into her shop either. He was filthy and she had no way of knowing how he would behave indoors. He had to be fed and cleaned up.

"You stay right here," she said and started across the alley to her back door. He followed. She stepped into her shop and picked a leash off a hook where she kept several. They came in handy in her animal-friendly enterprise. She clipped the leash to his collar without a problem and led him to her SUV that she always parked in the alley. When she opened the back gate, he jumped in without coaxing.

She walked back inside her shop, locked the front door and hung up the CLOSED sign. She hated locking the store during business hours, but with no one to watch it, she had to. One of her two employees, Betty Ann, had already been in early to help make Atomic Energizer, the homemade raw dog food LaBarkery sold in bulk, but Betty Ann was long-gone by mid-morning.

Like Sandi, Betty Ann loved animals. And like Sandi, she had gotten sucked in by Juanita Harper at We Love Animals, the no-kill animal shelter. Betty Ann now foster-cared for her own small menagerie.

Back in the alley, Sandi scooted behind the steering wheel. "We're going for a short ride." As she eased along the alleyway, her passenger sat calmly, so he was used to riding in an automobile.

A dog-grooming parlor, the Pampered Pooch, was located at the end of the strip mall. Sandi had become friends with the owner, Prissy Porter, and they referred customers back and forth. The new dog continued to behave well as Sandi drove toward the grooming parlor. She rounded the end of the strip and parked in front of Pampered Pooch, opened the SUV's back gate and reached for his leash. "Come on, boy. Let's go get a bath. Then you can have a nice lunch."

The dog hopped to the ground, his long tail swishing a steady beat.

As Sandi walked him into the grooming parlor, Prissy came from the back room. "Hey, Sandi. Whatcha got there?"

"This is my new best friend."

Prissy's brow tented. "Oh, no. Look how pitiful he is. Oh, bless his heart. I can't stand to see any animal like this. Where'd you get him?"

"In the alley, when I was taking out the trash. Isn't he sad? The way he acts, he must've belonged to someone and just gotten lost. He's very friendly and he seems to be trained. He jumped right into the back of my SUV and rode down here with no hassle."

Prissy squatted in front of the dog and began an inspection. "Oh, he's no stray. But he's been homeless a while."

"I'm going to try to find his owner, but first I need you to feed him and clean him up. Clip, shave, whatever you have to do. Just put it all on my bill."

"Oh, don't worry about that. We keep plenty to eat around here for our boarders." Prissy took the leash from Sandi's hand. "We'll be okay. You go on and do what you need to. This baby and I will be just fine."

The dog smiled up at her.

"Look at that," Sandi said. "I swear he smiles."

"Lord, he is full of personality, isn't he?"

"Any idea what breed he is?"

"He's kind of long-haired, so Collie and something maybe."

"I sure hope I can find his owner."

"I hope you can, too, because if this one stays around long, it'll be easy to fall in love with him."

Prissy led the dog to her back room and Sandi went outside to her SUV. Taking one last look at the grooming shop, she drove away feeling happy about the good deed she had done, but a little sad at recognizing herself in a lost dog. Alone and out of options weren't new emotions to her. A few years ago, she had been as lost as that dog and in some ways, she still was.

Well, fate had given her a break. What else could she do but pay it forward? She would see that the lost dog got a break, too.

☆ ☆ ☆

Back at her own shop, a regular customer waited at her front door. She turned over the CLOSED sign, then unlocked and opened the door. "Hi, Mrs. Arnold. Hope you haven't been waiting long."

"Oh, I just got here, honey." The customer stepped through the doorway. "I'm so glad you aren't really closed. I was scared for a minute. Where's your helper today?"

"She came in at five to help me make LaBarkery's Atomic Engergizer. We usually finish up by eleven and she goes home."

"Oh, that's your raw superfood, isn't it? Well, I'm just glad you're here. My darlings would be so upset if I didn't have a fresh LaBarkery treat for them every day."

Mrs. Arnold was married to a prominent personal injury attorney who made more money than both he and Mrs. Arnold could count, add up or spend on diamond rings. They lived large and Mrs. Arnold spared no expense in pampering their dogs and cats.

"I had to lock up for a minute," Sandi told her. "I found a stray dog in the alley. I took him down to the grooming parlor to be cleaned up."

Mrs. Arnold's brow tented. "Awww. I can't bear the thought of little homeless dogs."

"I don't think he's homeless, but I do think he's lost. He isn't exactly little, either."

"Awww. Well, you were sweet to help him."

"I'm going to try to find his owner. But if I don't, would you like to have him? He seems to be a really nice animal."

Mrs. Arnold pressed her palms against her cheeks, the multiple diamond rings on her fingers glittering under the fluorescent lighting. "Oh, my Lord, honey, I couldn't. My husband thinks four dogs and twenty cats are enough. Three of our doggies are Labs, you know. We've given one whole bedroom to them."

She leaned closer to Sandi and spoke in a whisper. "I don't tell just anyone, but the kitties have taken over the pool house, which upset my husband terribly. When he tells people he spends his weekends herding cats, they think he's crazy."

Instantly, Sandi thought of Jake, her African Grey parrot. She'd had to give him his own bedroom. Well, actually, Jake's room was the spare bedroom she had used for her office. So now, she conducted LaBarkery's clerical chores at her kitchen table and kept her files in the dining room. Beyond taking over her house, the bird had taken over her life and she sometimes found herself having conversations with him and following his advice.

He had been added to her little throng a few months back. As a registered foster parent at We Love Animals, she often got a call when they had a hard-to-place resident. Having spent some time—maybe his whole life—in a biker sports bar, he had come to her with a colorful vocabulary. He was so smart that after living with him for a few weeks, Sandi wondered if he had cognitive abilities. And after doing some research on African Greys, she was convinced he did.

"I know what you mean," Sandi said. "Mention him to your friends if you don't mind. Maybe someone might need a dog that's already trained."

"I certainly will," Mrs. Arnold said, "and I'll put a note on the bulletin board at church."

Sandi stepped behind the counter, quickly washed her hands and turned back to her customer. "Well, what can I get for your babies today? I've got lots of Energizer, made fresh this morning."

"Hmm. I still have plenty. I'll save that for later. I haven't treated everyone to Bare Paws in a couple of months. Let me have a dozen of those and a dozen of those cute little mice for the kitties."

Sandi reached inside her display case, removed a dozen Bare Paws from their paper containers. "Did you say a dozen of the Mousekins also?"

"I'll tell you what. Make that two dozen. The kitties come and go, but I want to be sure I have enough for everyone to have one."

Sandy counted out twenty-four little oval salmon cakes she decorated to look like pink mice with big white-and-black eyes and black noses. She carefully placed all of the treats in two bakery boxes that bore a LaBarkery logo.

"Oh, and let me have one of your birthday cakes. Mikey, my youngest is turning two. We're having a little party with six of his friends."

Sandy gave Mrs. Arnold a wide smile. "Oh, how cool."

She sidled along the long display case and lifted out one of her two-layer cakes filled with beef, chicken and vegetables and frosted with nutritious frosting that looked like chocolate. "Would you like the candles? They're really beef sticks, you know."

"Oh, by all means. Nothing's too good for Mikey. But two won't be enough. You'd better give me seven candles so everyone can have one."

"Coming right up." The corners of Sandi's mouth tipping up with another huge smile, she plucked seven doggie treats she had molded to look like birthday candles out of her display case and bagged them.

She packaged the cake in a fancy cardboard box worthy of a human gourmet bakery, handed it and the boxes of goodies across the counter to Mrs. Arnold and collected $158.76.

"Thank you, dear," the woman said. "I'll see you next week."

"Thank you, Mrs. Arnold and don't forget to spread the word about the dog I found."

Another happy customer strolled out the door, leaving Sandi humming. Yes, indeedy. 48-million Americans might be on food stamps, California might be out of water, Colorado might be going up in wacky-backy smoke, but tonight, in Midland, Texas, a pooch named Mikey was having a birthday party with six canine friends all chomping happily on birthday cake and candles made of healthy homemade dog food.

And for that, Sandi was ecstatic.

As she wiped the front of her display case, her mind spun backward to the beginning of LaBarkery and its exclusive pet treats that looked like fine gourmet bakery wares. Just four years ago, she had held a good job in a Midland bank where she had gone to work right out of college. On a fast track, she had moved up to a low-level vice-president and loan officer and was in line for another promotion when a mega-bank bought her employer and laid off more than half the staff, including her.

Sandi hadn't loved that job, but she had been good at it. Interacting with people — the bank's customers — seemed to be what she was meant to do, not to mention the bank paid her well and offered great benefits.

Though disappointed by being laid off, she took it in her stride because she was one of the lucky ones. At home she had a loving man who had a good job with an oil company and who supported her in all things. She would simply stay at home, tie on her apron, clean her house to spotless perfection and have elegant meals waiting for him when he came home in the evening. After feasting on her mouthwatering cuisine and washing it down with fine wine, she would slip into her sexy black nightie and allow the rest of the evening to take its course.

She hadn't even finished her unemployment application before Ken Coffman declared that their marriage no longer worked for him and moved out of the house, leaving Sandi reeling.

In a matter of two weeks, she learned the number one contributing factor to the "unworkable" part of her marriage to Ken was a pierced and tattooed nineteen-year-old who had flunked out of college in Lubbock and moved home to live with her parents, who happened to be neighbors. That information squelched any notion Sandi might have had that she and Ken could put things back together. It hadn't done much for her relationship with her neighbors, either.

She had known every nook and cranny of the bank that had employed her, but she'd had no clue what had been going on under her own roof.

Two weeks after that revelation, she found herself not only unemployed, but headed for divorce court for the second time.

She had filed for divorce, instructed her lawyer to clean Kenneth Coffman's clock and at the same time, petitioned to have her name changed back to her maiden name. She had never liked that stupid name, Coffman.

She was through with men. Period. Exclamation point.

After all of that, all she'd had to do was swallow her pride, get back on her feet, find a job and a new place to live. Meanwhile, for a social life, she had joined Book Wranglers, a local reading club whose members had taken on the lofty goal of reading all one hundred of the books everyone should read in his lifetime. She was now sandwiching *War and Peace*, *Fifty Shades of Grey* and the *Crossfire Series*, which made *War and Peace* infinitely more entertaining.

She had arranged to meet with the elderly ladies at the Glen Cove Retirement Home for crocheting lessons one night a week and had produced half a dozen intricate tablecloths and an untold number of afghans that nested in a neat stack in a corner of her bedroom. When she needed a gift for someone, she simply plucked something from her stack.

She had bought a gym membership and worked out, took Yoga classes and forced herself to think positive. She was honed into the best physical shape of her entire life. She might be thirty-two, but she had the body of a twenty-year-old.

But the most productive thing she had done back in the dark aftermath of her divorce was enroll in a Wilton course in cake decorating. With her mother working in the Walmart bakery in Big Spring, she had learned a little about cake decorating through osmosis, so she had a penchant for it. Now, daily in LaBarkery, she used what she had learned about cake decorating from Wilton and from her mother.

☆☆☆

Just then, the front door chimed again and Sandi turned around to see her mother pushing the heavy plate-glass front door open with her butt, struggling with her purse and balancing two Starbucks cups. Sandi strode forward and lifted the two cups from her hands. "Hey, Mom. I wasn't expecting you."

Her mother heaved a great breath and waved her hand in front of her face. "Whew. That was a handful."

Sandi studied the cold cup. Not being a regular consumer of Starbucks drinks, she couldn't identify its contents. "Whatcha got here?"

"Caramel Frappachino."

"Yum. Let's go into the back room." Sandi led the way back to her tiny kitchen where she concocted and baked the goodies she sold in her shop. Here, she kept a small table and two chairs. "What are you doing in Midland?"

"My hours got cut. I ended up with the day off, so I decided to drive over to see you. I thought you might like a pick-me-upper. Lord, I can't believe what I had to pay for these two drinks."

Sandi and her Mom sat down together. "Your shop looks so pretty," her mother said. "And you're so busy. I can't get over how this business has turned into such a success. You've been really lucky."

"I know, right?"

"But luck runs out, you know."

Sandi did a mental eyeroll. Her mother had barely said hello and she was already criticizing. She always counterbalanced a positive with a negative, thus Sandi herself had grown up with a foot firmly planted in each camp.

LaBarkery was successful. More so than Sandi could have imagined in her wildest dreams, but it wasn't just a matter of dumb luck. "Mom, I wish you'd stop saying that. I've got a college degree in business and marketing, for crying out loud. I worked my ass off to get it."

Her memory zoomed back to her student days when she had worked at an array of bad minimum-wage jobs. Not intending to let herself get sidetracked, she continued, "I've researched. I've studied trends. Do you know what I read just this week?"

Her mom's wide-eyed look came across the rim of her plastic cup. Her head shook.

"This year, the citizens of this country will spend forty billion dollars on their pets. Forty *billion*. And a piece of that fruit is there for my little business to pluck."

Her mother set her cup on the table, still shaking her head. "You can't believe stuff like that, Sandi. People make it up. Forty billion? Why, I don't even know how to write a number like that."

Mom had no concept of a billion dollars, Sandi knew. How could she? She hadn't finished high school, had worked for low wages her entire life, still worked for low wages though she had been employed by Walmart for almost twenty years.

"When you graduated from college, I was so proud of you," her mother said. "I hoped you'd get a good job and earn a good wage with a big company that would give you benefits. Like I've got."

Sandi stared at her a few beats, considering again the different wavelengths on which she and her mother functioned. Owning her own business would never occur to the woman sitting across the table.

"Benefits." Sandi said acidly and gave a huff. She had a hard time glossing over the bitterness she felt over her former bank employment and layoff. "Mom, read my lips. I had a good job with a big bank. I was there more than five years. And look what happened to me."

Her mother sighed.

Sandi sighed, too. "We've had this conversation more times than I can count. I always wanted to own my own business. You know that."

"But it's such a risk. If you weren't so tied down by all of this"—she gestured around the room with her hand—"you could still be out looking for another job with a big company. Look at me. I'm coming up on twenty years. I've got health insurance. A 401(k). Stock, too." Her mother leaned forward. "And when I do retire, because I've been there so long and been a loyal employee, I'll have a lifetime discount."

"That's what you've worked twenty years for?"

Her mother's mouth pursed. "Don't be so smart-alecky, miss know-it-all. You're a single woman now and you're over thirty years old. You need to be thinking about things like that."

Sandi had only one of those benefits her mother had just ticked off—a health insurance policy for which she paid a fortune. Even with its coverage, a serious illness or accident could destroy her. And retirement? She had cashed in her 401(k) and used the money to start LaBarkery. Was her mother right? Should she be out pounding the pavement looking for a "big company" job?

"Thirty-two isn't ancient, Mom. If you'll recall, when I decided to start LaBarkery, I had used up all of my unemployment and I wasn't hitting a home run with job hunting. You know how many resumés I sent out. It must've been five hundred. I traveled to a hundred fruitless interviews. You know all of that. And you also know I had reached a point where I had to do something."

"But you're a college graduate, Sandi. The only one in our family. You could've found a job if you hadn't been so particular."

Everyone in Sandi's blue-collar family stood in awe of her graduating from college, but at the same time, they felt resentment. "Wanting a job I liked was being particular? There were plenty of times I hated that job at that bank, Mom, but I believed it wwould take me somewhere. I worked hard and was a good employee, which got me nothing. I still work hard, but at least I'm doing something I love."

The idea of gourmet pet food had come to her from out of nowhere while standing in the Walmart pet food aisle in front of the refrigerator shopping for fresh food for her cats, Lucy and Ethel. She had always loved cooking and creating in the kitchen, considered herself a good cook. Once, she had loved cooking for her man.

Lesson learned: *Pets were more loyal than either of her men ever had been.*

The second idea of serving highly nutritious pet food as hand-decorated treats had rushed at her as if it was meant to be. She had gone home and spent the next three days studying dog and cat nutrition. By the end of the next week, she had experimented and developed half a dozen recipes and figured out how to decorate them.

Since then, with no help or encouragement from her family, she had daily filled her display cases with fancy treats so artfully decorated they tempted even humans. Her customers' pets ate healthier than most people.

"You know, Mom, I'm starting to add special healthy treats for other pets besides dogs and cats. And I'm in the process of copyrighting all of my recipes and trademarking the names. Eventually, I'm going to market them online."

Her mother's head shook again. "I don't know, Sandi. I just can't imagine people paying the kind of money you charge for fancy pet food. It's so unnecessary."

That was the crux of her mother's misunderstanding. Growing up, Sandi's brothers and sister, even Sandi herself, had always had dogs and cats around. While their parents had never abused or mistreated the various animals, they would have never spent the money for gourmet treats or homemade dog food for them.

"How can you say that? Healthy animal food is not unnecessary. It gives pets more energy and saves pet owners money on vet bills."

"Well, I don't want to argue," her mother said righteously.

"Animals deserve good food the same as people do. How would you like to eat that crap they sell in grocery stores or some of the pet stores?"

"Sandi. I do eat that crap they sell in grocery stores. Every day. And you ate it, too, all of your life. You're still eating it. So don't act so high and mighty."

"You know what I mean," Sandi grumped. "Why can't you be glad I came up with something that's working?"

"I just know I'd never pay what you charge for dog food.

"Really? You bought that Starbucks drink, didn't you? You could've brewed coffee at home, put it in a blender with ice and a little milk and added a little bit of caramel sauce and turned it into exactly what you're drinking. It would have cost half the money you paid for it at Starbucks. Maybe less than a dollar."

Her mother gave her a pursed mouth look and sucked up the last of her Caramel Frappachino. "It's a special treat. I don't do it every day."

"Well, some people do. Whether you like it or not, pet owners like giving special treats to their animals. And they aren't hesitant in spoiling them. They're willing, even eager, to lay down cold hard cash or credit cards to pay for those treats and special food for their four-legged children. And the price seems to be no obstacle. Nor is a lack of money."

"Maybe so, but I don't understand it."

"I do. Pets love you unconditionally. Stop and think about it, Mom. Did Morris ever steal your checkbook and overdraw your checking account? Has he ever called you in the middle of the night for bail money?"

"Now you're being silly. Morris is your dad's dog."

"Silly or not, that's exactly what Jason did. I remember it. You had to take money out of savings to cover those checks he wrote. And you and Dad had to borrow money to get Jimmy out of jail."

Now, Sandi was on a roll. "And here's another thought, Mom. If you have your female pets spayed, they don't come home unmarried and pregnant, covered with tattoos and with more holes in their bodies than a sieve."

Sandi might not have children, but her two older brothers and an older sister had done all of the above.

Her mother's face flushed and her mouth flattened. "That's a low blow, Sandi. Jason's paid me back every dime he took from me. Your brother Jimmy ain't even got a speeding ticket in more than a year, much less been arrested. And your sister? Jamie loves her baby. She ain't got any more tattoos or body piercings since Kaylee was born. She's moved in with this guy who's got a steady job at the Jiffy-Stop."

"Doing what?"

"He's a cashier. And it sounds like they're gonna get married."

Sandi had nothing left to say that wasn't insulting.

Her thoughts and opinions didn't matter to her family anyway. She had little contact with her siblings. All three were years older than she. She never visited them or vice-versa. They didn't even exchange birthday cards. Other than sharing the same parents, she had almost nothing in common with them. Considering the difference between her age and theirs, Sandi didn't doubt she had been her parents' Saturday night mistake.

"I'm not bad-mouthing my sister and brothers, Mom. I'm just trying to make a point. My life's starting to look good again. I don't want to ruin it working at a job I hate."

"Well, just don't get too comfortable, young lady. You know what your grandmother always says. A storm follows the calm."

Crap. There was that annoying conflicting philosophy again. "I hope not. My galoshes are still damp from the last downpour."

Chapter 3

Two months later...

THE CALENDAR MIGHT say September, but the daily temperatures were still hot enough to fry an egg on the sidewalk. Even so, the holidays were just around the corner. Sandi had been studying confections of all kinds and experimenting with how she could turn some of the traditional-looking holiday dishes into healthy pet treats. For Halloween, she could do something with tiny pumpkin faces made of ground chicken, carrots and sweet potatoes, she decided.

She applied the final flourish to a pastel pink rose petal on the Petits Furs she had removed from the oven earlier in the day. The little bite-size cakes looked almost like the fancy petits fours seen in gourmet bakeries, but the similarity stopped with appearance. Her creations were made of premium lean beef, vegetables and nutritious supplements.

A cold nose pressed against her leg and she looked down. Waffle had brought his dish and placed it at her feet.

"Waffle, you can't have another one. I've already given you two. This is my livelihood you're gobbling up."

The dog's mouth stretched wide, baring his huge canine teeth in what Sandi was sure was a smile. He was such a con artist. She chuckled as she always did when he pulled that trick and said a silent prayer of thanks for the day the dog had come into her life as a stray.

"Waffle" she had named him, because of the beautiful honey-colored coat Prissy had discovered under all of the filth and matted hair he'd had when he had first shown up in the alley. He had gained weight and no longer had a sad look about him. And he had won her heart and soul. She had even gone so far as allowing him to stay in the shop with her, a privilege she hadn't allowed any of her other pets.

Waffle was a great PR dog. Everyone who came into the store fell in love with him. Even her pets at home — all six of her snobby cats; her two big dogs, Ricky and Fred; the hens, Sophie, Snow White and Dominique. Even Christian Grey, her bossy rooster, had taken to Waffle. The dog's happy spirit was infectious. Sylvester had stopped hissing and spitting at him and trying to box him. Pablo had ceased growling and snarling when Waffle walked through the house. And Jake loved riding on Waffle's back. Though Sandi had found him only two months ago, she couldn't remember what her life was like with all of her pets when Waffle hadn't been part of it.

The jingle of the bell attached to the door drew her attention. Prissy entered, her ample hips jiggling, her hands flapping about from her obvious agitation.

"What's up with you today?" Sandi asked.

"Oh, Sandi, I'm so sad. Margaret's babies are going to be leaving me. They're six weeks old now. I've found homes for all of them except one. In a couple of weeks, it'll be time to let them go." Prissy turned away, hiding a sniffle with the back of her finger.

Margaret was a sweet little mama dog Prissy had groomed. The owner never returned for her. Prissy had intended to find her a home, but ended up keeping her. Soon after, Margaret had given birth to seven puppies.

"Aww. What are you going to do with the one that's left?"

"A guy is coming in this afternoon to see my last little boy. Hopefully, giving away all of these puppies will bring me a string of new customers. Come up and see them. They are, hands down, the cutest things you've ever seen."

Too busy to drop into the Pampered Pooch, Sandi had seen the puppies only a few times since their birth. "I'd love to see them before they go." She looked at Waffle. "I'll be right back. Watch the store for me."

She flipped the sign on her front door to CLOSED and walked behind Prissy's short stride. Being tall had its advantages, but even long legs were tested when trying to match the steps of a vertically-challenged person in a hurry.

When she entered the Pampered Pooch, she heard the puppy barks and yelps coming from the back room. "Ooh," she squealed, "let me at those puppies!"

Prissy had put a soft circular bed for the new mom and her litter in the corner of the room. The puppies were nursing when Sandi approached. Sandi and Prissy oohed and aahed. As if Margaret knew her offspring were the objects of human admiration, she wagged her tail.

"Oh, Prissy, they are so precious. I'm glad you've already given them away. I don't know if I could've resisted one. And God knows, I cannot handle another pet. The only thing missing from my life now is an ark. I even got a gerbil the other day."

"Where'd you get a gerbil?"

"The kid down the street didn't want it anymore. He came to my house and knocked at my door and asked me if I wanted it. His dad was going to hit it with a hammer."

Prissy's palms flew up, her fingers splayed. "Oh, no! Thank God you saved it."

"I know, right? It's cute. It's black and white and the cats are fascinated by it. I think, or I should say I hope, it's a male. I named him Hammerhead."

Frowning, Prissy pressed a forefinger against her cheek. "Hm. Well, under the circumstances, that seems appropriate. I'll bet Jake had plenty to say about him."

"I'll say. You know what he said when I first brought him home? He squawked and said 'Lunch.'"

"Did that mean he wanted to eat him? I thought he ate vegetables."

Sandi shrugged and laughed. "We didn't discuss it. He might've been talking about the cats. His relationship with them is different from how he behaves with the dogs. He plays with the dogs, but he pesters the cats."

Prissy laughed, too. "That Jake. He's such a card."

Just then, one of the puppies wriggled free. "Oh, look," Sandi said. "That one is the same color as Waffle. What a cute pair they'd make."

"Hell, Sandi, Waffle might be the father for all I know," Prissy said. She placed a cupped hand to her mouth and whispered, "I don't think Margaret was very selective."

The sound of the shop's front door opening interrupted the conversation. "I'll be right back." Prissy turned and left for her front room.

One of the puppies had finished nursing and ventured to the side of the dog bed. Sandi picked him up, giggling at the sight of his little pink tongue sticking out. "Just look at you. Aren't you sweet?"

Prissy re-appeared. Sandi knew Prissy only casually, but reading her oh-my-God facial expression wasn't hard. Close on her heels was the reason for the expression.

It was definitely a man worthy of the Oh-My-God response. He was tall and well built. Sandi was five-feet-eight herself, so men who exceeded six feet always caught her attention. He wore a starched button-down shirt, starched and ironed Wranglers that hugged his trim hips, cowboy boots and hat, the uniform of the area. But on him, it looked better than on most. He had striking strong features, but his crystal blue eyes set off by thick dark brows and lashes sealed the deal.

His mouth tipped into a lopsided grin and he touched the brim of his cowboy hat. "Ma'am."

"Sandi," Prissy gushed, "this is Nick ... er, uh, I'm sorry." She giggled and batted her lashes. "I forgot your last name."

"It's Conway, ma'am."

Oh, God. He had a devastating voice. It dripped with honey. A drawling Texas twang added to it.

"Did you, uh, come to see your baby?" Sandi asked, returning the little one in her arms to its mother's side.

"No, ma'am. I came to see a dog."

Oh, no. Was this who was going to take the last little boy? Sandi didn't expect him to react to the puppies the way she had, but he could show some kind of emotion. What kind of person could look at a bed full of squirming puppies and not want to hold every one of them?

Sandi looked at Prissy, but she was still staring up at the stranger, awe-struck.

"Prissy said you're interested in a male?" Sandi said to him.

"How many males did she have?" the man asked Prissy.

Prissy snapped her attention back to the present. "Males?...Oh, yes, males. Several. But there's just the one that isn't spoken for. I've found homes for all the others."

Prissy squatted beside the bed and picked up the golden puppy Sandi had just put down. Shrill little puppy barks came from the others. Prissy allowed Margaret to sniff her baby then turned to Nick. "This is him. He looks like a brick of gold, doesn't he?"

"Yeah, I like his color. I had a dog sort of that color once."

"Do you think your, uh, wife will like him? I mean, I wouldn't want to give him to a home where everybody didn't like him."

"Don't have a wife."

I don't wonder, Sandi thought.

"Oh, I see," Prissy gushed.

"I can take him with me now," he said.

"Oh, not yet. Like I said on the phone, it'll be a couple more weeks before they're ready to leave their mama."

"I'll be back in two weeks then." He touched the brim of his hat again. "Nice to meet you."

Prissy followed him to the entrance. Once he was through the doorway, she closed the door and fell back against it. "My God, that is a good-looking man. And he's single. Where do you suppose he's been hiding?"

"Humph. Where's he hiding a personality is more what I was thinking," Sandi said. "It's a good thing he's got looks."

"I thought he was nice."

"You should've seen yourself, Prissy. You wouldn't have cared if he had robbed you. I don't think you should let him have that puppy."

Prissy frowned. "Why?"

"He didn't strike me as having a lot of compassion for dogs. Or concern for their welfare."

"He wants a ranch dog. He's a cowboy. Cowboys like dogs."

"Who knows what ranch dog means or what he might expect a dog to do? I don't think that guy likes anything. I just think you shouldn't let him have something as precious as that darling little puppy."

Listen to yourself, Sandi told herself. Why was she setting up an argument for Prissy not to give away the last dog that she really needed to part with? The poor woman already had a house full of dogs and cats at home.

"Listen, I've got an idea," Prissy said. "Tell that friend of yours about him. Ask her if she's ever seen him."

"Who?" Sandi asked.

"Your neighbor. The one who gets around."

"Fiona? She doesn't get around. She just—"

"Dates a lot," Prissy filled in.

"Well, yes, she does date a lot. I'll ask her, but I'm more concerned about the wrong person taking one of these precious babies. Didn't you notice how cold he was?"

Prissy's mouth twisted into a smirk. "Cold? I thought he was hot."

"He didn't even hold him," Sandi said. "What kind of pet owner is he going to be?"

"Not everybody brings their animals into their beds to sleep, Sandi. That doesn't mean they're not good owners. Being a cowboy, he'll probably use the dog to help with cattle."

"Use. That's exactly my point. This little guy is a living creature with feelings and love to give. Being used sounds so, so..."

"Normal." Prissy said. "Honey, we live in cattle country. Lots of dogs are used to help with livestock and, I might add, the dogs love it. I was raised on a ranch myself. Our dogs were important members of our family, but they were working dogs."

"I guess so," Sandi grumbled, "but he could have held him."

"Men don't warm to the babies the way we girls do. I've seen grown men quake in fear at the thought of holding a baby."

"You're right, Prissy. I should shut my mouth. But there was just something about him that didn't sit well with me."

"Well there was plenty that sat well with me." She heaved a sigh, her heavy bosom rising and falling. "Good thing I've got my sweet ol' Charlie waiting at home. But I'm still curious. Don't forget to ask your friend about him."

"I won't," Sandi promised, "Thanks for letting me see the puppies. I'd better get back to Waffle. He's probably trying to figure out how to open the display cases so he can have more goodies."

Prissy laughed. "As smart as he is, I'm surprised he hasn't already done that."

Stepping outside Sandi was surprised to see Nick Conway again. He sat behind the steering wheel of a beat-up pickup that looked like its next stop might be some wrecking yard. He was talking on a cell phone. He looked directly at her for a few seconds, then looked away again.

"Screw you, buddy," she mumbled.

She'd had enough of self-centered men to last a lifetime. Tossing back her long hair, she lifted her nose a bit higher and strode toward her store. Still, she was unable to stop thinking about the damn cowboy. She didn't like him and if those puppies had belonged to her instead of Prissy, she would've told him to take a hike.

☆☆☆

Nick watched the redheaded woman stalking up the sidewalk. His reaction to her had caught him off guard and left him tongue-tied. He hadn't even asked the questions he wanted to ask about the dog breed. He supposed it didn't matter because it was obviously a Heinz57.

The redhead was tall, about chin high to him. Her hair was thick and shiny and she smelled flowery and feminine. The sight of her holding that puppy against her breast had washed over him like nothing had in a long time and sent a longing all the way through his system. He had heard the expression "thunderstruck." That was what he had experienced in those few seconds, but now he was confused. He liked the feeling, but at the same time, he feared it.

A voice on the phone interrupted his thoughts.

"Well, hello, stranger," his friend Sylvia said. "You in town?"

He visualized Sylvia, with her thick black hair and long tanned legs. "Hi. Yeah. Came to see the pup I told you about. I can't pick him up for a couple more weeks. You home for the day?"

"Just closed up shop."

"Okay if I come by?"

She chuckled seductively. "Have I ever said no?"

"Guess not. See you in a little bit."

The redheaded woman had disappeared from his sight. With his attention focused on his phone conversation, he hadn't noticed where she had gone. Just as well. He didn't have time for the foolishness of women who made him think of anything more profound that what he had with Sylvia. A woman like that redhead would leave. They always left. Everything he had ever cared about left, even his dog.

He snapped his phone shut, cranked his old Ford's engine and backed out, thinking he had better pick up a six-pack and some snacks on his way to Sylvia's.

Chapter 4

DEBBIE SUE TOSSED her purse onto a hair dryer chair and set a Hogg's Drive-In sack holding a hamburger and fries, two peach fried pies, a Snickers bar and a chocolate milkshake on the payout counter. "Here's your lunch," she told her skinny partner, Edwina-Perkins Martin. "If you eat all this, I don't see how you'll keep from exploding."

"Thanks, girlfriend." Edwina put the final touches on Bervena Mayfield's carrot-red hairstyle and fogged it with a cloud of hairspray. "What do you think?" she asked Bervena, passing her a hand mirror. She blew a huge bubble and popped it against her vivid red lips, then sucked it in and continued smacking her gum.

"Edwina Perkins-Martin, I swear you're a genius," Bervena said. "After the mess that kid at that five-dollar-hairstyle place made of my hair, I thought it would never be the same. I'll never go up to Odessa to get a haircut again."

"Just goes to show, Bervena, you get what you pay for. And I'm throwing in the color touch-up for free."

"Looks good, Ed," Debbie Sue said, flopping into her own styling chair. She was the one who was full to the point of exploding. She had eaten an Elvis special at Hogg's, which was far too many calories. That meant supper would be salad even if Buddy wanted a steak.

Her dear Buddy would never look at another woman, but Debbie Sue believed a girl should never let herself go. If she did, the next thing to go might be the husband. And losing Buddy Overstreet twice in her lifetime was something she did not want to think about. Their divorce hadn't occurred so long ago that she had forgotten the misery of life without him.

Edwina collected money from Bervena and said good-bye, leaving the beauty shop empty of customers. She picked up the sack of food, moved to her own styling station and began to lift out her lunch. "What'd you bring me?"

"I can't even remember all of it," Debbie Sue said.

"So did you ask them if they knew who new hand is out at the Flying C? I saw him at the grocery store last night. Lord, he gets better looking every time I see him."

Debbie Sue and Edwina knew everyone in Salt Lick, Texas, and almost everyone in Cabell County. The new good-looking man, who appeared to be unmarried, had all of the single women and half the married ones in a tizzy. With Debbie Sue and Edwina being licensed private detectives and with the Styling Station being the town's A-Number-One source of information, both true and false, they both felt it their duty to learn all they could about him.

"I forgot. I'm gonna call C.J. and ask her," Debbie Sue said, getting to her feet. A call to her old high school friend, Carol Jean Carruthers, was long overdue anyway. A few years back, C.J. had married and started having kids and Debbie Sue no longer saw her as much as she used to.

To say that C.J. had married well was an understatement of colossal proportions. Her husband was one of the wealthiest men in Texas, but being around her, you'd never know it. Having money hadn't changed her one bit. She now had three small kids that she took care of herself. No nanny. She maintained a beautiful home and the only help she had was a housekeeper who came in three days a week. C.J. often claimed that she couldn't cook a meal worth eating, nevertheless, she did the cooking for the family.

Debbie Sue walked to the payout desk, picked up the phone and punched in C.J.'s stored number.

"Hello?" C.J.'s soft country twang was unmistakable.

"What in the hell are you doing, C.J.?"

"Oh, Debbie Sue. I've been meaning to call you. But it seems like every time I stop to do it, something happens that I have to take care of first. I've missed you and Edwina so much. How are you?"

Now Debbie Sue felt guilty for calling to ask about the new ranch hand rather than to check on her old friend.

"We're both fine," Debbie Sue answered. "Just finished a ridiculous amount of fattening food from Hogg's. 'Course Ed doesn't have to worry about getting fat."

"Oh, my goodness," C.J. said. "I haven't been to Hogg's since I was pregnant with Jaden. I just absolutely craved their fried green tomatoes my last trimester with him." She laughed. "Come to think of it, I'd kill for a plate of those right now."

"You don't mean you're —"

"Oh, heavens, no. At least, I don't think so. Harley and I think three is enough. Of course, if another came along, neither one of us would be upset."

Still feeling guilty for not calling C.J. sooner, Debbie Sue saw an opening and decided to go with a little white lie to spare her old friend's feelings and glean information at the same time. "Speaking of Harley, I saw a Carruthers ranch truck in town yesterday. I thought it might be Harley running an errand. I intended to say hi, but--"

"Harley's in Fort Worth this whole week," C.J. said.

"Yeah, I soon saw it wasn't him. In fact, I didn't know who the guy was. Y'all letting just any ol' somebody drive your pickups these days?"

Debbie Sue waited for her friend to comment about the pickup's occupant, but instead, C.J. stopped talking and answered one of her kid's questions. When she came back to the conversation, she said, "I'm sorry Debbie Sue, what were you saying?"

"I said that I didn't know the guy in the pickup and I thought I knew all the hands at the Flying C."

"Hunh. Say, is Buddy in town? Maybe the two of you could come for supper this weekend. I can ask Martina to help me fix something special. Does Buddy still like enchiladas?"

Debbie Sue sighed, she was getting nowhere, but then the information was nothing that couldn't wait until the weekend. "He sure does. A taste for enchiladas never goes away. He's in town now and we'd love to. We've got a lot to catch up on, girlfriend."

"Then it's all set," C.J. said happily. "Saturday night. Sorry, but I need to run. The kids have gotten really quiet and I don't like the sound of that."

Debbie Sue hung up and stared blankly at the phone. Sometimes a person needed a map to have a conversation with C.J.

"What'd you find out?" Edwina asked.

"Harley's in Fort Worth, and C.J. craved fried green tomatoes when she was pregnant. She doesn't think she's pregnant now, by the way. They don't want any more kids, but she and Harley wouldn't be upset if they had another and she doesn't like the sound of kids when they're quiet. Oh, and Buddy and I are going out to the ranch for enchiladas Saturday night."

"You got all that in less than two minutes?"

"It's an art, Ed. Talking to C.J. is kind of like walking through Saran Wrap. You have to know how to do it."

"But you still don't know who the new guy is."

Debbie Sue shrugged.

"Well, it's nothing that can't wait for the weekend," Edwina said, unwrapping a peach fried pie.

Debbie Sue gave her a look. It was frightening to think about, but Edwina knew her better than she knew herself. "Right," she said.

"He must be a foreman," Edwina added. "Or a manager or something if Harley's letting him drive one of the ranch's newer trucks."

"Must be," Debbie Sue said.

☆☆☆

Sandi wrapped a rubber band around the day's deposit and dropped it into the side pocket of her satchel. Another profitable day. She couldn't keep from being self-satisfied. She had gambled on a venture that had done well.

"C'mon, Waffle, let's go home."

The golden dog rose and trotted to the back door, looking back at her as if to be sure she followed.

Her affection for this dog was more than she had ever had for another pet. He was more than a pet; he was a companion and a friend. The only thing lacking was speech. He was so smart, if he suddenly started talking, she wouldn't be surprised. In fact, she often wondered if he and Jake communicated.

Outside, she opened her SUV's back door and Waffle dutifully jumped in and seated himself squarely on his haunches in the middle of the bench seat. She assumed that position gave him maximum visibility and the opportunity to sniff the air from the open window or to lay his head on her shoulder as she drove.

"Let's run by the bank," she said, looking at him in the rearview mirror. "I'll go the long way."

Waffle gave her a whine of approval. He loved a car ride, even lingered behind in the car occasionally after they got home, not eager to leave his comfortable spot or the wonderful smells that came to him as they moved along. Sometimes she had to coax him into the house.

Sandi lowered all windows, allowing the cool autumn late afternoon to enter. Turning the radio volume higher, she sang along with a Carrie Underwood tune. She couldn't wait to get home and chill out. And she had to call Richard.

Taking one residential street, then another, she slowed as she spotted the pickup truck she had seen earlier in the day occupied by the good-looking Nick Conway. It was parked in Sylvia Armbruster's driveway. That woman was the most accommodating female in the whole area. Sandi's mouth slid into a sneer. *Typical man.*

Sandi and Sylvia had been classmates in college and even then, Sylvia's reputation for sharing her attributes had been well known. Twelve years hadn't whetted the woman's appetite for collecting males, only now her trinkets were men instead of boys.

She might be even prettier now than she had been in college. She was also smart and well-educated. She was a CPA and had recently opened her own practice.

Sandi still intended to ask Fiona about Nick Conway, but seeing him at Sylvia's told her all she needed to know.

She turned into the commercial deposit lane at the bank.

"Hi, Miz Walker," the young teller at the window said. "How's Waffle today?"

Everyone knew Waffle. H e had been a fixture in both her store and car only for only a couple of months now, but inquiries about his wellbeing came regularly.

"He's good, thanks. He's enjoying his ride in the car."

"I can see that." The teller returned the deposit cartridge with a receipt. "Y'all be careful out there."

"You, too," Sandi called back as she drove away.

The brief exchange brought to Sandi's mind how much she loved Midland and why, after losing her job and getting her second divorce, she had chosen to stay here instead of moving back to Big Spring. It was the people. Over a hundred thousand residents lived in the city of Midland, but it still had a small-town feel with small-town values.

Since she had lived here for years and formerly worked at a major bank, she felt she knew everyone, which made the good-looking stranger all the more puzzling. If she knew everyone, how had he slipped under her radar? Perhaps it was because she was loyal to her boyfriend, Richard, and rarely noticed anyone else.

If her neighbor Fiona, on the other hand, had encountered the hunky Nick Conway, she would have talked about him for weeks. A new, good-looking single man was always good for weeks of gossip.

As Sandi pulled into the drive of her two-bedroom vintage home—built in 1955 to be precise—she spotted her pal and neighbor sitting on her front porch step, cigarette in hand. She was wearing her perennial favorites—T-shirt and shorts and four-inch high-heels.

Fiona, barely five feet tall, insisted that high-heels and shorts made her appear leggy and therefore, taller. Sandi had pointed out numerous times that a height of five feet was still five feet no matter how you tried to rearrange it.

Sandi had known Fiona only as a customer of the bank until after she and Ken Coffman divorced and she had been forced to find a more affordable home. By the end of the first month after Sandi had moved into her place on Buffalo Way, she and Fiona had become fast friends.

Sandi enjoyed going out and having a good time, but Fiona was flat-out crazy when it came to socializing. She loved to party and rarely encountered anything in life to drag her down or stop her momentum. Fiona did things Sandi would never dream of doing, said things Sandi would like to say, but usually remained mute. Thus, Sandi reveled in her company.

"Hey girl," Fiona yelled, hoisting a margarita glass. "Come on over! It's happy hour on Buffalo Way!"

Laughing, Sandi yelled back, "Give me a minute."

"Hell to the yeah!" Fiona answered. "I've been home since two o'clock. Made my first margarita at two fifteen."

Fiona owned a busy, successful beauty salon and she was rarely home as early as five, much less two. Sandi noticed a slur in her speech. "You've declared the whole city block your bar?"

"What time 'zit now?"

"A little after five. Save me a margarita. I've got a bone to pick with you. I'll be right back."

As Sandi started toward the front door with Waffle trotting along with her, she could hear her friend still talking. "Me? You got a bone to pick with me? What'd I do? I didn't do it, whatever it is."

The minute Sandi walked into her own house, a screech came from up the hall. "Helllp! Helllp! Lemme out! Lemme out!"

She rolled her eyes. The screamer was Jake.

Along with his screeches, a distinct odor met her. When she had agreed to take him, she hadn't considered that he would make her whole house stink. Thus, she left the door to his room closed all day. He made a big enough mess in his room. No way did she want him flying around and pooping at random in the other five rooms. She had watched a video on YouTube about potty training a parrot, but so far, she hadn't had much success.

"Just hold on, Jake."

Waffle trotted up the hallway, anxiously looked up at the closed door, then swung his gaze back to Sandi, his tail wagging. Waffle and Jake were pals. Jake liked riding on Waffle's back.

She opened the bedroom door, checked the floor in case Jake might have left something for her to step in and walked in. She opened the window to let fresh air into the room, then snapped one end of a tether around Jake's leg and the other around her wrist.

"Waffle's a pretty boy, Waffle's a pretty boy," Jake squawked. "Move your hand. Move your hand. Don't touch my knee. Don't touch me."

Sandi arched her brow and sighed. She could only conclude that Jake had learned sentences like that listening to the goings-on in the bar from which the SPCA had rescued him.

Waffle barked and whined.

With Jake riding on her shoulder and Waffle following, Sandi walked through the house to the kitchen, gathered a plastic bowl full of treats and continued on through her back door. Waffle bounded to the middle of the back yard. She let Ricky and Fred out of their pen and they joined him in rough and tumble play.

Once, her backyard had a nice lawn, but no more. With so many animals passing through, she had given up on lawn maintenance. A full quarter of the yard was fenced off with chicken wire to make a pen for the various large dogs that had passed through her life. In the other back corner, she'd had a small aviary built for Jake. On her days off, she parked him in it so he could be outside and get fresh air.

She moved through the yard petting and scruffing heads, checking water levels and handing out treats.

"Where's mine? Where's mine?" Jake squawked.

"I've got a muffin for you," Sandi said and handed him a small muffin she made herself just for him.

Fred, her lab-Rottweiler mixed breed, and Waffle, an unknown mix of breeds, darted around, ducking behind tree trunks as if they were playing tag. Out in a corner of the yard, Sophie, Snow White and Dominique pecked for bugs while Christian Grey, her one-eyed rooster, pecked at Dominique. Pablo, her poor little jittery Chihuahua sat trembling beside her.

Sylvester, her tuxedo cat, sat on her opposite side, calmly bathing and grooming himself. The poor thing had been starved, losing his hair and only minutes away from being euthanized when Sandi rescued him. Now, after living in a safe environment and eating a diet of healthy food, handmade by Sandi herself, and a daily dose of vitamins, his coat was soft and glossy and he looked like a show cat.

From her shoulder, Jake watched the cat and cooed sweetly. "Pretty pussy. Pretty pussy."

Sandi's brow arched. She didn't know if Jake's words were directed at the cat because after all, Sylvester was a pretty cat. She sighed. She would never know what Jake meant, which probably was just as well.

Back inside the house, she tethered Jake to a perch she kept near the back door, then started to leave the room for her own bedroom. Jake made a haunting sound as if he were in agony. "Nooo. Don't leave me, don't leave me. Torture, torture. I'll talk, I'll talk."

"You are not being tortured, Jake. I'll be back in a minute." She started for her bedroom again, shaking her head as she walked. She had to relocate Jake to a new home. No way could they share a house long-term. She didn't have the time he required and he was worse than a nagging husband.

In the bedroom, she changed into her comfy jeans, a T-shirt and a pair of flip-flops, at the same time, watching the animals play from her bedroom window. She so longed for a place in the country and a few acres. Then the animals she already had would have more room and she could take on larger animals. A small city home was too crowded for as many animals as she had and Richard always complained about the smell.

Richard! Ohmygod! She was supposed to have returned his call hours ago. Oh, well, he could wait until later. She needed to go to Fiona's house and quiz her about Nick Conway.

She left her house and crossed the front lawn to her neighbor's, who was singing along with Michael Bublé. "Let me go hooome…"

"Fiona, child, leave the singing to Michael and gimme me some of what you're drinking," Sandi said.

"Done," Fiona replied, reaching behind herself and producing another plastic cocktail glass. She tilted the pitcher and filled the glass to the top. "Oops, got it too full. Here, let me sip a little off the top." She leaned and sucked deeply on the green froth, then thrust the glass to Sandi. "Here. Have a margarita, neighbor."

"Uh, okay, thanks." Sandi took the glass.

"How's Jake?" Fiona asked.

"He's fine. Why do you ask?"

"You know ol' bubble-butt up the street? Jake whistled at her today and called her a sweet piece."

Bubble-butt was the name Fiona had given to Stephanie Cummings, their cranky neighbor who constantly complained about Fiona's partying and Sandi's pets. Stephanie even sometimes called the cops when Fiona and her friends were especially loud.

When Sandi had taken in Sophie and Snow White, Stephanie had made an issue with the city council, but Sandi had pleaded for sympathy for the rescued homeless hen with a broken wing. Fortunately, Stephanie's complaint had been dismissed. The adoption of Anastasia and Christian Grey a few days later brought on another confrontation. Christian Grey crowed loudly and repeatedly at five a.m. every morning without fail.

And now that he had been around for a while, Jake had picked up his crow. But Jake didn't confine it to sunrise. He might crow at any time of day or night.

Sandi closed her eyes and shook her head. "I wish he wouldn't call her names. If she can figure out what he's saying, next thing you know, I'll be going to a City Council meeting again."

"I don't get it. I don't think he's heard me call Stephanie "bubble-butt" more than two or three times."

"I know, but you have to be cautious what you say around him. All he has to do is hear something one time and it becomes part of his lexicon."

"Is he mimicking me? Or does he really know that Stephanie is overweight?" Fiona looked at her with a serious expression, her drink poised midair. "Do you think he knows what "overweight" is?"

Sandy chuckled and sipped her drink. "Your guess is good as mine. I'm constantly amazed at how fast he learns words and uses them in their correct context. We could almost have a conversation.

Sometimes, if I absent-mindedly asked a question outloud, he answers."

Fiona tilted her head. "I wonder if he's really as smart as anyone else I know."

"Maybe I'll have to start closing the window," Sandi mused, staring into her margarita. "I was just trying to air out his room a little and let him get some fresh air." She sighed. "I've got to find him a good home. My house smells like a toilet."

"Why don't you keep him outside in that aviary thing you had built?"

"I can't when I'm not home. I'm afraid someone will steal him and I'd never stop worrying about him."

"If I didn't work all time, I'd take him," Fiona said. "Me and him would be good roommates. He could teach me a thing or two. I think he's better edju— educated than I am."

"I know what you mean. All the time I wonder if he's smarter than I am. But don't worry about it. I think my aunt down in Salt Lick is going to take him to give to her husband."

"The one who's a hair stylist? Like me?

"Right. Aunt Ed and her husband both are a little daffy, so Jake would fit right into their household."

"Aww, that's sweet," Fiona slurred. "Two daffy people and a daffy bird."

"Why are you home so early?" Sandi asked and sipped her drink.

"I scheduled my day light. I decided I work too hard. Don't you think I work too hard? I needed some *Me* time, so here *Me* is, sitting on the front porch, smokin' and drinkin'. Quality time. Yessiree. It's not

what you do with your time that's important, it's the
important things you do with your time."

Sandi gave her the squint-eye. "What?"

Fiona's brow scrunched into a frown. "Did I
screw that up?"

Sandi laughed and shook her head and sipped
more of the salty sour tequila mixture. "Be sure to give
your car keys to me. You don't need to be driving."

"No worries, neighbor. But if you were a real
friend you'd ask me for my cell phone. After a few
drinks, I do a whole lot more damage with that damn
thing than I do with a car. They should write tickets for
calling when drinking. That would be a CWD or a CUI.
Right?"

Sandi was about to agree when her friend said,
"What bone do you have to pick with me?"

"Oooh, yeah," Sandi said slowly, deliberately
dragging out the moment. "I met a good-looking single
man today and I find it hard to believe I've never heard
you say a word about him."

"Well, I do know them all. Slept with some of
'em, too. Who was it? Oh, God, don't tell me. No, wait.
Do tell me."

Sandi leaned back against the porch support
post. "Nick Conway is his name."

Fiona sat straight up, coughing and sputtering
and holding her glass level to keep from spilling it.
Sandi waited several seconds for her to recapture her
wind. "You okay? What is he, a criminal or
something?"

"That was the last name I expected to hear you
say. The absolute last. I've been trying to get a peek at
that guy for six months. Where'd you see him?"

Sandi related the encounter at the Pampered
Pooch and the cowboy who came in to see his puppy.

"He was cold as ice," she said in conclusion. "Never even looked at the little--"

"Did you check him out below the belt?" Fiona broke into a spasm of giggling.

Sandi gave her a look.

"His fly, I mean? Did you check it out?"

"You're drunk. I never check out a man's fly."

"Tell me exactly what he looked like. Don't leave out anything."

Sandi tilted her head, recalling. "Well, he's definitely your type."

"You mean breathing."

"No, I mean rugged. You know, really manly. Tall. A good foot taller than you."

"Who does he remind you of? Living or dead."

"Umm, Chris Hemsworth."

"God almighty. A Chris Hemsworth look-alike walking among us? And I haven't met him?"

"How come you haven't met him is what I want to know and how do you know about him?"

"All I know is from Sylvia Armbruster. For the past four months, every time she comes into the shop, it's Nick this and Nick that. She's head over heels, which, by the way, is her favorite position. I've asked her to bring him by the shop so I can meet him, but she won't do it. She's cowardly like that."

"You'd think she'd want to show him off. How did *she* meet him?"

"How does Sylvia get to meet any man? She stands at the city limits and stops every car that's got a male alone in it. She wants to be the first to check 'im out."

"And that's all you know about him, that he sees Sylvia and she's crazy about him?"

"You know Sylvia's mouth. I know absolutely everything about him, and I mean everything. I even know the size of his ding-dong. That's why I asked you if you checked out his fly. Why do you think I'm dying to meet him? A guy who brings that much to the party? Well...what can I say?... Wait a minute. Why do you care? You're taken." She slashed the air with a hand. "Off the market."

Sandi felt a flush crawl up her neck. "I'm not interested for myself. It's uh, it's that sweet little puppy. I'm worried about him going to a good home."

Fiona leaned closer and laughed softly. "Why, Sandi Walker. Pretty boy Nick Conway's got your juices flowing."

She reared back and swallowed another swig of her margarita. "And that amps him up for me. I have just got to meet him."

Sandi's carnal juices had indeed flowed when she met Nick Conway, but the new and successful businesswoman Sandi Walker had no intention of delving into that fact. The last thing she needed in her new life was an inarticulate cowboy in a worn-out pickup truck who was probably being pursued by a string of willing women. She lifted her chin indignantly. "Are you implying that my juices don't flow?"

Fiona tilted her head back and laughed and lost her balance, nearly overturning herself and her drink. She righted herself again. "Sandi you're the nicest person I've ever known and I know you've been married and divorced and I'm sure ol' Richard does something for you, but if what Sylvia says is true — and I gotta think it is 'cause she might be a lot of things but she's not a liar and she's bound to be an expert — then this guy is out of your league."

One thing Sandi had observed about Fiona. When she was drunk, she talked without commas and periods.

Her inebriated friend hadn't meant to hurt her feelings, but old insecurities weren't buried so deeply in Sandi's subconscious that she didn't feel a sting. Losing two handsome and charming husbands to other women could do that, even if both of them had been underachieving dullards. Lesson learned the hard way: Relationships with good-looking men came with a price.

In terms of fidelity, she had lucked out when Richard Townsend had come along. He might not be the most handsome man she had ever met, might not have the most sparkling personality, but he wouldn't even look at another woman.

After this conversation with Fiona, Sandi's only hope for the sexy-looking Mr. Conway was that he wasn't a dog abuser.

Chapter 5

FIONA'S CELL PHONE warbled and she launched into an animated phone call. Sandi mouthed the words, "Gotta go."

As she trekked from Fiona's porch to her own, she finally returned Richard's call. They made a plan for him to come by in an hour. She needed to shower, shave her legs and pretty herself up for the evening ahead. Lately, more often than not, an evening with Richard meant staying in, eating dinner, having sex and him departing early. He didn't even stay over anymore. If she could find the time, she might worry about that. In truth, at the end of the day she was as exhausted as he was and she was happy to have him go home and sleep in his own bed.

She really couldn't fault him for being worn out. As a criminal defense attorney, his time was not his own when a big trial was pending and in Midland, the current murder trial couldn't get any bigger.

John Wilson and the crime he had committed stayed in her mind. Sandi understood criminals had a right to legal representation, but Richard approached his career as if it were a game in which the tally of wins and losses took precedence over all else. She had a hard time accepting that the man with whom she had an intimate relationship was exploring every possibility to set this Wilson creep free. Especially after the evil bastard had bragged about how killing the elderly woman had been as easy as swatting flies.

For Sandi and Richard to fall into heated debates about his profession wasn't out of the ordinary. And with him coming over, she needed to shake those negative thoughts from her mind.

Reaching her house, she went to her spare bedroom and picked Jake off his perch, then proceeded outside. She sat down on her porch to watch her children play in the backyard. Another vision of a huge fenced area with acres of room scrolled through her mind. Someday, when her business became more profitable, she would have it. She just had to be patient.

Sudden tears welled in her eyes. She loved these defenseless, cast-off animals so much and she would protect them with the fierceness of a mama lion. Every one of them was defective in some way and if not for her giving them a place on the planet, all of them would now be gone. She had been their savior.

Suddenly, Jake flapped his wings and screamed, "Get that sonofabitch!"

Language from the sports bar, no doubt. "Jake! Watch your mouth … er, beak."

"Waffle! Waffle!" Jake squawked. "What the fuck?... What. The. Fuuuck?"

"Jake! You're outside! You cannot talk like that outside the house."

Sandi gave herself a mental eyeroll. God, had she lost it? He was a dumb bird.

"Bubble-butt, bubble-butt," Jake squawked.

Sandi's gaze swerved to her neighbor's house. Sure enough, Stephanie Cummings was in her backyard watering her flowers. "Jake! Cut it out! I mean it! You're going to get me in so much trouble."

The silly parrot cocked his head to the side and studied her for a long moment, "Jake's bad. Jake's bad." A soft garble came from his throat that sounded like a coo. "Kiss Jake. Kiss Jake."

He always knew how to get out of trouble. "Oh, no, you don't. I'm not letting you sweet talk me. It's time for you to go inside. You've been ugly and I have to get ready for Richard."

Jake shifted and squawked. "*Aarwk!* Dickhead! Dickhead!"

Richard's name was the only word that prompted that particular euphemism from Jake. "You have stop calling Richard Dickhead. It hurts his feelings."

Feelings? Crap. What had she just said? Sandi dropped her forehead against her fingers and shook her head. How was it possible that a human being's feelings could be hurt by a bird? The question hanging in her mind, she carried Jake back inside, toward his bedroom.

As they neared the bedroom door, Jake flapped his wings and screeched. "No! No! Help! Help! Call nine-one-one! Nine-one-one!"

He never wanted to be put away. "You cannot have free rein in the house. You poop on everything. You're a poopy bird." She was in the process of tethering him back to his perch when he said, "Dickhead. Dickhead."

Sandi hadn't heard Richard come in, but since he was the only person Jake greeted with that particular salutation, she knew her fiancé was behind her. A laugh burst out. Laughter was an improper reward for Jake, but she couldn't help it. She turned to face Richard with the moisture of mirth in her eyes.

Richard stood there with his eyelids narrowed. "I'm going to kill that fuckin' turkey." On a growl, he thrust his face toward Jake's beak. "Turkey! Turkey!

Jake cocked his head and cooed and Sandi could almost believe he was smiling except that parrots couldn't smile.

Richard straightened and gave her an accusing look. "Where did he learn a word like "dickhead"? And what's more, what does he mean when he says it?"

Sandi suppressed her amusement. "I'm not sure about that one. He only says it when you're around."

"The sonofabitch hates me. He'd look good stuffed and mounted."

"Call the cops. Call the cops." Jake squawked.

"Now, don't be mean, sweetie," Sandi said to Richard. "You know Jake's history. Life in a biker sports bar couldn't have been an ideal environment for a talking parrot."

"Biker sports bar? Have you thought about how dumb that sounds? Do bikers give a shit about sports?"

"I don't know. I just think Jake was rarely around any people except rowdy drunk men. I'm teaching him new things. Listen to this." Sandi turned her attention back to the parrot. "Jake, who does Sandi love? Come on, now. Tell me. Who does Sandi love?"

Jake walked back and forth on his perch, his head bobbing up and down, "Sandi loves Jake. Sandi loves Jake."

"See?" she said to Richard. "That's something new he's learned."

"Hey, Dickhead," the bird piped.

"Put him in his cage and throw a blanket over it," Richard said, sliding his arms around her waist. Her arms automatically went around his shoulders and their lips joined in a sweet kiss.

"Wanna fuck? Wanna fuck?" Jake said.

Unable to stop a guffaw, Sandi laughed against Richard's mouth and pulled away.

His face flushed a deep crimson, Richard shook his head. "Sandi, dammit…"

She wiped tears from her eyes with a fingertip. "I think he heard someone say that when he lived in the bar. He understands things. I think he knows that when you come over, we sometimes have sex."

"Bullshit, Sandi. How the hell does a damn bird know what fuck is? Or sex, for that matter?"

"My goodness, Richard, you think baby parrots just fall out of the sky?"

"You know what I mean," Richard groused. "Besides that, I hate a damn bird knowing my private life. And repeating it."

Sandi continued to dab away tears of mirth. "You scared me to death, by the way. I didn't hear you come in. I haven't even had time to shower."

"It's no wonder." He shot another disapproving glare at Jake. "I called out to you, but it's hard to be heard over your critters."

Richard's attitude about her pets was just one of the reasons Sandi's relationship with him might never go further. Though he had casually talked about getting married, she doubted she would ever marry him even if he became serious. If he had more power over her, he would complain even louder about her pets, might even try to make her get rid of them. She would never admit it aloud, but her animals were more important to her than Richard. And her deepest self knew that was no way to start a marriage.

She gave him a peck on the cheek, "Oh Richard, don't be a grump. I'm glad to see you."

Jake fluffed his feathers and cocked his head. "Wanna fuck? Wanna fuck?"

"Don't be surprised to find that sonofabitch missing one of these days," Richard griped. He turned to Jake and pointed his finger at his beak. "You hear that, you mouthy bastard? Hear that? You could come up missing."

"Richard, you're talking to a bird," Sandi reminded him.

"What did your aunt say? Is she going to take him?"

"I think so. She says her husband will love him. But I swear, I'm going to miss him."

"Good riddance, I say. How soon can you get rid of him?"

Jake ruffled his feathers and squawked. "Help! Nine-one-one. Nine-one-one."

"When she has time to come and get him," Sandi said, starting for the kitchen. "Come on into the kitchen. Are we eating out or in?"

"Don't leave me," Jake screeched. "I'll talk. I'll talk."

"No time to eat," Richard said. "I just stopped by to say hello. I'm headed home to change into something more comfortable. I'll grab something there and go back to the office."

"You work too hard, Richard. I've hardly seen you in weeks."

"I know. And I promise to make it up to you." He caught up with her and kissed the tip of her nose.

"It's this case. I've been reading and re-reading the arrest reports and I think I'm onto something—"

"Oh, no." Sandi looked squarely at him. "I hope it isn't a way to get that monster off."

Richard sighed deeply. "We've been over this too many times, Sandi. My job—"

Sandi raised her palms and stopped him. "I know, I know. I'm sorry. I promised myself I wouldn't say anything, but Fiona did Mrs. Bean's hair. She says she was one of the sweetest women she knew."

"I'm not paid to argue that, Sandi. I'm paid to make sure the man accused of killing her gets a fair trial."

Sandi bit her bottom lip. It was pointless to continue with this argument. Richard was undaunted in his defense of John Wilson. He couldn't change his position and Sandi wouldn't be moved from hers.

"Honey," he said softly, moving closer to where she stood, "this whole thing will be over in a matter of weeks. Maybe less. Let's make a plan to get away to San Antonio or Santa Fe. Or maybe down to the coast. How about St. Thomas? Wherever you want."

Instantly, Sandi thought of her animals. If she were gone for an extended period, who would take care of them? "I'd love to go anywhere with you, Richard. You know that. But we can talk about it later. You'd better go on home so you can get back to work. The sooner you get that trial over, the better."

Sandi let him pull her close. Richard planted a kiss on the top of her head. "You're right about that. I'll call you later."

As he drove away, Sandi stood at the door watching, the same question she had dismissed so many times going through her mind. Could her relationship with Richard Townsend withstand John

Wilson's murder trial? And if it did, what about the next trial?

☆☆☆

"It's Raining Men" by the Pointer Sisters interrupted Sandi's TV surfing. Grinning broadly, she keyed into the call on her cell phone. "Aunt Ed! What a great time for you to call."

"It is? Why?"

"My boyfriend just left and I'm alone. I can't think of anyone who can cheer me up more than you."

"Well, thanks, hon. Listen, you still looking for a home for that parakeet, the one that talks?"

"You mean the African Grey. He's a parrot, Aunt Ed. Not a parakeet."

"Whatever," Edwina said. "Birds are birds."

"Well, not exactly," Sandi replied, glancing in the direction of the Jake's room and biting down on her lower lip. Dammit, she hadn't intended to get attached to him.

Of course, she had that attitude in the beginning with every one of her foster pets, but after a few weeks or months, she hated to see them go. Ultimately, a good and loving home was what she wanted for all of them, including Jake. She was convinced being a foster parent to an animal—or fowl—and then letting them move on carried the same emotional upheaval that parting from a child would. Love was love, two legs or four. Or in Jake's case, two large feet and a dirty mouth.

"I do have to find a home for him, but I'm particular about where he goes. You know me, Aunt Ed. I get attached and—"

"Now don't get upset, hon. It won't be going that far. You can come to see it any time. I can't wait for Vic to see it. Is it still cussin' with every other breath?"

"I'm afraid so. I've tried to break him, but I haven't had a lot of luck. Sorry."

"No problem. I think it'll remind Vic of his days in the Navy."

Sandi couldn't imagine anyone better suited for the foul-mouthed fowl than a former sailor. The fact that she would still get to visit Jake was a plus.

"He's picked up some new cleaner words, but he hasn't forgotten the old ones. I hope that won't — "

"Perfect." Edwina said. "I wouldn't have it any other way. Vic will think he's talking to one of his old Navy buddies. Can I come get him tomorrow? The landlocked sailor is out of town and I want to surprise him when he comes back."

Sandi's heartbeat picked up, but she had been through this before and knew it would pass. She was born to be a mother and like all good mothers, seeing one of her children leave made her anxious.

"Sure, tomorrow is fine."

"After lunch?"

"Perfect, see you — Wait, Aunt Ed. My helper is going to mind my store tomorrow so I can have a day off. I could ask her to also babysit Waffle and I could bring Jake down to Salt Lick. Maybe I could get my hair trimmed while I'm down there."

"You sure could, hon. I just happen to know somebody who's an expert at trimming pretty long red hair."

Sandi hung up, went to Jake's room and opened the door. "Looks like you're getting a new home tomorrow, Jakey. But you don't mind, do you?"

He gave no reaction. As far as Sandi could tell, he was devoid of emotion or affection. She walked into the room and extended her hand. "Come to mama. It's almost time for me to open the store. Time for school. Time for your vocabulary lessons."

"*Awrrk!* Hate school, hate school."

Hmm. Maybe he wasn't devoid of emotion.

Chapter 6

THE NEXT MORNING, Edwina was already at the Styling Station when Debbie Sue arrived. "Hey, Ed. Early appointment?"

"Nope. I got up early to watch my TV show on Netflix. It ended, so I just came to work. It's lonesome in that trailer house without Vic."

"I wish you'd stop calling your home a trailer house, Ed. It's a beautiful double-wide. It's bigger and prettier and more modern than the old house I live in."

Just then, the cowbell on the front door clattered and Burma Johnson came in. She seated herself at Debbie Sue's station and Debbie Sue covered her shoulders with a black plastic cape. "What are we doing today, Burma?

"Just the usual, honey."

Debbie Sue walked her back to the shampoo room. They soon returned and Debbie Sue began to dry and style Burma's hair.

Edwina plopped into her styling chair, crossed her long skinny legs and began swinging her foot.

"Ooh, your shoes," cried Burma. "I love them. Wherever did you get them?"

Edwina stuck out her leg and flexed her foot, showing off the straw platform sandals with bunches of glittery butterflies adorning the toes.

"Online. Butterflies on my toes. Cute, huh?"

Debbie Sue stuck out a foot covered by a Tony Llama boot. "Mine might not be cute, but they're comfortable. And I can walk, even run, when I'm wearing them."

"Where am I gonna run to?" Edwina asked.

"You never know when you're going to have to run," Debbie Sue replied solemnly.

Burma laughed heartily.

"Guess what, Burma," Edwina said. "I'm getting a talking parrot for Vic. It cusses like a sailor. Won't that be a hoot?"

"I'll say." Burma tilted her head for Debbie Sue's convenience. "You know anything about taking care of a bird like that?"

"What's to know?" Edwina blew a bubble that hid her face, then sucked it back into her mouth. "You give 'em seed and water. Easy enough, right?"

"Seed?" Debbie Sue gave Burma a wink in the mirror's reflection.

Burma piped up right on cue. "Those talking birds are a whole other breed of fowl. They don't eat seeds. They're carnivorous."

"That's right," Debbie Sue added. "I looked it up on the Internet last night."

Giving them the squint-eye, Edwina halted the swing of her foot. "Okay, you two. What the hell do they eat, dogs and cats?"

"Spiders. The big hairy kind."

Edwina gasped, got to her feet and straightened to her full five-feet-nine, standing tall on her platform sandals. "No, they don't. Everybody knows birds eat seeds."

Debbie Sue assumed a serious expression. "But this is an exotic bird." She blasted a cloud of spray net on Burma's silver hair.

Burma turned in front of the mirror and petted her new hairdo. "Debbie Sue's right. Spiders are what they eat. Big, hairy, live spiders."

Debbie Sue unclasped the cape from around Burma's neck. "Yes, ma'am. That's what they eat,"

"You mean tarantulas?" Edwina huffed a loud gasp. "Oh, hell no, I'll burn that trailer house to the ground before I bring live tarantulas into it."

She picked up her phone, pressed a number, waited a few seconds, then shouted, "Sandi! This is your Aunt Ed again. Listen, honey, I can't take that bird after all. Sorry to have bothered … No, honey, it's the tarantulas. Fuckin' live tarantulas in my house. I can't even think about it without getting queasy."

Debbie Sue hid a grin while following Burma to the payout counter. One of the pleasures in her life was giving Edwina a hard time every chance she got. She felt no remorse for the orneriness. It was a game she and Edwina had always played and the very cornerstone of their tight relationship.

Debbie Sue said to Burma, "Sweetie, do you want me to put you down for next week, same time?"

"Honey, I'm talking about the ones they eat," Edwina said into the phone. "If Jake finds them, that's great, but I'm guessing when he can't find treats, I have to provide them myself and there is no way in hell…"

Burma kept her eyes on her purse and Debbie Sue bit her lip as Edwina paused. "They don't? Are you sure? Debbie Sue was telling…"

Debbie Sue burst into laughter. Burma, too, laughed so hard, she couldn't find her money in her purse.

Edwina scowled in Debbie Sue's direction. "Never mind, Sandi. I think some people are having a good time at my expense. I'll see you this afternoon."

Edwina paused again, then said, "Of course. I understand, darlin'. I know you get attached to all of your animals. You've told me several times."

Edwina disconnected. "Okay, you two. Sandi just told me he eats vegetables."

Burma squelched another laugh.

"You're going to get him this afternoon?" Debbie Sue said. "I am not going with you. Don't even ask. I've got things I need to do."

"Just cool your jets, smarty-pants. She's bringing him down here. But if I wanted you to go with me, you damn should would. That's the price for scaring the shit out of me."

"Ed—"

"That's my last word on the subject," Edwina said, raising her palm like a traffic cop. She picked up a lollipop and peeled off the wrapper. "Haven't you ever heard pay back is hell?" She stuffed the red bulb of candy in her mouth.

☆☆☆

Sandi's go-to employee, Betty Ann, came in early on Thursday mornings to start on the cooked dog and cat food. That way, they could make sure the cases were filled with plenty of freshly-made goodies for which pet owners could shop on the weekend and Sandi wouldn't have to try to do it while customers browsed in her store. The other employee, Jessica showed up late morning to help Betty Ann and watch the store in the afternoon so that Sandi could have a day off.

After lunch, Sandi gave Jessica some last minute instructions, then drove home. She gathered all of Jake's treats, toys and other paraphernalia and loaded all of it in the back of her SUV. Next, she put Jake in the travel cage she had bought for him and belted it onto the SUV's cargo area.

As she motored southwest toward Salt Lick, Texas, the parrot sat on the trapeze swing in his cage, squawking or whistling occasionally. She didn't know what those sounds meant, but she assumed he was happy and liked the car ride. She opened one of the back windows slightly so he could enjoy the crisp fall air.

She looked at him in the rearview mirror. "Hey, Jake. How does that fresh air feel?"

Jake screeched an uneven rendition of "God bless America, land that I love ..."

Those were the only words he knew of the song, but each time he sang them, Sandi sang with him. Man, she was going to miss him.

Soon Jake grew tired of singing. "Where's Waffle? Where's Waffle?" he squawked.

Being separated from Waffle these days was rare, but Sandi had reluctantly left him at home in case the other animals might need his company to compensate for Jake's absence. He was good to keep everyone out of mischief.

From behind her, the roar of a large motor caught her attention and she glanced into the rear view mirror. A big gray pickup was way too close to her back bumper.

To her surprise, she recognized the driver's silhouette—broad shoulders, cowboy hat. Nick Conway. What was he doing on this highway? He must have bought a new pickup. The vehicle behind her wasn't the wreck she had seen him in before.

"Crap." She glanced again in the mirror, but this time, she took a critical look at her hair and makeup. At the same time, she chastised herself for such teenage behavior, for even caring about how she looked. He hadn't noticed her the day they met in the Pampered Pooch and a chance encounter on a highway would mean nothing. He would pass her without a glance. Even if he did glance, he probably wouldn't recognize her.

Sure enough, he did just that, his bigger engine growling like a mad cat. He never so much as glanced her way, "Why would he?" she muttered to the air. "I'm just another car on the road."

Jake let out a squawk.

Coming out of a sharp blind curve, Sandi met a large Hereford cow and her calf standing in her lane and blocking her path. She slammed on the brakes, swerved to the shoulder and stopped. The cow looked at her with lazy eyes.

Luckily, she had slowed for the curve, but what if some driver behind her didn't? He or she would plow into the pair, which could result in the death of the animals and possibly the driver. She looked in her side mirror at the two of them still standing in the middle of the road seemingly without a care in the world.

"What am I going to do, Jake? I can't just let them get run over. And why in the hell didn't Mr. GQ Cowboy stop and get them off the road? What an asshole."

"Mr. GQ Cowboy," Jake squawked. "What an asshole. What an asshole."

She killed her SUV's engine, stepped out and eased toward the cow and calf, making a palms up shooing gesture with her hands. She hadn't taken a dozen steps before her feet began to burn. She was wearing thong sandals that weren't the ideal footwear for hot asphalt, but she couldn't let defenseless animals stand at risk in the middle of the highway. "Shoo, mama. Move now. Come on."

The cow continued to look at her with blank brown eyes and stood perfectly still. Sandi stamped a hot foot against the pavement and clapped her hands. "Get off the road! Hurry! Hurry!"

The cow lifted its head and bawled, but didn't move its feet. The calf bleated.

Why didn't the damned things move? Exasperated, Sandi hung her head.

"What an asshole. What an asshole," Jake piped from back in the SUV.

The engine's loud growling sound split the air again. Sandi looked frantically at the cow and calf, then toward the sound. The pickup that had passed her moments before was barreling backward toward her at the same speed it had been traveling forward, the driver expertly handling the wheel. It stopped on the shoulder only feet away, the door opened and Nick Conway stepped down.

He strode back to the pickup bed, lifted out a lariat and walked toward her, forming a loop as he came. "We meet again. Best move back and let me do this."

He continued past her, toward the cow and calf.

She should slip into a Scarlett O'Hara flirty mode and say something cute and charming, but instead of acting coquettish, she couldn't keep from being hostile. After what alpha men had put her through, they had that effect on her.

She lifted a defiant chin and hollered behind him. "I'm not afraid of a cow. I've been around cattle my whole life."

Giving her a look, he walked right up to the cow and slid the loop over her head. "Then you oughtta know that mamas can be ornery when it comes to strangers around their calves. I've seen many a man put on the fence because he got too close."

He tugged and sweet-talked the cow, coaxed her toward the edge of the pavement. The calf followed.

"Well, at least I stopped," Sandi called after him.

"I was checking to see if I could spot where she got out," Nick yelled back. "I didn't notice a break in the fence before that curve, so I figured it must be ahead of me." He flashed a grin in her general direction.

Every female cell in her body swooned. She hated that her body reacted this way.

"Did you find the break?" she finally asked.

"Yes, ma'am, I did."

Silence as he walked the two animals past her and up the side of the road.

"Are you going to fix the fence?"

Good Lord, why don't I just shut up and be on my way?

"Yes, ma'am," he called back over his shoulder. "That's my plan."

She couldn't help admiring the excellent view of his backside. Tight Wranglers hugging his tight bottom. He was the stereotypical cowboy. She was the first to point out, having lived in West Texas all of her life, that there were cowboys and then there were damn fine cowboys. The one leading a cow in front of her definitely fell into the latter category.

"Always good to have a plan," she yelled.

Nick stopped suddenly and turned to face her. He thumbed his hat back, hitched his hip and cocked his knee. *Oh, my God. John Wayne.* Seconds turned into an eternity. "Speaking of plans," he drawled, "is it your plan to stand in the road and get run over? Do I need to get another rope?"

Sandi's jaw dropped. Her cheeks flamed. *The very nerve!*

She flung back her hair, turned sharply and stomped back to her SUV. "What an asshole." She jerked the door open and slid behind the wheel. "Did you hear him, Jake?"

"What the fuck?" Jake squawked.

"You're exactly right, Jake. He talked to me like I didn't have enough sense to come in out of the rain."

Jake fluffed his feathers. "Don't let me get wet. Don't let me get wet."

She started the engine, jerked the SUV into gear and roared past Mr. Nick Conway as Jake squawked loud enough to wake the dead, "What an asshole! What an asshole!"

☆☆☆

Nick watched the SUV growing smaller against the horizon. He could have sworn she had called him an asshole. Not the first time a woman had expressed that opinion. It usually resulted because he kept attractive women who were the type to be looking for a steady attachment at arm's length. He could spot them a mile away.

His heart had been broken twice—once in the fifth grade when Miss Taylor had come back from Christmas break showing off an engagement ring and again ten years ago when he'd come home from work early and caught his former wife in bed with a former friend. Both times, he had sworn he was finished with women.

He had gone back on the first vow when he met his ex-wife, but when he had made the vow the second time, he meant it.

He didn't need a woman nagging and bugging him. He had everything a man could want. He had a truck that ran most of the time, a couple of good horses and a trailer to haul them in. In his work, he had other fellas around him for interactions with human beings. He had a woman sixty-five miles away in another town to slake his lust when need be. Sylvia's only expectation was to be satisfied in bed and Nick had no trouble in that department.

Most importantly, he had the ability and education to make a good living doing what he loved for a good boss. Harley Carruthers trusted him implicitly to do the right thing and gave him free rein to do his job. The Flying C was a solid ranching outfit that provided him with good pay, good medical insurance, a 401(k) and other small, but desirable benefits. It was a job that would serve his needs for as long as he wanted it to.

Yep, the only thing missing from his life was a good dog and soon he would have that, too.

Tugging on the rope, urging the cow to move along, he couldn't hold back a grin. Women like that redhead were so damn cute, trying to be cool and aloof. Tiptoeing toward this ol' cow and her calf, shooing at them with her hands. Damn cute, but she obviously didn't understand cattle. She could have made hand signals all day long and this ol' blister wouldn't have moved an inch until some car or truck came along and plowed into her.

The woman might be dumb about cows, but she was good-looking. Had hair the color of this baby calf and he liked that. Nothing was prettier than a Hereford calf.

Chapter 7

SANDI REACHED SALT LICK mid-afternoon. With the crash of the oil market in the '80s, the small town had almost turned into a ghost town, but the businesses that had been able to hang on were recovering and the little place again hummed with activity. A surge in new drilling had the entire Permian Basin enjoying a smaller scale version of a way of life that had been stalled for decades.

Sandi came to a stop near the Styling Station's front door and looked at her passenger through the rear-view mirror. "Jake, listen to me now. This is going to be your new home. You don't want to make a bad impression. No cussing. I'm serious. No cussing. You'll be around ladies."

The bird squawked and fluffed his feathers. "Hot damn."

"Jake! I am not kidding. Do not say anything ugly."

"Jake's a good boy. Jake's a good boy."

"What are the ugly words you can't say, Jake?"

"Tits, balls, fuck, shit. Tits, balls, fuck, shit. Tits—"

Good grief. Where did he learn those words? "Enough already! Those are the words you cannot say, Jake."

"Jake's a good boy."

Sandi dragged the big cage out of the backend, rested it on her hip, reached for his plastic tub of supplies and headed for the Styling Station's front door.

Though juggling her burdens, she still managed to open the front door. "Aunt Ed? Debbie Sue? We're here."

Edwina rushed to her, gave her a quick hug, then looked into Jake's cage. "Good Lord, Sandi. I thought parakeets were little birds."

Debbie Sue came over, grabbed the tub of supplies, then the cage and gingerly placed the cage on the nearest foot stool in front of a hairdryer.

"I don't know where you got the idea he's a parakeet, Aunt Ed. I told you, he's an African Grey parrot."

"My God, it's bigger than a chicken. I guess if I get hungry, I could cut its head off and have it for supper." She guffawed.

Jake squawked and hopped around on his perch. "Helllp! Call nine-one-one. Helllp!"

Sandi's heart leaped. She didn't believe for a minute that her aunt would really eat Jake, but on the other hand, the woman did have a reputation in the family for being a little...well, eccentric. "Aunt Ed! Oh, my Lord —"

"I'm kidding, babygirl. You know I pop off. I wouldn't really eat that thing."

Relieved, Sandi drew a deep breath. If she thought for a minute that statement had a ring of truth to it, she couldn't leave Jake here. "Don't talk about eating him, Aunt Ed. You'll scare him. He understands what you're saying."

"Riiight," Edwina said, backing away and eyeing Jake from every angle.

Sandi almost wished her aunt would reject Jake, which would give her an excuse to take him back to her own home. "If he's too big...if you want to change your mind—"

"*Aawrk.* Jake's not fat. Jake's not fat."

"See? I told you he understands what we're saying."

"That's amazing," Debbie Sue said, obviously fascinated.

"It's fine, Sandi, it's fine," Aunt Ed said. "Besides, it's not for me, it's for Vic. And I guess a larger bird makes sense for him. I mean, he's a big guy and all."

"Well, first off, Jake is a he, Aunt Ed. And he's very alpha. That's why his former owner named him Jake."

"Alpha?" Edwina said, her brow furrowed.

Debbie Sue had been circling the foot stool, studying Jake. The parrot, as if he knew he was being scrutinized, showed his acrobatic skills by climbing upside down on the travel cage's bars, then fluffed his feathers and strutted as much as he could in the cage's limited space. Debbie Sue finally straightened and placed her hands on her hips. "I love it. I think it's the prettiest thing I've ever seen."

"Really, y'all," Sandi said. "He's not an *it*. He's a he. I'm not sure he'll appreciate being called an it. He might be sensitive about it."

"Did you say it... er, *he* appreciates things?" Edwina asked.

"He's sensitive?" Debbie Sue followed up.

Sandi gushed like a proud mother. "Oh, yes. Sometimes I honestly believe he has feelings, as well as cognitive abilities."

"What does that mean?" Edwina asked.

"She just told you, Ed," Debbie Sue said. "It means he might feel human things. He understands human things."

"I truly believe he does," Sandi said. "A couple of months ago, the last time we had rain, I had him tethered outside to get some fresh air. I got tied up on the phone in the kitchen and when the rain started, I heard this voice from outside. 'Help. I'm getting wet. Help. Help.'"

"No shit?" Debbie Sue said, staring at Jake round-eyed. "And it was Jake talking?"

"That's some scary crap," Edwina added. "I mean, birds live outside. A little rain shouldn't bother him."

Jake piped up. "*Aawrrk.* Don't let me get wet."

Sandi had to laugh. "Jake, you are so funny."

She turned her attention back to her aunt and Debbie Sue. "I catch myself having conversations with him all the time. Just to give you a boring factoid, people who research these birds believe that the African Greys can learn up to a thousand words. And Jake does have quite a vocabulary. Of course, some of it isn't suitable for mixed company. I've been trying to teach him more appropriate words, but it's been challenging, given his history."

"What's his history?" Debbie Sue asked.

Sandi gently passed her finger over Jake's feathered gray head. "Poor sweet baby. He lived in a biker sports bar in Odessa until he was rescued by the SPCA and taken to We Love Animals. Everyone was amazed he survived in that environment. His owner let the customers buy him beer and pizza. On top of that, my friend at WLA told me the poor thing witnessed a murder. Apparently, that bar was a wild place."

"A real murder?" Debbie Sue said.

"Can you believe it? The cops actually questioned him and Jake told them all about it, even who did it. But the judge wouldn't let him testify in court. He ruled that testimony from a parrot wasn't credible."

"Wow," Debbie Sue said. "Why would he think that? I'd believe a parrot if he was an eyewitness and told me something."

"Well, yeah. Me, too." Edwina added. "I mean, this is a beauty shop. I'd come as close to believing a parrot as I would some of the human shit that gets shoveled in here every day."

"Shoveled shit. Shoveled shit," Jake squawked.

"Oh, my Lord, Aunt Ed. You just taught him some more dirty words. He seems to learn the bad words fast."

"If he lived in a bar, I'll bet he learned some great pick-up lines," Debbie Sue said, giggling.

"Uh-huh." Sandi turned to the parrot. "Jake, say something nice to the nice lady." She emphasized the word "nice," hoping he remembered her admonishment back in the car.

Jake whistled what sounded like a wolf whistle and cocked his head. "Hey, babe. Nice tits. Let's blow this joint."

Sandi's hand shot out to cover Jake's beak. "Oh, Debbie Sue, I am so sorry. I just never know what he's going to say. Tits is one of the bad words I told him not to use."

But evidently Jake hadn't offended Debbie Sue. She clasped her hands under her chin. "Oh, I love him. I wish you weren't taking him, Ed. I think I might have to."

"Fourth and ten, fourth and ten. Bring in the kicker," Jake chanted.

"Oh, my God," Aunt Ed said. "Those are football words. You say he lived in a sports bar?"

"Who's your favorite team, Jake?" Sandi asked him. "Who do you root for?"

"Go, Cowboys. Go, Rangers."

Jake was putting on a show. Sandi's chest filled with pride. She and Debbie Sue laughed together, but Aunt Ed hung back.

"Ed, what's the matter with you?" Debbie Sue asked. "You haven't said anything to him. This is such a good idea for Vic. He'll love him. Ed, come say something to him. Ask him something."

Edwina stayed across the room, watching closely, her arms crossed under her breasts. "Is that all he says? Stuff about sports? Vic isn't much of a sports guy. He watches the military channel."

As if he were auditioning, Jake squawked, "Mr. GQ Cowboy. What an asshole. What an asshole."

Debbie Sue straightened, a bemused expression on her face. "What does that mean?"

One thing that Sandi had learned about African Greys was that they were unique mimics and Jake had proved it. Sandi had feared he might repeat the words he heard her say out on the highway. Warmth flashed in her cheeks. "It was just someone we met on the road."

Edwina came forward. "Oh, really, niece-of-mine. So who's the GQ Cowboy? Anyone we know or better yet, anyone *you* know?"

Sandi told the story of the trip down from Midland and the encounter with the cow and calf standing in the middle of the highway. With her Aunt Edwina well known for her meddling and matchmaking, she left out the fact that she had seen GQ Cowboy before and he had left her weak-kneed. And that she even knew his name.

"He put a rope around her neck and led her away, end of story," she said in conclusion. "Not much to tell."

"I know that sharp curve," Debbie Sue said. "That fence runs along the Carruthers ranch. Must have been one of Harley's cows."

Edwina brightened. "Must've been one of Harley's ranch hands. It was him, Debbie Sue. I'll bet it was him."

"Who?" Sandi asked, looking from Debbie Sue to Edwina. "Who do you think it was?"

"We don't know." Edwina winked. "But we're working on finding out. Hey, speaking of men, how's your boyfriend doing these days? I read in the paper that he's defending the bad guy that murdered that elderly woman, Mrs. Bean."

"Allegedly, Aunt Ed. Innocent until proven guilty Richard keeps reminding me."

"But the bad guy confessed," Edwina said.

"He told Richard he only confessed because he was afraid the cops were going to beat him up." She shrugged. "Now he says he's not guilty."

"And I suppose him being seen leaving Mrs. Bean's house at the time of the murder, her belongings found in his car and his blood a DNA match to some that was taken from the crime scene is all alledgedly," Edwina replied.

Debbie Sue raised her head from studying Jake, "I heard Buddy talking to somebody on the phone. There's some problem with how the DNA was obtained. They may have to throw it out."

Crap, Sandi thought. *So that's what Richard is working on.*

Aunt Ed's hands rested on her skinny hips, her arms akimbo. "I sure as hell hope Richard doesn't get him off."

Jake fluffed his entire body and screeched, "Dickhead. Dickhead."

"Did he say dickhead?" Debbie Sue asked, round-eyed.

Sandi's face flushed with embarrassment. "I'm afraid he did. That's what he calls Richard. Don't ask me why."

Aunt Ed broke into peals of laughter. She grabbed a Kleenex from her station and wiped away tears, then moved close to the cage and squatted to eye level with the bird. "Maybe he's got a sixth sense. Maybe you'll do after all, Jake. A plain-spoken bird could come in handy. What do you think, Jake-O? Want to go home with me?"

Jake turned his head sharply and stared at her for several seconds. "Not tonight, Q-Tip. I ain't had that much to drink."

Sandi slapped her palm against her mouth. "Oh, my Lord, Aunt Ed. I'm so sorry. Like I told you, I never know what's going to come out of his mouth." She turned to Jake and pointed her finger at his beak. "Bad Bird. That was ugly."

Jake squawked. "Ugly. Tits, balls, fuck, shit…"

☆☆☆

Later, as her aunt snipped away at her hair, Sandi made eye contact with her in the mirror. "Where are you going to keep Jake, Aunt Ed?"

"In his cage, I guess."

"I was going to talk to you about that. He needs more space than that. At my house, he has his own room. I turned my guest bedroom that I was using for an office into his room. I was hoping that since you and Vic don't have kids living with you, maybe you'd have that much space to give him."

"Hells bells, it never dawned on me that he'd have to have his own room. I guess he could have my craft room. I'd have to move out all my stuff. I mean, I would want him crapping all over everything. He does crap like normal birds, right?"

"Of course, he does. There's nothing abnormal about him, Aunt Ed."

"You've got plenty of room, Ed," Debbie Sue said. "You've got one whole bedroom that has nothing in it but your clothes and shoes."

Edwina sighed. "Sandi, I don't want you worrying yourself about this bird. I'm a grown woman. I can figure out how to take care of it … er, him."

"And if she can't, I can," Debbie Sue added.

They were trying to reassure her, Sandi knew. But she couldn't keep from worrying.

An hour later, her red hair perfectly trimmed and shining, she prepared to leave the Styling Station. Even before they left home in Midland, she had steeled herself to say good-bye to Jake, but as she stood at the salon's front door ready to leave, a lump formed in her throat and tears burned her eyes. She might break into a wail any minute.

This was what happened when she parted from all of her foster "children." She formed a bond of love with each precious life she was appointed to watch over and each separation was a bittersweet event.

"Now, don't cry, hon," Edwina said, starting to sniff. "You know Vic and I will give him a good home."

Debbie Sue's eyes, too, had misted over. "And if they don't, I will."

Believing that her charges were going to homes that would give them as much love as she had given them had always been the only balm that made Sandi feel better. But today, that belief didn't lessen the pain of parting with Jake. "I know" — her voice hitched — "It's just that he needs so much attention and I'm afraid you'll run out of patience with him. And I'm going to miss him so much."

"Wellll," Edwina said, pulling her into a hug and patting her shoulder. "It'll be okay. Vic won't get tired of him. And if you want to come see him, he'll be just a few miles down the road."

"I know." Sandi pulled herself together. Barely holding her tears in check, she parted from Edwina's hug and picked up the plastic tub. "I've brought you his toys and the parrot mash he likes and some of the treats I sell in my shop."

"Parrot mash? Yuck. No wonder he went for beer and pizza."

"Oh, Aunt Ed, please don't feed him food like that. It's so bad for him. The parrot mash is organic. It's what he's supposed to eat. I get it from one of my wholesalers. I'll continue to get it and send it to you every month. It's the least I can do for Jake. And for you, too."

"That's all he eats, huh?"

"That and some vegetables. He needs a variety of things. I also put some homemade parrot bread in the tub. I bake it in my shop in the form of muffins and sell it to bird owners. I baked for Jake a couple of days ago, so he still has a few little muffins left."

"Wait a minute. You bake muffins for him?"

"Uh-oh," Debbie Sue said, looking as if she was deep in thought. "Ed uses her oven for storing her shoes. But that's not a problem," she added quickly. "She can use mine. Just be sure to leave us the recipe."

Sandi nodded. "I put the recipe in this tub. One a day is usually enough. He also needs salad greens every day. Organic if you can get them. No onions or garlic, of course. I shop for him at the farmer's market."

"My God. I have to make him a salad?"

"It only takes a few minutes, Aunt Ed. I buy the bagged broccoli slaw, then add some zucchini and yellow squash. Also, some kale. He loves kale. And nuts, like walnuts. Just give him a whole nut and he can crack it and get the meat out."

"My God. He's a gourmet?"

"You should feed him some fruit, too. He loves strawberries and kumquats—"

"Kumquats," Debbie Sue said. "When was the last time I saw a kumquat, much less ate one?" She turned to Aunt Ed. "Does City Market sell kumquats? Or kale?"

"Hell, we're lucky to get lettuce," Aunt Ed answered. "I see both my grocery bill and my gasoline bill climbing. What else?"

"Oh, some blueberries, grapes…any of the dark fruits that are high in antioxidants."

"Dark fruits. Antioxidants," Debbie Sue said. "I should get a pencil and take notes."

"I wrote it all down in a tablet and put it in his tub. Taking notes until you get used to his routine might help. A vegetable chopper is in the tub, too. It's just an ordinary Hamilton Beach brand I got at Walmart. It's perfect for chopping his food. I just put everything into the bowl and chop it up together. Takes only a few minutes.

"Oh, and you should sprinkle some of the parrot mash over his food when you offer it to him. It absorbs the fruit juices and enables him to get the benefit of the juice. Oh, and one more thing. At home, he has a table in his room to eat on. He seems to eat better if his food is sort of spread out on a table. In their natural environment, African Greys eat off the ground, like chickens do."

"Hells bells, Sandi. I thought I just had to put a few seeds in a little cup. You didn't tell me he was going to be a gourmet diner in his own room with his own table. Do we need to hire him a chef?" Aunt Edwina cackled.

"Here's an idea," Debbie Sue said. "You could simplify things if you and Vic started eating like he does, Ed. More veggies and less chicken-fried steak."

"Are you kidding? Veggies ain't replacing chicken-fried steak at our house. You know how Vic loves to cook. Now that I think about it, cooking for Jake will give him new purpose. On the other hand, knowing Vic, if Jake gets to be too much trouble, we'll be eating chicken-fried parrot."

Instantly she slapped her hand over her lips. "Ohmygod. I'm sorry." She bent down and looked eye-to-eye at Jake. "I'm was kidding, Jake-O, okay? Just kidding."

Jake cocked his head, closed his eyes and garbled something unintelligible.

"I'm not sure he has a sense of humor, Aunt Ed. I doubt he understands sarcasm."

Edwina flipped a palm in the air. "Whatever. Don't worry, I'm telling you. I'll find the stuff he likes."

"What else is in this tub?" Debbie Sue asked. She walked over and snapped the lid off the plastic storage tub. She lifted out the large spray bottle Sandi used to shower Jake. "What's this?"

"It's the spray bottle I use to give Jake a shower."

"Did you say shower?" Aunt Ed asked.

"It sprays a fine mist. Don't use the shower head, Aunt Ed. I think it's too much water all at once. I just put his perch in the shower, he stands on it and I spritz him. He really loves it. You need to do it, oh, about once a week, I guess. Oh, and sometimes I let him play in the kitchen sink."

"*Eww*. Yuck. The kitchen sink?" Her aunt stood there blinking, her dark brown eyes magnified by her thick glasses lenses. "I thought he said he didn't like getting wet."

"What he doesn't like is water pouring on him. He seems to enjoy the fine mist the most. He hops around, even spreads his wings so you can spray under them. It's so cute."

"You'd better get on the road," Debbie Sue said. "The longer you stay and talk, the more horrified your aunt gets." She turned to Aunt Ed. "Don't worry about it, Ed. Vic can shower him. Or maybe you could mist both of them together." Debbie Sue belly-laughed. "I can already see it."

Sandi managed a small laugh. "I guess that's everything." She gave a great sigh. "You can call me, of course, if you have any questions or any problems. And you can surf the Internet. There's a lot of information on the Net and some good videos on YouTube."

"I'm kind of a dinosaur when it comes to the computer, but Debbie Sue can look stuff up."

Sandi nodded. "I have to go." She turned to the cage, put her hand inside, brought Jake out and smoothed a finger over his head. "Mama's going to leave you now. Try not to miss me. I'll be thinking about you."

Jake cocked his head and garbled from deep in his throat. "Kisses?"

"Ooh," she whined. "Look at that. He knows I'm leaving. He's going to miss me." She sniffled and placed a gentle kiss on his beak. "Mama loves you, baby."

He cooed softly.

Debbie Sue began to whimper. "That's the sweetest thing I ever saw. He loves you, too, Sandi."

"I know."

Edwina sniffed, too. She grabbed another Kleenex out of a box on her station counter. "Don't you worry, Sandi. Vic and I'll take good care of him. He'll have everything he wants. Hell, I'll even hunt down tarantulas for him to eat."

Sandi restrained her tears for a moment and frowned. "Those big hairy spiders? I doubt if he likes tarantulas, Aunt Ed."

"Never mind. It was another joke. Obviously not a good one."

Sandi left the Styling Station in tears. Her aunt and Debbie Sue stood in the doorway, wiping their eyes and blowing their noses. Black mascara had made trails down Aunt Ed's cheeks. According to Sandi's mother, Aunt Ed had been blinder than a bat her whole life. Sandi had often wondered how she managed to cake on so much black mascara if she needed such thick lenses to see.

☆☆☆

Once Sandi was out of sight, Debbie Sue closed the Styling Station's front door and locked it. "Let's close this place up." She turned to Edwina. "Wow, Ed. You're going to be busy with ol' Jake here."

"He ain't exactly a goldfish, is he?" Edwina wiped her eyes and blew her nose. "When do I have time to take care of a bird that's this much trouble? I can see I should've gotten more information from my niece. I should've given this more thought. And I definitely should've discussed it with Vic."

"But it's supposed to be a surprise for Vic."

"Yeah. Kind of like one of those messages from outer space surprises."

"What happened to the idea of Vic taking him in the truck?"

"Oh, hell, Debbie Sue. That was BS. Vic won't take a damn parrot in the truck with him. He's gonna be busy driving and this silly bird's gonna be stuck at home with nobody to talk to all day."

"Who did he talk to in Midland? Isn't Sandi gone from home all day? Didn't he stay home alone?"

"Yes, but that was a temporary arrangement. I'm supposed to be what they call the permanent adoptive parent. I'm supposed to give him a loving home, a good environment and attention."

Debbie Sue squatted in front of the cage and studied the parrot. "He's really interesting, Ed. I love his red tail feathers."

Jake whistled. "Hello, pretty lady."

"We can get a handyman to build him a cage in the corner," Debbie Sue continued. "That way, he won't be alone."

"Yeah, maybe. Hells bells and Jesus Christ. I'll have to stay home three days a week just to fix his food. Look at his damn feet. Am I gonna have to give him a pedicure on top of everything else? Then there's the cat. Gus is like a part of the family. What will *he* think?"

"Last I heard, Ed, a cat doesn't get a vote in what goes on in someone's household. Since Vic likes to cook, maybe he'll fix his food and all of that."

"You're right about a cage here in the shop. Jake will have to come to the shop, that's all there is to it." Edwina threw up her hands. "Either that or I'll have to find somebody to babysit him."

"You're too stressed out, Ed. This isn't hard. He can come to the shop. It's okay with me. Just put him in his cage and bring him. The customers will love him. And I'll help you make his food."

"Jake's a good boy," the parrot said and fluffed his whole body.

"Yes, you are, baby," Debbie Sue said. "You're a good boy. And a pretty boy." She pushed her finger into the cage and rubbed his head.

Edwina gave the parrot a hard look, then turned back to Debbie Sue, her eyes brimming with tears. "I've really done a dumb-ass thing, haven't I? I hate like hell to disappoint my niece, but tomorrow, I'm gonna call her and tell her she has to take her bird back."

"No," Debbie Sue said firmly. "Vic's going to love him. And if it doesn't work out for y'all, I told you I'd take him."

"But Buddy—"

"Buddy will love him, too. I'll make him."

Chapter 8

SANDI HADN'T BEEN gone from the Styling Station three minutes before she was awash in a full-on, throat-hitching boo-hoo, her vision blurred by tears. Hogg's Drive-In was the nearest exit off the street. She pulled into the parking lot, barely avoided clipping the edge of Hogg's ELVIS ATE HERE sign. She came to a stop and fell over the steering wheel sobbing.

Aware of a presence at her window, she looked up. *Ohmygod! Nick Conway!* And he was seeing her with her eyes and nose swollen and red and, no doubt, smeared makeup.

He bent down at the driver's window, gesturing with a twirl of his finger for her to lower the window. She hesitated, then buzzed down the window.

"Ma'am, you need some help?"

"No. Just leave me alone." She turned toward the passenger seat and rummaged in her oversized purse, came up with a Kleenex and blew her nose with a loud snort.

"Where you headed?"

"What?... Not that it's any of your business, but I'm on my way home."

"Midland?"

"Well … yes, if you must know."

He pointed behind himself with his thumb at Hogg's building and the huge ELVIS ATE HERE sign. "You nearly ran over this outfit's sign."

Shit! The damn sign was as big as the side of a house and white lights raced around the outside edges. How could she almost run over it?

"You're kind of upset to be driving as far as Midland," he said. "I was just about to go inside for a bite to eat. Come inside with me and I'll buy you supper. Maybe eating something would make you feel better."

She drew a deep sniff. "I don't need supper. I'm not hungry. And I'm not upset."

"Okay. If you don't want supper, I'll buy you a cup of coffee. Or a Coke or something."

She stared up into the bluest eyes she had ever seen framed by the blackest lashes. The world tilted. After a few beats, she lowered her gaze to her tightly clasped hands. "Uh, well…I haven't eaten since breakfast. Maybe some food would make me feel better."

"Good." He opened her car door and held it for her to scoot out. Without pause, she started toward the entrance to the café.

"You're not gonna take your key?"

She stopped and gave him a glower, then strode back to her SUV, yanked the key out of the ignition and started for the restaurant's entrance again.

He followed. "You're not gonna lock your door?"

"This is Salt Lick. No one steals cars in this town."

She hardly recognized her own voice. Her nose was so plugged from crying, her speech was affected and she had to breathe through her mouth. Dear God. She had become a mouth-breather. And in the presence of the best-looking man she had met in years.

"'Zat right? If I were a car thief, I might think this is a pretty good place to practice my profession. The local sheriff is a joke."

Without more talk, he held the entry door for her to walk through and they settled into one of the pink vinyl-upholstered booths. A larger-than-life black and white portrait of Elvis Presley hung on the wall directly in Sandi's line of sight. Other '60s memorabilia decorated the walls. Black and white tiles covered the floor in a checkerboard pattern. Black metal chairs with pink padded seats were parked at white Formica tables.

Sandi took all of it in, amazed. She had eaten Hogg's food when Aunt Ed had provided it, but she had never been inside the restaurant. "This place looks like a cartoon," she muttered.

"Food's good though."

She diverted her gaze to him. He was looking at her intently with those blue, blue eyes, his forearms resting on the table and showing pronounced veins below his rolled-up sleeves. A little buzz zinged through her system.

He smiled, showing perfect straight teeth. He certainly had a good dentist. "You're staring at me. What's wrong? Is my eye makeup smeared all over my face?"

"Only a little."

She quickly wiped under her eyes with her fingertips. "Better?"

"You look great. We ran into each other yesterday at that beauty parlor for dogs up in Midland. My name's Nick Conway in case you forgot. But I didn't catch your name."

True. With all of the commotion of feisty puppies barking and milling and Prissy swooning, she hadn't introduced them. A memory of what Fiona had said about him and Sylvia Armbruster burst into Sandi's head: ...*I know absolutely everything about him, and I mean everything. I even know the size of his ding-dong. Why do you think I'm dying to meet him? A guy who brings that much to the party? Well ... what can I say?*...

Sandi's cheeks warmed at awareness of such intimate details about this man who was a virtual stranger. Was what Fiona had said true? Sandi couldn't keep a visual from forming. Then, there was the encounter on the highway earlier.

... Speaking of plans, is it your plan to stand in the road and get run over? Do I need to get another rope?...

She still smarted over that tacky remark.

After all of that, how could she not feel as if she knew him? But she wasn't sure she liked him. Why had she agreed to have a meal with a jerk, sexy with a big ding-dong or otherwise? "Did you fix the fence?"

"Nope. I don't fix fences. But I got somebody else to do it."

She waited for more information. When none came, she said, "My name's Sandi. I own LaBarkery a few doors down the mall from the Pampered Pooch."

"What's that, a dress store?"

Was he dense or what? "Who would name a dress shop LaBarkery? I sell gourmet food for dogs and cats. And a few other pets."

"You don't say."

She made a mental gasp. He had absolutely no interest in who she was or what she did. "I made up the name myself. Bark as in LaBarkery? Get it? It's supposed to be clever."

"I get it. I didn't know pets needed gourmet food."

"Gourmet might be the wrong word. What I sell, really, is fresh, healthy food I make myself."

"Sounds expensive. Speaking of food, what would you like to eat?"

She gave him a squint-eye, then swept her gaze up to the white menu with black letters and numbers hanging over the order counter. Hogg's was supposed to be a fast-food place, but their menu was widely varied.

When she didn't answer right away, he said, "Order whatever you like. I'm gonna have the Hogg's Special."

"What is that?"

"It's a burger." He pointed to the menu. "Look at Number One."

She read through the description of Number One: Double lean beef patties, three thick slices of bacon, two slices of cheddar cheese, grilled onions and jalapenos. And a fried egg. All of it topped off with a Texas-size helping of Hogg's homemade chili. It came with a pile of French fries drenched with Hogg's special sauce.

She turned back to him, her eyes bugged. "Oh, my Lord. If you eat all that, you might need an ambulance. And the last I heard, the nearest hospital is all the way up in Odessa."

"I like living dangerous. What would you like to eat? Go ahead and order."

She returned her attention to the menu. "Well, not much, really....Maybe some chicken tenders. Hm. Then again, maybe not. I don't know if I'm in the mood for eating fowl right now. And they're deep-fried. Still, they look like the only thing on the menu that isn't loaded with calories....Oh, wait, I know. I could have a Hogg's Chili Dog. I haven't had a chili dog in ages. But that's probably super fattening and they say hot dogs are so unhealthy. ... Hey, they serve breakfast all day. I could have —"

"Ma'am, please. I'm hungry. Pick something."

She gave him a glare and a gasp. "Look, you're the one who asked me in here. I didn't ask you."

He shrugged and arched his brow.

"You know what? A small plain hamburger is just fine. A child's size."

"Baby hamburger. Coming up." He scooted out of the booth and walked to the order counter, giving Sandi another excellent view of his very fine butt in his tight Wranglers. But after Fiona's drunken remarks, that wasn't the part that drew her.

Thinking of sex, her boyfriend floated into her mind. Had she ever seen Richard in a pair of tight jeans? The answer to that question was a resounding no. If he wore jeans at all, he wore "mom jeans." His body was a pathetic comparison to the one standing at the counter placing an order for hamburgers.

She pinched herself mentally. Richard might not be a hard body with a big ding-dong, but he was steady, with a good education and a good income. He didn't smoke, didn't do drugs and drank only moderately. They were as comfortable with each other as a brother and sister and nothing was wrong with that. Surely, long happy relationships were based on comfort.

Being around Nick Conway would lead to something different from comfort. Sex. Red hot sex. The kind that wakes you from a sound sleep. And that was anything but comfortable.

Nick's return to the booth interrupted those wayward thoughts. He carried a tray laden with food and two tall Styrofoam cups. He began to unload everything off the tray and set it on the table. Two baskets of hamburgers and fries and a couple of Hogg's locally-famous fried pies enclosed inside parchment wrappers. Folded over, they were not much smaller than a dinner plate.

She stared at the array of food. "That's a lot of food. I don't see a small hamburger."

"A child's hamburger is the size of a quarter. Not enough to eat. I got you a regular size."

Controlling jerk. Sandi made a huff of annoyance. "You also got fried pies. What kind?"

"Apricot. The kind my granny used to make when I was a little tyke. Hogg's uses lard in the crust, just like my granny did. That's why they taste so good."

She made a mental groan. "A fried pie made by these people probably has about five thousand calories."

His brow scrunched into a frown. "You're not gonna eat a fried pie after I got you one?"

She shook her head. "I am not. I did not ask for a fried pie. You obviously aren't concerned with your diet, but I try to limit the fat and carbs I eat. I don't want to have a heart attack before I'm thirty-five and I want to be able to pass through the front door of my shop."

He scooted the fried pie across the table toward her. "One little fried pie is not gonna give you a heart attack or put twenty pounds on you. Maybe a dose of sugar will put you in a better mood."

She hadn't eaten since breakfast. Now that food was before her, she really was hungry. She stared at the pie, tempted. "Welll...I know the fried pies are good. I've had them before. My aunt always buys them." She peeled back the wrapper, broke off a small corner, put it into her mouth and chewed the heavenly confection, its flaky layers rich with lard and butter and perfectly fried to a golden brown. She wanted to just grab it and gobble it up, but she couldn't let herself be so undisciplined.

He was looking at her as if he was eager for her to say something, so she complied. "Do you know that even after all these years, this place still claims that Elvis Presley loved their fried pies? And they claim they shipped them to him in Memphis many times."

Nick looked around at their surroundings, laughing. "I've been hearing those Elvis stories ever since I first moved here. You believe that stuff about him eating here?"

"Why not?"

"I don't know. I just can't figure out how and why a music icon like Elvis Presley ever even passed through a burg like this." Nick unwrapped his thick burger and bit into it, smearing chili all the way to his nose. He grabbed a napkin and wiped his mouth while he chewed.

"It was in the early days of his career. Before he got so famous." Sandi broke off another tiny bite of the fried pie and munched on it, barely restrained herself from moaning with delight. "They say his bus had mechanical problems and he had to stay here overnight. He fell in love with Hogg's food. He wasn't the healthiest eater, you know." She broke off a larger chunk of the pie and popped it into her mouth.

Nick's wide shoulders lifted in a shrug. "I've never kept up with Elvis. But if he ever really came in here, I can believe the part about him falling in love with the food."

She picked up a Styrofoam cup, lifted the plastic lid and looked inside. "What's this?"

"Iced tea. No sugar." He settled back into the seat and gave her another cute grin, as if he were proud of his cleverness, which did nothing to help her erase a naked Nick and a big ding-dong from her mind.

All at once, the coincidence of running into him again and in Salt Lick, of all places, dawned on Sandi. Located sixty-five miles southwest of Midland, the tiny town wasn't exactly on the beaten path. "What are you doing in Salt Lick, Mr. Conway?"

"I work here. Out at the Flying C."

Naturally, he worked on a ranch. He was obviously a cowboy. "Oh. That's the ranch owned by the local rich guy. My aunt and her partner know him."

"I imagine everybody in town knows Harley. Probably everybody in Texas. Yeah, he's rich. More oil wells than he can count. But he's still a good guy."

"I thought you lived in Midland."

"Not right now. I grew up in Midland though. I've still got my place up there. I'm here most of the time, but I go up there when I get a chance. Mostly on weekends."

"What kind of place?"

"Some grazing land and a house and a barn. What are you doing here?"

"Visiting a relative. I brought a parrot down to my aunt."

"A parrot," he said, a flat expression on his face. "You mean a big colorful bird?"

"I had to find him a good home." From out of the blue, a new spate of tears filled Sandi's throat and eyes and began to slide down her cheeks. "I took him in after the SPCA rescued him. I'm a...I'm a...rescue animal foster parent."

He gave her a quizzical look. "A what?"

"I'm a registered foster parent for unwanted animals," she wailed, her voice hitching.

She put down her fried pie and shook her head, turned to her purse and rummaged for a fresh Kleenex. After she mopped her eyes and nose, she glanced at him. He was looking at her with bewilderment. He probably thought she had lost her mind. She almost concurred. Why was she so grief-stricken over a parrot?

"Is that what's got you so upset?"

"I'm not upset." A new wave of tears burst out. "I just hate parting with him. I think I fell in love with him."

A long pause while he sat and watched her compose herself. Finally, he said something. "I can understand, I guess. I like animals myself. I lost my dog a few months ago and I'm still stewing over it. I feel like I lost a brother." He took another bite of his burger and gave her a long look as he chewed. "I've also got an old horse I've had since I was a boy and a couple of llamas my neighbor abandoned."

"You don't strike me as the llama type."

"I can't stand to see any animal starve to death. The sheriff's office was gonna haul them off. I knew what that meant, so I took them. At least they pay their way. I have them sheared and sell their wool. Come spring, I'll probably try to sell them. This parrot. Is he big? Little?" He formed his thumb and finger into a measuring gesture.

"Are you making a joke? He's an African Grey. On the vet's scale, he weighs two pounds, give or take. The size of a small chicken."

"Never heard of African Grey, but I know this much. Birds aren't like dogs. From what I know about birds, you're probably just as well off to be rid of one. Looks to me like a pet bird the size of a chicken could be a helluva lot of trouble."

"He is...was.... But he was fun, too." She sobbed again, sopping her cheeks and eyes with her napkin.

He heaved a sigh. "Ma'am, I don't think I'm gonna be able to let you drive back to Midland alone. You're in no shape—"

"My shape is none of your business. You're not—you're not the boss of me."

"You're too upset. If you had a wreck, I'd feel guilty."

He was right. She needed to pull herself together. Waffle and a herd of animals that depended on her waited at home. She drew a deep sniff and wiped her eyes. "If you're thinking of driving me to Midland, forget it. I'm fine now."

"Uh-huh. I can see that. Look, maybe you could think about it another way. Maybe you could be glad the parrot's gone. I'll bet he lived inside your house and I'm sure he made a hulluva mess. Now that he's gone, you don't have to clean up after him."

"Don't say that." She broke into tears again. "I didn't mind. He cooed to me when I left him."

"You loved him, he loved you. A real romance, huh?" He dragged a French fry through his puddle of Hogg's Special Sauce. "What makes you think he loved you? Birds aren't capable of emotion. They function from instinct, not intelligence. A two-pound bird's brain is probably the size of a marble."

Sandy gasped. "How do you know so much?"

"A lot of animal science in college. And logic."

"College? Oh, really. And what college did you attend? You're a ... you're a *cowboy*."

His pointed glare came at her like a spear. "I caught that sneer when you said that. What, you think cowboys can't go to college?"

She closed her eyes and heaved a sigh. "I didn't mean that. I went to college in Odessa and there were plenty of cowboys who were students."

"Then what did you mean?"

"All I meant was I didn't think...I mean, I assumed...You just don't strike me as a college man."

"I don't strike you as a llama man, either, but the two I've got aren't a mirage."

"Did you ... graduate?"

"Sure did. Got a BS. And that doesn't stand for bullshit. Went to Texas Tech on a football scholarship. Got a degree in biology. Been through A&M's range management program. Studied grasslands enhancement with Dow Chemical. I've got a Masters in animal nutrition. That enough education for you?"

Her mind blanked out. Now she felt foolish and embarrassed. He knew more about nutritious food for animals than she did. "Okay, okay. I apologize for stereotyping. I shouldn't have jumped to conclusions." She toyed with her napkin. "I'm not thinking clearly. Maybe you're right. Maybe I am a little upset. You're the manager of the Flying C Ranch?"

"Yep. All of what I just told you and a few years' experience qualifies me to be the general manager of just about any spread in Texas. And that's what I do. A man's gotta make a living."

"Managing a big ranch must be a good job."

"It is. It's like being a CEO. And I like it. Provides me with damn near everything a man could want."

"Believe it or not, I know how you feel. I like what I do, too. I'm not making a fortune in my little business, but I'm making enough. And the personal satisfaction would be hard to give up. I suppose it depends on your priorities."

He nodded, chewing on another bite of burger. He had eaten more than half of the super-size burger.

She looked down at her own food. The fried pie had disappeared. Without even realizing it, she had eaten all of it. He tilted his head toward the empty wrapper that had held it. "You must've decided that fried pie wasn't too fattening after all. Want another?"

She ducked her chin, glared at him from beneath her brow and drew a long breath. "Please do not patronize me."

"Wouldn't dream of it, ma'am." He shrugged. "But you obviously know that old saying."

"What old saying? And don't call me ma'am."

"The one that says, 'Life's uncertain. Eat dessert first.'" He nodded toward her hamburger. "I hate to see you waste that hamburger. Somewhere in the world, some little kid would —"

"Please. Are you deliberately trying to annoy me?"

"Just trying to put you in a better mood."

"Well, stop trying. I don't want to be in a better mood."

"I had them cut that burger in half. If you can't eat all of it, you can take the other half home with you. Growing up, I was taught not to waste food."

She composed herself and wolfed down half of the hamburger. He went to the counter and returned with a to-go box in which he placed the other half of her hamburger.

Soon, they were leaving Hogg's, her with a half of a hamburger in her satchel. Daylight had already turned to twilight. He walked her to her car door. She scooted behind the wheel and looked up at him. "Thank you for supper."

"You're welcome. Sure you're okay to drive now?"

"I'm fine, I told you."

"Okay, then."

He closed her car door and she started the engine. He stood back and touched the brim of his hat. "You be careful, you hear?"

Without giving him another look, she backed out and drove out of the parking lot.

☆ ☆ ☆

That woman's crazy, Nick thought. And he hated thinking that because appearance-wise, she was the kind of woman he liked—pretty hair and eyes, tall, well-built and healthy-looking. Biologically speaking, except for the fact that she was a few years older than eighteen, she was a perfect specimen for propagation. And she was passionate. No more time than he had spent around her, he had seen that much. In his mind, passionate trumped crazy. In his experience, passionate women liked red hot sex and that was mostly all he wanted or needed from a woman.

☆ ☆ ☆

That guy is even better looking than I remember, Sandi thought. And he was intriguing. But the word "intriguing" didn't explain her visceral reaction every time she had been in his presence. She'd had two husbands and she couldn't say that she had ever found either one of them intriguing nor had either of them made her stomach tremble.

As she neared the curve in the road where she had encountered Nick earlier in the day, she eased her foot off the accelerator and slowed to a crawl, scanning for livestock that might have escaped the fence. She saw nothing but a panoramic expanse of flat pasture, mesquite trees and sage brush and several seesawing pump jacks. Plenty of oil, but no cow. And no cowboy.

Chapter 9

THE NEXT MORNING, before daylight, a cold nose and a whine awoke Sandi from a troubled sleep. She sat up slowly. Her eyes felt scratchy and sore after yesterday's crying jag. Waffle darted to the doorway and stood wagging his tail and anxiously looking at her. When she didn't rise immediately, he ran back to her and placed a paw on her knee.

"What is it, boy? What do you want?"

On a canine whine, he started out of the bedroom, stopping once to look back at her. With a groan, she got to her feet and followed him. He beelined to Jake's room and began to whine and spin in front of the closed door. He typically went to Jake's bedroom door first thing every morning, but he didn't usually appear so fretful. Then it dawned on Sandi that he must be able to tell that the parrot wasn't inside the room.

"He went to a new home, sweetheart."

She opened the door, instinctively holding her breath. Sometimes the smell when she first opened Jake's door took her breath. Nick's words from last evening rushed at her:...*Maybe you could be glad the*

*parrot's gone. Now you don't have to clean up after him. I'm
sure he made a hulluva mess. ...*

A little part of her that she hated acknowledging
clapped with glee at seeing the empty room. She shut it
down. She had been Jake's savior. Who could say what
would have happened to him if she hadn't been willing
to act as his foster caretaker. "See? He isn't here," she
said to Waffle.

She had never seen anything that looked as
lonely as Jake's empty room. When she had given the
bedroom over to him, she had removed everything that
didn't have a hard surface that she could wash,
including the carpet. She had spent money she couldn't
afford to spend on laminate flooring that was easy to
mop. This morning, seeing dollar signs with wings
made her even gloomier.

The bird's shoulder-height perch stood in the
middle of the room. The square white Formica table
where he ate looked bare and cold. The small table
where she had tried to teach him to go potty most of the
time stood in the corner, its surface clean. The cabinet
where she kept his supplies and toys stood open-
doored, its shelves empty. She had taken everything of
Jake's to her aunt in Salt Lick. New tears burned her
eyes.

Waffle walked in and looked around, sniffed
everything, then looked back at her with big
questioning eyes, a keening sound coming from his
throat.

"Oh, Waffle..."

Stop it, Sandi!

She had no time for this. What was she doing
grieving over a damn bird? Having him gone was going
to free up hours of her time. When she agreed to take
him, the plan had been for her to keep him for a short

time while the SPCA found him a new home. She would have stuck with it except that the SPCA appeared to have made little effort to relocate Jake. WLA had found him a place with her, so everyone stopped worrying about him. That was what was annoying about the SPCA and the animal shelter. Half the time, they failed to follow through. That was how she had ended up with a menagerie. And now poor Betty Ann, her employee, was finding herself in the same boat.

Sandi quickly dried her eyes. "We have to hurry, Waffle. Betty Ann and Jessica are already at the shop making raw food. Come on, now, and eat your breakfast." She grasped the dog's collar and dragged him toward the kitchen.

In the kitchen, she found that Waffle had already nosed into her bag, opened the Styrofoam box in which the half a hamburger she had brought home from Hogg's had been stashed and helped himself. She fed him anyway, then threw together a quick breakfast for herself.

While she ate, she watched the local news on the small TV she kept in the kitchen. The news anchor came on with a mug shot of John Wilson and a report that the damning DNA evidence against him had been illegally obtained and might be thrown out of court. Any minute now, she expected to see a picture of Richard grinning at the camera. Disgusted with Richard and his client and the whole situation, she clicked off the TV.

She hurriedly showered and shampooed, dressed in jeans and a T-shirt and pulled her long hair back in a ponytail. When she returned to the kitchen, Waffle was lying prone, his chin resting on the floor. "Oh, baby." She squatted and pulled his head to her chest. "I know you're sad. We just have to get through it."

☆ ☆ ☆

At LaBarkery, Sandi went through the motions. While Betty Ann and Jessica ground and mixed the raw food to be sold in bulk, Sandi mixed, molded and baked cookies she labeled "Barkies." Made of fresh ground turkey, eggs, cooked brown rice, a chopped broccoli-carrots-cauliflower mix, a smidgen of dried rosemary and tiny chunks of peeled apple for natural sweetness, her customers' pets loved them.

She liked them herself, even ate a few. These days, instead of buying lunch or bringing it from home, she often grazed on her homemade pet food. The recipe fit into the healthier lifestyle she had adopted after her divorce and with no flour, the baked items were gluten-free.

In the beginning, she had baked a couple dozen Barkies a day and had an empty showcase at the end of the day. Responding to demand, her production had now grown to fifteen dozen a day. Thus, every morning, she found herself in the kitchen in the back of her store baking Barkies. Sometimes she was there before daylight.

At this pace, soon she would need more space for a bigger kitchen and even another employee. She was in the process of copyrighting her recipes and looking into packaging the various items she baked for mail order. If she started marketing on her website, she could definitely need more hired people and space.

"Are you upset about something?" Betty Ann asked.

"A little. I took Jake to his new home yesterday."

Jessica chimed in. "Aww. I'm sorry. I know you're going to miss him. I'm going to miss hearing stories about him."

Sandi nodded as she used an ice cream scooper to place another Barkie on a cookie sheet. "But he had to go. My home is only a temporary stopover for most of my animals. Finding them a new place is what I'm supposed to do." Tears welled behind her eyes again. She shook her head. "I can't talk about it. It makes me sad and I've got too much to do to let it distract me."

"Okay, we won't mention it again," Betty Ann said.

"But who knows what might have happened to him if it hadn't been for you," Jessica said. "He went to live with your aunt, right?"

Sandi made a mental huff of frustration. "Girls, come on now. We aren't going to talk about it, okay?"

She had just pulled the first sheet of cookies from the oven when the phone rang and she picked up. Richard. He didn't even say hello. Instead, his first words were, "Well, did you get rid of him?"

She burst into tears and hung up. "Why do I tolerate Richard and his attitude about my animals?" she asked the air. "He has no soul. He only cares about criminals."

Betty Ann and Jessica exchanged knowing looks.

Seconds later, the phone rang again. Neither Betty Ann nor Jessica, up to their elbows in raw meat, was in a position to answer the phone, so Sandi picked up again.

"I'm sorry, Sandi," Richard said. "I didn't mean to sound mean. I've just got a lot on my mind."

"Oh, really? Well, I heard on this morning's news that the court might throw out the DNA evidence on John Wilson, so that should make you happy."

"Oh, baby, it does. I'm waiting to see if my man goes free."

"But you know he's guilty. He's already confessed."

"A coerced confession. Not worth the paper it's written on. I've never asked him if he's guilty and he's never told me."

Sandi's eyes rolled involuntarily. How many times had she heard Richard say he never asked his clients if they were guilty? "That is nonsense. You know he confessed. You're being dishonest, Richard, and endangering the citizens of Midland."

"Whoa! What is this? I'm trying to get the guy a fair shake. You're beating me up over what?"

"You know what. We've talked about this a dozen times. I'm in no mood to deal with it today. I'm too upset."

"About what? A friggin' bird? Is it too much to expect a little support from the woman who's supposed to be my girlfriend?" After a long pause, a huge sigh came over the line. "We need to talk about those animals, Sandi. I'll be honest. I've been wondering how your menagerie is going to mesh with our future. One loud-mouthed bird was only part of the problem."

"You know what, Richard? Maybe I've got a few problems myself. Maybe I'm not worried about meshing with our future. Maybe I don't want a...a heartless, soulless...*lout* in my life!"

"Lout? Did you say lout? Sandi, you don't mean that. Just a minute—"

"Do not "just-a-minute" me. You think you'd have a hard time living with me and my animals? I don't have enough pens and papers to write down all of the things about you that get on my nerves, Richard." She hung up with a loud *Clack!*

Waffle looked up at her anxiously, as he always did when she raised her voice. She had never had a dog that was so intuitive. "That's that, boy," she said to him. "The next thing he'd be telling me is he doesn't want me to have *you.*"

Chapter 10

Friday, a week later...

SANDI WAS ON the way to putting put her grief at parting with Jake behind her. Still, she hadn't altogether abandoned concerns about him. After sliding three dozen Barkies to be sold over the weekend into the oven, she called her aunt to check on him.

"Sandi," Aunt Ed said first thing. "How are you, hon?"

After they exchanged how-are-yous, Sandi said, "And how's Jake? Are all of you getting along?"

"Great. Doing a little remodeling, but —"

"Remodeling for Jake?"

"We're ripping the carpet out of his room. You must've forgotten to tell me how well his bowels work."

Oh, hell. Indeed she had neglected a discussion with her aunt about how messy Jake was. "I'm sorry, Aunt Ed. I just assumed you knew...I mean, well, he's a bird. And birds poop on things. I'll admit I didn't think of that when I first agreed to take him. After I figured out they might never find another home for him, I started to realize I had to make some changes."

"Like what?"

"I had to re-do the bedroom. I added only hard surfaces that could be washed. Then I hired a cleaning service to come in once a week."

To Sandi's relief, her aunt cackled. "My God, he not only eats like a gourmet, he has to have a maid. This parrot might turn out to be a more expensive pet than a horse. Don't worry about it, hon. The important thing is that Vic loves him and they're getting along great. You should see the big cage he's built for him at the Styling Station."

Her aunt followed up with a long description of an elaborate set-up that Sandi couldn't quite picture.

"I'd love to see it. I'll drive down one day pretty soon."

Sandi disconnected, her thoughts channeled in a new direction. Just because her aunt was pleased with Jake now didn't mean she would still want him a few months from now. Sandi thought about the painter she had gotten quotes from for re-painting the walls in Jake's room. Maybe she should hold off on having that done, just in case her aunt suddenly had a change of heart and Jake ended up moving back to Midland. She had planned to locate her office back in that room, but she might continue to use the dining room table a little longer.

Otherwise, her life was finally settling down. She had made up with Richard. He had brought her flowers and chocolates and an apology. He had taken her to dinner at the best steakhouse in Midland. He had even taken her to Tag Freeman's Double-Kicker Barbecue & Beer, one of the hottest fun spots in town. She had accepted his gifts and extra attention, although she wasn't sure why. She was more certain than ever that their relationship had nowhere to go.

He was in a great mood. The story of John Wilson's botched DNA test in Midland had made headlines across the country. Richard had even done an interview for the local CBS-TV station that had filtered to the affiliates in major cities. He and the case had briefly been the talk of the town.

John Wilson's trial appeared to be on a track to be thrown out of court and he would soon be released on bail. Mrs. Bean and all the good she had done in her long life had gotten lost in the legal haggling. A woman who would be hard pressed to find the will and strength to kill a mosquito had been savagely beaten and her throat had been cut. An extreme act when all it would have taken from the intruder was a firm reprimand to 'keep quiet' about the theft that had occurred.

Then, in the blink of an eye, everything had changed. Yesterday afternoon, the judge had ruled that the DNA evidence was acceptable after all and rescinded Wilson's bail. When Sandi heard the news on TV, she had cheered. Richard would be devastated, but she wasn't sorry to see a monster return to jail. She should have called Richard and consoled him, but she could not. And the fact that she couldn't and didn't had probably done untold damage to the fragile relationship that they had just put back together.

☆☆☆

Debbie Sue arrived at the Styling Station early, toting the *Odessa American* newspaper. She spread it on Edwina's work station with the headline obvious: "Midland Man Held Without Bond." And the story went on from there.

Edwina soon came in the back door. "Morning," she sang.

"Did you see the news this morning?"

"If you're talking about John Wilson, yes, I did. Is there a reason I should care?"

"Ed. He's guilty."

"Debbie Sue, I know where you're headed. And I'm repeating this has nothing to do with us."

"But it might. They might need us. We should be ready in case they do."

"Why, on God's green earth, would the Midland PD need us?"

"I'm just saying—"

"Well, don't be saying, Debbie Sue. This is one time I'm putting my foot down. I've got all I can handle with dealing with this damn parrot. You know what he said to me this morning? He told me my lime green glasses didn't look good and he bit my finger when I fed him a grape. I nearly slapped him."

"You can't slap the parrot, Ed. Your niece would come down here and take him back."

"I can only hope."

"And what would you tell Vic?"

"That damn bird would make a nice meal. As much money as he has cost me, he would be the most expensive poultry we've ever had.

☆☆☆

Nick had heard that the two women who owned the Styling Station were excellent barbers. His hair, being naturally wavy, required skillful cutting to keep it simple and manageable. Having taken the day off, he headed to the beauty salon for a haircut.

The salon obviously had formerly been a gas station. He couldn't guess its age, but a pair of round gasoline pumps stood outside the red limestone rock building. Today, the antique pumps were dressed up in Halloween costumes and surrounded by pumpkins and black and white skeletons. The scene looked odd, but in the few months he had lived in Salt Lick, he had learned that a lot of things in this town were odd.

He was gradually growing accustomed to the place's eccentricities. The hand-painted sandwich sign that stood near the beauty shop's front door, for instance:

GOT A CHEATING SPOUSE OR SIGNIFICANT
OTHER?
DON'T GET MAD, GET EVEN.
CALL THE DOMESTIC EQUALIZERS.
555-1212

Harley Carruthers had told him the two women who owned the salon called themselves detectives and had actually solved the mystery of his former wife's murder. That piece of information had left Nick stunned. He had never known anybody associated with so violent a crime. That it had occurred in a desert burg like Salt Lick was incredible enough, but to learn the victim had been the wife of one of the nicest guys Nick had ever met as well as one of the richest fell into the realm of pure fiction.

Salt Lick appeared to be the epitome of an all-American small town. Not quite the Norman Rockwell type, but still as wholesome and clean as a desert town with a shortage of water could be.

Walking into the salon, the first thing he noticed was the far corner and what looked something like a cramped jail cell, except that it was made of new two-by-twos. It housed a mini-jungle.

A parrot sat perched on a round bar that spanned the width of the structure. This must be the bird the weepy redhead had told him about. He walked over to what could only be called a cage. Other than having the basic look of a parrot, the bird didn't look like anything special. Gray and white and a couple of red tail feathers. Typical parrot's head and thick beak.

"Mr. GQ Cowboy," the bird squawked and ruffled its feathers. "What an asshole."

Nick frowned. He had heard that bird before. Did the damn thing recognize him? "Did he say what I think he said?"

"He did," the younger hairdresser said.

That would be Debbie Sue Overstreet. She was a good-looking woman who appeared to be close to his age. Her husband, a Texas Ranger captain, was a local legend, but Nick had never met him. The locals rarely saw him. He was usually down at the Mexican border chasing drug traffickers and people smugglers.

Debbie Sue walked up beside him. "That's Jake. He's got a potty mouth, but we're trying to re-train him."

"Oh, yeah? Good luck with that. I can't imagine how you would go about training a bird in the first place, much less re-training one."

He stared into the cage at a snarl of branches and perches, obviously put together with skill and care. "Who built the fancy cage?"

"My husband," the tall skinny one said. She, too, crossed the room to look into the cage at the parrot.

That would be Edwina, the redhead's aunt. She had a few years on Debbie Sue. Nick guessed her to be around forty-five. Harley had told him about her husband too, but Nick had never met him either. He was eager to meet a true military hero.

He turned and faced the two women. "I need a haircut."

"You've come to the right place, cowboy," the aunt said. "You're the general manager out at the Flying C, aren't you?"

"I am." Nick put out his right hand. "Nick Conway. And you are?"

She took his hand. "Edwina Perkins-Martin, at your service. You're the guy my niece met on the highway a couple of weeks ago, aren't you? The day she brought Jake down here." She tipped her head toward the cage.

Nick's memory spun backward two weeks. How could he forget seeing any woman wearing a dress and sandals trying to shoo a cow and her calf off the highway, especially if the woman was a gorgeous redhead?

Debbie Sue laughed. "The one Jake calls an asshole." She, too, put out her right hand. "I'm Debbie Sue Overstreet."

Not knowing if Sandi had revealed she'd had supper with him the day she brought the parrot down, he chose not to mention it. "I remember running into her. So she just up and left her parrot with you."

"Oh, it isn't her parrot any longer," Edwina said. "My husband would take a machete to somebody who tried to take that bird away from him. Me, on the other hand, I might take a machete to the bird. He craps on everything in sight."

Nick laughed. "That's a bird for you. Keeping one this size penned up indoors would create a lot of work for somebody."

"In spite of what Ed says about him, everyone loves him," Debbie Sue said. "Her husband is taking him to the football game tonight. He used to live in a sports bar, so he's a football fan."

Ah, yes. High school football and Friday nights. Legendary in Texas. "Who, the parrot? Or her husband?" Nick followed up with a chuckle.

Debbie Sue ducked her chin and gave him a deadpan look. "The parrot. Ed's husband couldn't care less about a football game."

Nick made another quick stroll down memory lane. He had played football from eighth grade forward until he graduated from college. He had been blessed with the smarts and leadership skills as well as the physical size, strength and coordination to win a full-ride scholarship and play quarterback. He thanked his Maker every day. Being able to hold his own among the best of them had bought him an education at Texas Tech University and an opportunity to escape the debilitating poverty into which he had been born.

"I haven't yet made it to a Salt Lick Steers game," he said. "I'm not familiar with six-man football's rules."

"Jake loves football. Ed's husband has been teaching him some of the cheers the cheerleaders do. He's going to take him down to the sidelines and the girls are going to do cheers with him."

"*Awrrk,*" Jake piped. "Go Steers. Get that sonofabitch! Break his fuckin' leg!"

"Ain't that a hoot?" Edwina said. "So, cowboy, are we gonna cut your hair today or play with the bird?"

"What the fuck? What the... *Fuuuck?*" Jake squawked. "What an asshole."

"Oh, my God," Edwina said. "I'm so sorry. We have absolutely no control over what he says."

"He does say a lot of words, doesn't he?"

"He more than *says* words," Debbie Sue said. "He knows what they mean and he can solve problems. He's even got opinions on everything."

"Debbie Sue and I are teaching him about politics," the aunt said. "Some of our customers have started asking him for advice, so we're coaching him to tell them who to vote for. We figure we can influence elections that way."

Was she serious? Casting her a skeptical look, Nick took a seat in her chair. A newspaper lay on the counter with a headline about John Wilson not being released from jail after all. Nick had seen that report on this morning's TV news, but he hadn't seen it in a newspaper. He picked up the paper.

"Do you know that guy?" Edwina asked, draping him with a black plastic cape.

"I know about him and the murder he's accused of. Midland is more like a small town than a city. Home invasion and murder are a big deal."

"The dude's confessed," Debbie Sue said.

"But he's recanted his confession." Nick replied. "With all of the publicity the case has had, a jury might find him not guilty."

Debbie Sue assumed a sagely demeanor. "Just because he might get found not guilty doesn't mean he's innocent."

"True enough," Nick agreed. "He sounds like a tough customer. The evidence against him was pretty damning even without the DNA results. You ladies are interested in that crime?"

"We're interested in all crime," Debbie Sue said. "We're detectives. Didn't you see our sign out front? Your boss's former wife was our customer a few years back. Pearl Ann Carruthers. She was murdered and we found the killer."

"You don't say."

"Are we shampooing you today?" Edwina asked.

Uh-oh. That was an abrupt change in direction. Evidently the aunt didn't want to discuss their adventures as detectives. "Nope. Already did that at home. I can't see myself getting my hair washed in a beauty shop."

"Too bad.," Debbie Sue said. "Ed would give you a shampoo you'd never forget."

Edwina picked up a squirt bottle and doused his hair with water. "You're out early."

"Headed for Midland. I'm getting my new pup today. I want to spend the weekend bonding with him. Already got him a new doghouse, a new bed, some new toys and dishes and a new collar.

Nick had bought new puppy supplies that would stay at his place in Midland. With a heavy heart, he had thoroughly cleaned his old dog house at the Flying C for the new puppy to occupy when they were at the ranch. Buster was gone. It was time to move on.

"Aww. Really?" Debbie Sue said. "That's sweet. I love dogs. I've got three myself."

"Oh, yeah? What kind?"

"Strays. They just showed up and I kept them. Now they're like my kids."

"I know what you mean. Yep, the new dog's gonna be a good one. Still haven't thought of a name for him though." He had been trying for days to think of a name to give the new puppy, but nothing had come to him yet.

"Male or female?"

"Male."

Snipping away at his hair, Edwina looked at her partner and said, "Okay, we gotta come with a name for Nick's new dog."

From the wooden cage in the corner, the parrot said, "Awrrk! Felix. You're such a dog, Felix."

"Felix?" Nick said. "Did he say Felix?"

The bird followed up with what could only be described as gasping. "Felix. ... Oh, yes, that's it. Touch me there. ... Yes! Yes! Yes! Right there ..."

A pregnant pause followed. Warmth crept up Nick's neck. He angled a look toward the parrot.

Finally, Debbie Sue spoke. "See? We told you. He knows what we're talking about. I mean about naming your dog," she added quickly.

Nick laughed, relieved to get past the awkward moment. "Get outta here. A parrot might learn a few words, but no way does he know what they mean."

"Seriously," Debbie Sue said. "He's scary smart. And he mimics everything he hears. Dogs barking, coyotes howling. He yowls like Ed's cat and makes her think Gus is hurt. She drops everything and chases after the cat. We've already made a pact not to discuss anything confidential in front of him. The last thing we need is for him to repeat what he hears in here. Our customers do talk about secret stuff from time to time."

Nick laughed again. He left the Styling Station with a good haircut and an upbeat mood. Sandi's aunt and her partner were fun. As he drove, he idly wondered if he might run into Sandi again. She had seemed to

be friends with the woman who owned the Pampered
Pooch.

Chapter 11

BEFORE OPENING HER shop every day, Sandi sprayed her display cases with a mixture of vinegar and water and wiped them down so that they sparkled. She and Waffle played a game. He pressed his nose to the case, leaving a nose print. Swiping it away with her cloth, she laughed. "Waffle, did you know you're my best friend?"

The dog began to wag his long tail furiously, stretching his grin even wider. Sandi laughed so hard she barely heard the phone behind the counter.

When she picked up, Prissy greeted her with a whispery, out-of-breath voice. "He's here. He's picking up the baby."

Sandi's insides lurched. She didn't have to be told that the "he" was Nick Conway, even though she and Prissy hadn't had a conversation about him since the day they both met him. Scarcely a day had past that Sandi hadn't thought of Nick, but she had deliberately avoided passing on to Prissy the gossip Fiona had told her. She hadn't want to share such intimate details.

Keeping him in her mind as an erotic escape was one thing, but knowing he was a few doors up from where she stood sent a tremble from her head to her toes.

"Are you going to come up here and see him?"

The insistence in Prissy's voice brought her back to the moment. "Heavens, no. Why are you whispering?"

"Because he's in the next room. Come on up here."

"Why would I do that, Prissy?"

"Because when I told you he was here you stopped breathing, I mean you stopped breathing. I could hear it. I remember feeling that way when I was your age. I ended up married to him."

Sandi gave a little grunt of impatience. "I don't know why you think that. Trust me, I'm still breathing. I don't like him, Prissy. Have you forgotten I have a boyfriend? I'm not coming up there. Gotta run —"

"If you're not gonna come up here, I'm gonna send him down —"

"Prissy, no. That isn't necessary."

"Yes, it is. I'm sending him and Randy down to your shop for some treats."

"Who's Randy?"

"He named the puppy Randy. Isn't that sweet?"

"Randy, the cow dog? Wow. That has a real poetic ring to it."

Sandi heaved a sigh, accepting the inevitable. "Well I'm here and I'm open and I want to sell my stuff. He can come shopping any time just like any of my customers. But, I warn you, Prissy. He'd better not waste my time. He'd better buy something."

The minute she hung up, Sandi dashed to her tiny bathroom, ran a brush through her hair, checked her eye makeup and touched up her lipstick. The last time Nick had seen her, she had been a bawling, makeup-smeared mess. She intended for him to see her as the bank's customers used to see her — an attractive, well-put-together professional woman who had control of her circumstances.

She was bothered that a cowboy with whom she had nothing in common caused such a reaction within her. Not because there was a possibility of anything developing between them, but because a woman with a boyfriend shouldn't have those thoughts about another man.

Even if her ex-husbands hadn't been fully vested, in their relationships, she had been. If you truly cared about someone, another person couldn't make you feel things. Sexual things you should share only with your steady beau. Was it just John Wilson's trial that had cooled her attraction to Richard? Or was it a total lack of chemistry between them. God, she wished she had some answers.

Next, she grabbed a leash from the hook beside the phone. "Come on, Waff. You need to go outside and potty."

Once outside, Sandi led Waffle to a grassy area in the vacant lot behind the strip center where he could relieve himself.

A deep male voice came from inside her store. "Hellooo? Anybody here?"

Damn that Prissy. "Hold on," she shouted back. "I'll be right there."

Sandi walked briskly through the back doorway, unhooked Waffle's leash and closed him in the back room. Then she entered her showroom. She recognized the customer immediately. It was him, all right. Damn it all to hell, it was him. Hard body, tight jeans, cowboy hat and boots. And cradled in his arms was the golden puppy and it was sound asleep.

She mustered her composure and tried to speak as if her heart weren't pounding. "Hi. Can I help you? I was out back with my dog. I see you have your baby, uh, I mean puppy."

She had momentarily forgotten the sweet loveable puppy was only a dog to him.

"Yep," he said, looking down at the sleeping puppy. "He's taking a nap. The lady at that grooming shop told me you might have some stuff I'll need. You weren't feeling well the last time I saw you. You okay now?"

"Yes, yes, of course. I was just upset that day. I get attached to all of the animals I care for."

He looked around. "So this is your store, huh?"

"Indeed it is." She gestured around the showroom. "What would you like?"

"Maybe we could try some of that homemade dog food you were bragging about."

"Absolutely." She whisked a menu and price list from a holder on the wall. "LaBarkery pet food has no chemical additives. It's good for puppies as well as adult dogs. I also sell treats. Very healthy, easily digested—"

He pointed at her refrigerated display cases and the layer cakes that looked to be frosted with chocolate. "This looks like human food. Is that cake really for an animal?"

"Sure is. But you could eat it, too, if you were so inclined. We can discuss what it's made of if you're interested."

"All homemade, huh?"

"Every day. By me and my two employees." Sandi couldn't tell if he was impressed or making fun.

"The decorations are more for the owners than the pets. Not to eat themselves. I mean, they could, but they like them for their dogs and cats. Some of my customers have a special bond with their pets and they get a kick out of spoiling them."

"Uh-huh," he said, looking around the store again. "And I guess all these clothes and hats and such are the owners' idea too."

He wasn't the first customer to come into her store and scoff at the costumes on the shelves, some adorned with ruffles and bling. In this part of the country, some men in particular saw dogs as ranch hands or guard dogs and cats as barn cats. Others enjoyed dressing their pets in costumes. She usually took the mocking in stride, but this guy was yanking her chain.

"Tell you what," she said schooling her voice to be steady and laying the menu aside. "Let's look at some plain leashes for this little guy. You don't want to lose him. He'll be in the running away stage until you get him trained."

"I already got a leash. How about a muzzle? I forgot to get one when I was in PetSmart the other day."

Muzzle! Had he said muzzle? Surely she had heard wrong. Sandi steadied herself. "Why would you need a muzzle? He's only a puppy."

"And he'll be a dead puppy if he gets around horses or cows and starts barking and raising hell. I've got to train him not to bark around the pens that have livestock in them. It's for his own safety."

The sound of the back doorbell and the unmistakable click of Waffle's toenails on the tile floor caught her attention. Of course he could open the door.

His entrance was the only thing that saved her from breaking into a tirade against this dumb cowboy for what she felt were cruel methods of training.

Looking back, she smiled at her dog. "Hey, Waff, come see the baby."

Without warning, this stranger stepped toward Waffle. "Buster? Buster, is that you?"

Waffle let out a pitiful whine. He looked up at her, then back at the cowboy as if he was confused. His long tail began to whip and before she knew it, the puppy's new owner had handed her the sleeping baby and dropped to a squat near her knee. "Buster? Buster? C'mere, buddy."

Waffle charged forward as if he'd been shot from a cannon. He reared up and placed his front paws on Nick's shoulders, licking and whimpering and pushing him onto his back. He began to feverishly lap at Nick's face.

Nick scruffed his head and neck, wrapped his arms around his neck and hugged him. "It *is* you, buddy. It's you. Where have you been?"

Sandi had to take a step backward to keep from getting caught in the fray. In her wildest imaginings, she could not have foreseen what was taking place before her eyes. "Waffle! Waffle! Stop that! Bad dog!" She grabbed his collar and with great effort, pulled him back. "What are you doing? Bad dog."

Barking, the dog broke away from her and barked and danced and bounced around the room, then returned to Nick, who lay back on the floor propped on one elbow and laughing. "I taught him to do that little dance. He still remembers."

Sandi stood glued to the floor. Clearly Waffle knew Nick, but the lout couldn't possibly mean anything to her precious Waffle.

Still cradling the sleeping puppy, she reached down and yanked her dog back by his collar again. "Waffle! Settle down, boy, settle down."

Nick got to his feet, still laughing. He had lost his hat and she noticed his dark blond hair, mussed and slightly wavy. And he did have the nicest eyes and they showed a glimmer of wetness. *Tears?*

She thrust the puppy back to him, his hands came out reflexively and he cradled it in one arm. "I'm sorry he did that," she said. "He loves everyone who comes in the shop, but I've never seen him get so excited. He must have smelled—"

"Ma'am. Stop." Nick raised a hand, showing her his palm. His eyes held an intense look. "Just stop."

A feeling of dread crept up Sandi's spine. Some kind of nightmare was unfolding.

"Ma'am, that's my dog. The one I told you I lost. It was about nine months ago, just after I went to work for the Flying C." He bent and picked up his hat. "Man, I can't believe this. I'd given up ever finding him." He clapped the hat on his head, then pulled a handkerchief from his back pocket and dabbed at his eyes. He shook his head, then looked at her, his beautiful eyes alight with utter joy. "How long have you had him?"

Sandi could not let herself be distracted. She tilted her chin. "For a while. Quite a while, actually. Since he was a puppy."

He shook his head again. "Man, oh man. To think he's been this close all this time."

What? He didn't believe her? "You have to be mistaken. Waffle's my dog. He's part of me and part of my store. You can ask anyone."

"You saw his reaction—"

"I saw him get excited. That's not exactly something I haven't seen him do before."

A lie. Waffle never acted out. Lying was the only defense in this desperate situation.

Nick's handsome face morphed into a stare of incredulity. Then he smiled a killer smile. "Tell you what. I'm extremely grateful that you found him and that you've taken such good care of him. This little puppy's the same golden color. He's gonna be a pretty dog when he grows up. And you obviously like him. How 'bout you take him? I'll take Buster off your hands and we'll call it an even trade."

"I would never trade Waffle to someone like you," she snapped, a death grip on Waffle's collar.

Nick's fist reflexively jammed against his hip. "What do you mean, someone like me?"

"I've never muzzled him or left him to sleep outside or treated him like an... an..."

"Like a dog?" Nick finished.

Close to sputtering, all Sandi could manage was, "I love Waffle and he loves me."

"Look, I apologize for coming across wrong. I got overexcited when I realized I'd found my dog." His deep voice almost became a purr. Sexy and seductive. "I know that women who are alone tend to get involved with their pets, especially if they don't have much social life or kids to take care of and —

"What? You know nothing about me. About my life."

"Now don't get upset. I asked the woman who gave me this puppy about you. She told me you're divorced and don't have any kids, so you give all your love to animals."

Such a rage raced up Sandi's spine her head might explode and her eyes might burst from their sockets. She squelched the powerful urge to grab her head with both hands in case that very thing happened. She would kill that Prissy dead, dead, dead the very next time she saw her. "Prissy Porter discussed me and my personal life with you?" Her voice had become as shrill as a harpy's. "Why, in all my life, I've never been—"

"Now, calm down." Nick patted the air with his hand. "I didn't mean to upset you. What I mean is, you said you were in love with a parrot, too. What that says to me is you throw that "love" word around pretty freely. Maybe you need a boyfriend or something."

That was the last straw. "What?" She sank to the floor on her knees beside Waffle and wrapped protective arms around his neck. Summoning her dignity, she set her jaw and lifted her nose. "I'd like for you to leave my store, Mr. Conway."

"But —"

"I'd hate to call the police, but I will." She leveled a searing stare at him that said she meant business. But it was hard to be tough when she was sitting on the floor and he stood six feet tall above her. Their stares locked.

"Okay, I'll leave," he snapped. "But I'll be back. Buster is my dog and you can't refuse to give him to me." He reached down and stroked Waffle's head, putting only inches between her face and his. "Don't worry, Buster," he said to Waffle. "I'll be back to rescue you."

He straightened and stepped back. Waffle sprang forward. Even with all her strength, Sandi barely held him in check. She scrambled to her feet, still hanging onto his collar. "We'll see about that. Have you ever heard possession is nine-tenths of the law?"

He glared at her. "Oh, yeah? Have you ever heard a picture's worth a thousand words?"

He turned and stalked out of her shop. The minute he cleared the doorway, she shoved the deadbolt into place and hung up the CLOSED sign. Her heart pounded as she watched him climb into his pickup, still holding the puppy as he drove away. Waffle whined and fidgeted and barked.

Anxiety roiled Sandi's stomach. For a few seconds, she thought she might throw up. "God, Waffle," she stage-whispered. "You aren't really his dog, are you?"

He looked up at her anxiously, his long tail whipping.

"Whatever. You're happy here now. You've got playmates."

... But I'll be back. Buster is my dog and you can't refuse to give him to me. ... Don't worry, Buster. I'll be back to rescue you. ...

Rescue? Had he said RESCUE? The bastard. No dog could have a better home than Waffle had with her.

"Don't worry. I won't let you go and be a work dog. You deserve better. I'll put up a fight for you. I'm tired of people walking all over me. If this guy plans to take me on, he'd better pack a lunch."

She eased away from the door.

Suddenly a weekend at Aunt Ed's house seemed like a great idea. She stalked to the back room and found her cell phone on the counter, pressed in the Styling Station's number. Her aunt answered.

"Hi, Aunt Ed. Waffle and I miss Jake so much. We'd love to come and see him. You wouldn't like a house guest for the weekend, would you?"

"Abso-fuckin'-lutely, babygirl. You haven't spent the night at my house since you were a little girl.

Bring some rubber gloves and cleaning supplies when you come. After we swamp out Jake's room, we'll open a bottle of wine and cook up a big steak. Just put your little butt in that SUV and come on down.

"Listen, I'm going to do that. I just have to throw some things together. Is it okay if I bring Pablo and Adolph, too?"

"Who's that? We've only got two extra bedrooms now that Jake moved in."

"They're little dogs. At home, I keep them separated from the big dogs and Waffle sort of protects them. Without him there, I'm afraid they'll get hurt."

"Sure. We'll just have an animal party. As long as they don't beat up my cat."

Sandi had to laugh. "Aunt Ed, Waffle loves cats. And Pablo and Adolph together don't weigh fifteen pounds. Neither one of them could beat up a cat if he wanted to."

Next, she called Betty Ann and arranged for her to mind the store tomorrow. As she drove home, she called Juanita, her friend at WLA and asked her to go to her house tomorrow and do the morning feeding.

At home, she threw some toiletries and a change of clothing in a duffel, grabbed a small tub of dog food and beds and loaded all of it, including cleaning supplies, into the SUV. As she worked, she couldn't keep from thinking that though she loved all of these animals, they were certainly a lot of trouble. Finally, she loaded a snarling Pablo and a yipping Adolph into an oversize pet carrier and headed for Salt Lick.

☆☆☆

Nick sat in his truck in Wendy's parking lot finishing up a hamburger and deciding what to do next.

He had planned on spending the afternoon at Sylvia's house, but now that idea held no appeal. He called her and told her he wouldn't be stopping by after all.

He needed a different strategy to get Buster back. He had made a mistake barreling over Sandi and insisting on taking him. Of course she was attached to the dog. He was a loveable animal and she had obviously had him a few months. Long enough to bond with him. Nick was known as a patient man and good negotiator who usually persuaded adversaries to his way of thinking. If he ever wanted his old canine pal back, that was what he had to be now.

He disposed of his trash, then started back toward LaBarkery, intending to take a different tack with the store's owner.

Parking in front of the store, he saw a CLOSED sign hanging inside the front door. But just because she had put that sign up didn't mean she wasn't inside. He walked up to the door and knocked on it. When no one came, he gave the door a rattle. Peeking inside, he saw that the place was dark except for the night lights. Shit. Nobody in the retail business would close their store at three o'clock in the afternoon on a weekday.

Sooo....did Buster's pretty and perky dognapper intend to play dirty?

Nick returned to his truck and started the drive to his place ten miles out of Midland. He glanced over at the sleeping puppy on the passenger seat. *Sweet little dog,* he thought with affection. He would train him to be a good dog the same way he had trained Buster. Then, when he got Buster back, he would have two good dogs.

☆☆☆

On Sunday, before returning to Midland, Sandi donned heavy rubber gloves that reached her elbows and helped her aunt and Vic clean the room they had given Jake in their mobile home.

"I'm just glad we moved Mama Doll's craft supplies out of here," Vic said, as they washed bird poop off the walls and hard surfaces. "I'd have a helluva time getting bird shit off all of her beads."

"I'm so sorry, y'all. I should've told you more about Jake. From the beginning of my association with him, I tried to figure out a way for him to wear diapers."

"That diet he's on," Aunt Ed said. "Maybe you could come up with something that's a little more binding."

Sandi broke into laughter. "Oh, Aunt Ed, you're so funny."

"Yeah, I'm a real card. Some of my funniest moments are when I'm up to my elbows in shit."

Leaving Jake in Vic's care, Sandi and her aunt moved to the beauty salon to clean Jake's sanctuary.

After they had situated Pablo and Adolph in the storeroom, Aunt Ed grabbed Sandi's elbow and dragged her into the salon. "Look what Vic built for Jake."

Her aunt had told her on the phone about Jake's digs at the beauty salon, but in her wildest imagination, Sandi never would have pictured what stood in one corner of the salon. Made of wood, extending from floor to ceiling, filled with both artificial and growing plants and even a small fountain that looked like a waterfall, it appeared to be a tiny jungle retreat. The only thing missing was Jake. "Oh, my God. Vic built that?"

"He sure did," Debbie Sue said. "Isn't it great? It even has climate control."

"A lot of it's plastic," Aunt Ed added. "We can take it outside and hose it off."

Sandi tried to wrap her mind around maintaining climate control in a corner of a large rock building and dismantling the cage and its contents to take it outside. "What a lot of work. Vic must like Jake then."

"Hon, I told you he did. I've never seen my honey get so attached to anything so fast. Even Gus likes that silly bird. You should see them. Vic puts Jake on the floor and Gus peeks around the corner of the doorway. Jake scratches the floor at him, then Gus humps up and dances in a circle. They do that over and over and Vic laughs like a crazy man. It's a hoot."

Able to picture the scene, Sandi laughed. She was so glad Vic and her aunt had learned to live with Jake and love him.

All the way back to Midland from Salt Lick, she thought about her visit with her aunt and Vic Martin. She should spend more time with them. Both of them were fun, unconventional and fearless. Nothing like her parents. They paid little attention to what other people thought. They were an inspiration. Fun was in short supply in Samdi's life and lately, she seemed to fear everything—love, marriage, life itself. The weekend at her aunt's house had been uplifting.

Jake had indeed found a good home. The mini-jungle Vic had built him in the corner of the beauty salon was awe-inspiring. Vic had researched African Grey parrots—their native habitat, what they ate, what scientific studies had revealed about them. Aunt Ed had said he was the best gift she had ever given her husband and she thanked Sandi for bringing the parrot into their lives.

Jake apparently loved his new environment as well as his new owners. He sent Aunt Ed into giggles by wolf-whistling at her. When Vic was at home, Jake rode on his shoulder everywhere. Vic's attempts to teach him not to say "fuck" resulted in squawking arguments and roaring laughter.

Jake even sat on Vic's shoulder while he barbecued chicken on the grill and Vic told him those chicken parts could be him if he didn't behave. What was hard to believe was that the parrot seemed to know Vic was kidding. Every time Vic said that, Jake flapped his wings and squawked, "I can say fuck if I want to."

Debbie Sue had taught him to play peek-a-boo, with him hiding out among the plants in his Styling Station aviary, Debbie Sue calling to him and Jake popping out from behind the foliage.

With the beauty shop's customers, he had an audience, which he probably loved since he had spent his life performing for his fans in a bar. Hopefully, those women in the beauty shop would be teaching him a more socially acceptable vocabulary and would not be feeding him beer and pizza.

Sandi's biggest challenge now was dealing with Waffle's former owner, which presented a quandary. Her better angel told her that indeed Waffle was really Buster. Should she just give him back to Nick? She loved Waffle so much, would miss him so much. And he was so much better off with her than he would be working as a cowdog for a cowboy.

Should she discuss what had happened with Richard? He must know what was legal when it came to lost and found animals. Of course, Richard's solution would be to just give Waffle to Nick and be done with it. One less aggravation with animals. No, she didn't want Richard's opinion.

Maybe she should call Juanita and question her. What to do, what to do.

Chapter 12

MONDAY MORNING, 8:00 A.M. If Nick were in Salt
Lick, he would be on the job, doing the work he had
been hired to do. Instead, he was still in Midland. He
had made a decision. The woman holding Buster had
no intention of letting him go. Getting him back
required stronger measures.

He called the Flying C and told Harley he was
delayed in Midland, but would be back to the ranch as
soon as possible. Harley didn't complain. The cattle sale
had gone better than it had in years, thanks to Nick's
organizing skills.

Nick's old high school friend, Jason Webster,
was now a Midland County deputy sheriff. Jason and
his wife and Nick and his former wife used to be social
friends. Now that Nick was single, he and Jason didn't
connect socially that often, but they had continued to be
buds. Nick had called him when the llamas next door
had been abandoned. He called him now and explained
the situation with Buster.

"You're sure it's your dog?" Jason asked.

"Stake my life on it."

"You say she found him while he was lost? If she didn't steal him, there isn't much my office can do."

"I understand that. I'm not calling to file a complaint. She appears to be a high-strung person. She might respond if you just show up and scare her a little."

"I guess we could drop by and see her. Most people, even if they're blustery at first, tend to get more cooperative when the cops come." Jason gave a wicked chuckle. "What's her name?"

"Sandi. I don't know her last name. Listen, Jason, I don't want trouble. All I want is for her to give my dog back."

"Is she mistreating him?"

"No. He looks good, like she's taking good care of him. She owns this store where she makes and sells health food for dogs and cats. It's got a goofy name. La-something."

"LaBarkery? I know that store. Either I or my wife go into it occasionally to buy a treat for our dogs. That's a real cool store. Your dog is probably eating great."

Suddenly, it came to Nick that though he hadn't taken a close look at Sandi's little operation, he admired what she was doing. With in-depth knowledge of animal nutrition himself, he could see she was conscientious and caring.

"Tell you what," Jason said. "I've been here all night. I'll be off in about half an hour. I know right where LaBarkery is. I'll meet you in the parking lot. We'll go talk to her. I'm a firm believer that a little conversation solves a lot of problems."

Half an hour later, Nick drove to the parking lot and came to a stop away from the front entrance to LaBarkery. After Jason had sung the store's praises,

Nick had a dubious feeling having him be the one to talk to Sandi about Buster.

Jason soon drove up, interrupting Nick's thoughts. Nick stepped down from his truck as Jason parked beside him and scooted out of his county car. "I looked up her business license," he said. "Her last name is Walker. Sandi Walker. Let's go see what she has to say. When she sees me in my uniform, she'll probably hand your dog right over."

As they approached the store's front entrance, they saw Buster barking and wagging his tail on the other side of the front door. "See?" Nick said. "He knows me. He's glad to see me. He's my dog."

They walked into the store and the aromas of freshly cooked meats surrounded them. Buster barked and danced and bounced. Tail whipping, he rose on his hind legs and put his paws on Nick's chest. Nick hands reflexively went to scruff the golden head and ears. Man, he loved this dog. "Hey, boy. Howya doing today?" Nick couldn't keep from smiling. "See how glad he is to see me?" he said to Jason.

Sandi came from the back room wearing a green butcher's apron and wiping her hands on a towel. She stopped in her tracks, her breath catching.

Instantly, Nick saw a storm of emotions in her pretty green eyes, including fear. He felt like a chickenshit and wished he hadn't called Jason. There was something about her that made him not want to quarrel with her.

"Waffle. Come here," she said firmly.

The dog obeyed, but reluctantly. He looked back at Nick. She bent forward and clutched his collar. "You stay here with mama, boy. Be a good dog."

Nick could see she wasn't going to let Buster escape her. She looked up at him. "How can I help you?"

Jason removed his uniform cap and held it in front of his chest. Nick, too, removed his own cap.

"Miz Walker, I'm Deputy Webster. First, let me tell you this isn't an official visit. The truth is, I'm one of your customers. I was hoping you and me and Mr. Conway here could have a conversation about his dog" —he nodded toward Buster—"that's obviously in your possession."

Nick winced, even more profoundly sorry for what he had set in motion.

"Sit, Waffle, sit," Sandi told Buster. The dog parked his butt between him and Sandi, looking first at one, then the other.

Two young girls came out from the back room, their faces lined with worry. Sandi lifted her chin defiantly. "I do not have his dog."

Again, Jason tilted his head toward Buster. "The dog seems to know him, ma'am."

"That doesn't mean anything. Waffle is friendly to everyone."

Buster began to whine and strain toward Nick. "See?" Nick said. "He wants to come to me."

"I have to agree, ma'am," Jason said. "The dog seems to want to be with Mr. Conway."

Sandi's eyes glistened with tears and Nick felt worse. "That isn't possible. I've had Waffle since he was a puppy."

Jason turned to Nick, a bewildered expression on his face.

Any idea that this woman was going to easily give up Buster just because a cop was on the scene fled. Now Nick was even more uncertain that he was doing the right thing, but his ego demanded that he stand his ground. After all, she had just told Jason a bald-faced lie. "That's not true, Jason. I got him when he was less than a week old. I saved his life."

The two girls stood silently in the background, their faces in a scowl, their arms crossed over their chests. If looks could kill, Nick was sure he would be a dead man.

Buster pranced and whimpered and strained against Sandi's grip on his collar, his toenails clicking on the tile floor.

"As I said, ma'am," Jason continued. "This isn't an official visit. I want to try to mediate something between you and Mr. Conway."

She sniffled. "What, you just automatically believe what he says, without even considering that I just told you I've had Waffle since he was born?" She turned to one of the girls. "Betty Ann, please bring me Waffle's leash."

The petite blonde quickly left the room.

"No, ma'am. I mean, yes, ma'am," Jason said. His jaws puffed and he blew out a breath. "Look, here's an idea. Why don't you and Mr. Conway here share the dog and let it decide where it wants to live?"

Nick didn't want to share Buster with Sandi Walker or anybody else. He glared at the deputy. The expression on Sandi's face could be explained only as a look of horror. She was as stunned as he was.

The blonde returned with a dog leash and handed it to Sandi.

She snapped it onto Buster's collar and held a solid grip on it. Though poor Buster looked up at her with pleading eyes, she said, "That's the dumbest idea

I've ever heard. Dogs don't get to decide where they want to live. Only cats do that."

Jason pulled a handkerchief out of his pocket and wiped his brow. Now Nick felt guilty, not only for badgering Sandi, but for putting a friend in an awkward spot.

"I wouldn't know, ma'am. Don't have any experience with cats. All I'm saying is if you both like the dog and want him to be around you, I don't see why Nick here can't keep him a while, then bring him back to you and you keep him a while. Kind of a back and forth situation"—he made a rocking gesture with his hand—"know what I mean?"

Now Nick was as confused as Jason. His head shook involuntarily. "I'm not sure that solves the problem, Jason. Buster's a trained working dog. I need him with me at the ranch to—"

Sandi's mouth dropped open and she huffed. "Oh? Nick and Jason, is it?" She looked up at Jason, her eyes snapping with anger. "You two are on a first-name basis? What is this? Are you using your job as a law enforcement officer to harass me on your friend's behalf? I guess that explains why a county cop is in my store inside the city limits throwing his weight around."

Inside, Nick winced. He hadn't intended for her to know he and Jason were even acquainted, much less friends. And it hadn't occurred to him that Jason, as a county employee, might not have jurisdiction in the city or that she might know that.

Jason's eyes rolled toward the ceiling. Nick could tell he hadn't intended for Sandi to know that fact either. "That's not what's happening here. Mr. Conway, er, Nick and I knowing each other doesn't keep me from trying to be an honest broker in this deal."

Sandi planted her fists on her slim hips and gave Jason the squint-eye. *Uh-oh.* Nick hadn't anticipated this.

"Sharing definitely doesn't do it for me, Deputy. Didn't you hear what he just said? He's a dog enslaver and an abuser. Since you know him, you must know that about him."

Dog enslaver? Abuser? Nick grunted a loud gasp.

"Ma'am, using a dog to help with cattle isn't enslaving the animal and it isn't abuse either," Jason said. "The dog probably likes it."

Sandi crossed her arms over her breasts. "Hah. That's what *you* say. Are you a dog mind-reader, too?"

"Wait just a minute." Enough was enough. Nick cocked his head and raised his palms. "I've had just about enough here. I've never abused an animal in my life."

He turned to Jason. "You know that, Jason. I love animals. I've always loved animals. Don't I take care of a broken-down horse that's not good for much except eating up feed? Don't I feed every stray cat that comes along and let them sleep in my barn? Didn't I take those llamas to keep them from being put down? I damn sure didn't do it because I needed two glorified goats in my life."

"Oh, really," Sandi said, fire in her eye and her arms crossed under her very attractive breasts. She turned to Jason. "Mr. Conway takes care of cattle that are set to be slaughtered because he loves animals? Y'all must think I just fell off a turnip truck."

"That's different," Nick said firmly.

"How is it different?"

Nick growled and threw up his hands. "What are you, nuts? You wanna go through your life without beef to eat?"

"Of course not. And I'm not —"

"Just hold on." Jason plopped his cap back on his head and stabbed the air with his finger. "Listen, you two. Y'all aren't trying."

Sandi flipped a palm in the air. "There's no point. You're already prejudiced against me. Even if that weren't true, Mr. Conway" — Sandy pointed a finger at Nick — "lives down in Salt Lick and I live here. Sharing will not work."

Jason pushed the bill of his cap back. "Sure, it will, ma'am. Look, Nick's place is just out of town a short distance from here." He leaned forward and opened his palms, his eyes holding hers. "I'm sure he'd let you go out there and look around. You can see for yourself it's a good place for a dog to live." Jason turned toward Nick. "You'd do that, wouldn't you, Nick?"

Sandi didn't relent, maintaining her pinched-mouth expression. She wasn't buying Jason's conciliatory tone or gestures. Mental eyeroll. Nick wished he had never called the deputy. "Uh, sure. I guess so."

Jason's's face broke into a toothy grin. "See? A little talk always solves problems. Look, I need to get home, so I'm going to leave you two to work this out."

With that, the deputy readjusted his cap. "See ya, Nick." He walked out of the store, leaving Nick speechless.

Buster whined, but Sandi hung onto his leash.

Seconds of silence crept by. As much as he hated to do it, Nick caved. "Did you want to go out to my place now?"

"I thought you worked in Salt Lick. Why are you in Midland on a weekday?"

Nick's mind flew back to the supper at Hogg's and how he had prompted her several times to place an order for food. "Ma'am, you've got a way of not answering a question and taking a conversation off in a direction it wasn't intended to go. I'm not going through this again. Just a simple yes or no. Do you want to take a ride out to my house?"

She ducked her chin and glared at him from beneath her brow. "For the record, I do not consider this a satisfactory resolution to this problem. If you hadn't gotten the law involved, I wouldn't even consider it. Even if I go to your house and inspect it, Waffle is staying here with my two employees."

"Okay, fine. My place is about ten miles out one-fifty-eight."

"Where, pray tell, is that?

Nick couldn't stop the are-you-stupid expression he felt overtaking his face. "It's the highway going north out of town. You take one-ninety-one, then turn right on seventeen-eighty-eight. When you get to the four-way stop, turn left on twenty-four twenty-five. My place is on the left side of the highway before you get to one seventy-six going to Andrews. Do you want to follow me? Or would you rather ride with me?"

She returned a sour look. "I am not in the habit of riding into rural areas with men with whom I'm not acquainted."

She was the most exasperating woman he had ever met. He set his jaw and summoned his patience. "Fine, then. I'm leaving now. If you intend to follow, you'd better get it in gear."

He plopped his cap onto his head and stamped out of the store.

☆☆☆

Sandi had no intention of making a ten-mile trip over a bunch of confusing roads with only numbers for names to look at Nick's house when Waffle was never going to live there. Besides, she could get lost forever in that maze of highways and connections going north. Good grief! She could end up in Wyoming!

The minute Nick cleared the door, she yanked off her apron and turned to her two employees. "Girls, I'm going to be out for the rest of the day and tomorrow. If anyone calls for me, just say you don't know where I am."

She was already pressing in the number of Juanita, her animal shelter friend who soon connected with a "Hey, Sandi."

"Hi, Juanita. How are you today?"

"Busier than that well known cranberry merchant. What's up?"

"Listen, I have to make an unexpected trip out of town. I'll be gone overnight. Can you arrange for someone to go to my house and feed the animals tomorrow morning?"

"Sure can. What about tonight?"

"I'll take care of tonight. I have to run by my house and pick up a few things before I leave, so I might as well feed everyone while I'm there."

"Don't worry. I'll do it myself. It's the least I can do for somebody who's as friendly to unfortunate animals as you are."

"You know where everything is. You know I've found a home for Jake, so you won't have to worry about feeding him. He was the one who took up so much time. Thank you so much, Juanita."

The minute Sandi disconnected, she looked up and saw Betty Ann's brow tented with concern. "You aren't going to look at his house?"

"I am not."

"But he's so good-looking."

"Which has what to do with the price of tea in China? Remember this, Betty Ann. Looks are only skin-deep. Ted Bundy was good-looking, but that doesn't mean I would want to go visit him."

"Where are you going now?" Jessica asked, her eyes wide and questioning.

"Waffle and I are going to my aunt's house in Salt Lick. I'll be back tomorrow. You girls will have to close the store tonight and open it tomorrow. You have my cell number if you need me."

They could manage without her until tomorrow. Sandy had confidence in Betty Ann, her go-to employee who had a key to the store.

"Remember, if he calls, you don't know where I am."

"But you said Mr. Conway lives in Salt Lick," Jessica said. "If you're down there, too, won't it be easier for him to find you?"

"But he's not in Salt Lick now. I don't want him to come back and catch Waffle and me here in Midland. He might go to my house. Even if he goes back to Salt Lick today, he won't figure out that Waffle and I are there. Besides that, my aunt's husband is a retired Navy SEAL. He's six-feet-five and weighs over two hundred pounds. Aunt Ed says he knows three hundred ways to kill you quietly and he liberated Kuwait. We'll just see if Mr. Nick Conway wants a confrontation with *him*."

"Wow," Betty Ann said.

"Holy cow. I hope no one gets hurt." Jessica bit down on her lower lip.

Sandi rushed home. Adolph barked and stalked around as she gathered Waffle's bed and a couple of his toys. Then she picked up Pablo and Adolph's beds and toys. She put the two miniature dogs into the oversize pet carrier and was on her way to Salt Lick.

Chapter 13

SANDI ARRIVED IN Salt Lick soon after noon. The Styling Station was closed, but circling the block, she saw Edwina's blue classic Mustang and Debbie Sue's red pickup in the back parking lot. She parked beside it, picked Pablo and Adolph's carrier off the passenger seat and set it on the ground, then let Waffle out of the SUV's backseat. After they all did their business, she picked up Pablo and Adolph's carrying case and walked around the building to the front door. Waffle followed like the well-trained dog that he was.

She tapped lightly on the front door. "Aunt Ed? Debbie Sue?"

"We're closed. Who's there?"

She recognized her aunt's voice. "It's me, Sandi. Can I come in?"

The door swung open. "Well, great day in the morning. Where did you come from?"

"Why are you closed?"

"Mondays are light days. Sometimes we just close and catch up. What are you doing all the way down here today, girl?"

"Oh, I just thought I'd visit Jake."

"On a Monday? Who's taking care of your store?"

"My two employees are there. I'll bet you don't want my dogs inside—"

"We can't let them into the salon, hon, but they can go into the back room. Take them around to the back door."

Sandi trudged around the building again. Her aunt met her at the back door. She secured the three dogs in the back storeroom, then walked into the salon. She didn't spot Jake in his corner home. "I don't see Jake."

"My honey's home today, so he and Jake are having a boys' day. Vic's teaching him about patriotism."

"He's okay then. He's still healthy and—"

"Oh, hell, hon, he's already gotten acquainted with the vet. We know the vet and his wife, Paige, personally. When she spotted him, she had a fit and dragged Spur all way out of his office to come and see that Jake do his thing. The whole town is talking about him. We could sell tickets."

"It'll be interesting to hear what the state inspector says when he comes around the next time," Debbie Sue said.

Sandi frowned. "Oh, my gosh, I hadn't thought of that. I guess I didn't realize he'd be living in the salon."

"Well, we aren't worrying about it yet," Aunt Ed said. "Salt Lick is so far off the beaten path those Austin folks might not know this town's got a beauty shop. Hell, they might not even know we're anything but a ghost town." A thoughtful frown creased her brow. "I wonder if they'd notice if we stopped sending them sales tax."

"You wouldn't believe how our business has picked up since he's been here," Debbie Sue said. "We've got customers who want to come in just to talk to him. But since his cage is near the manicure and pedicure corner, we don't let them unless they get manicures or pedicures. That way, they're happy and we're making money. And a crowd doesn't gather. Also, the smell of the nail products masks the odor coming from Jake's cage."

Sandi gave Debbie Sue a look. "You're making money off of Jake?"

"That bird is a real ham. He craves attention. Some of the customers ask him to pick a color for their nails. He's learned colors and he's learned to say red and pink and even blue. If they choose a color he doesn't like, he'll make a noises and say 'not that one, not that one.' And some ask his advice on other things, which, by the way, he gives freely."

"Oh, I know he has opinions on everything." She turned to her aunt. "You haven't had any trouble with his diet then?"

"Oh, hell no. My honey's on top of it. I suspect Jake eats even fancier than he did at your house. Vic drives all the way up to Odessa to buy him stuff. I passed around the recipe for parrot muffins so that the customers can bake them for him."

"Oh, my gosh. Sounds like Jake has never had it so good. I hope their homemade muffins don't have sugar. He gets enough sugar in the raw fruits and vegetables he likes."

"Listen, I told them, 'If it ain't in the recipe, don't put it in there. And that includes sugar.'"

But Sandi was skeptical. Well-meaning cooks might think a cup of sugar would make the muffins better.

Stop it, Sandi, she told herself. Jake was no longer her responsibility. Only after she got over parting with him had she realized just how much of her time and attention he had consumed. Not having to take care of his daily needs or cope with his personality or clean up after him was almost like being on vacation.

☆☆☆

Four o'clock. After cooling his heels for six hours waiting for Miz Sandi Walker to appear, Nick's temper stewed at a simmer. He had about a million chores he could have been doing down at the Flying C instead of waiting for her up here in Midland. He had called her shop several times, but her employees said she wasn't there and refused to give him her cell number. He had found her name in the phone book and called her house several times, left messages each time.

Now he had run out of time. He had to get on the road back to Salt Lick. One day was all he was willing to take off work to try to reason with Sandi and rescue Buster.

An hour and a half later, he drove into the Salt Lick city limits. He had to follow the highway through the middle of town and pass by the Styling Station on his way out to the Flying C. Parked in front of it was a silver SUV that looked way too familiar.

Dammit, that's her!

She had lied to him again. She'd had no intention of following him out to his house and looking it over. Instead, she had run down here to her aunt's place where she thought she could escape him. Except for his ex-wife, he couldn't think of a woman he had known who had wanted to escape him.

Of all the human frailties Nick hated, the one he hated the most was lying. He hit the brake, slowed and circled the block, deciding how to handle the situation, his anger so close to the surface his skin burned. Finally, he decided to confront her.

He pulled into a parking slot beside the SUV. A CLOSED sign hung on the front door, but he knew she was in there. He stepped out of his truck and stalked to the door, gave a heavy *rap-rap-rap* with his knuckles on one of the glass panes in the upper part of the door. When no one responded, he knocked again.

"We're closed," a voice sang out.

"I need to speak to Sandi Walker."

Silence. He knocked on the wood frame with his fist and rattled the door knob.

The door opened a three-inch crack. The older skinny hairdresser's face and her lime green glasses showed through. "Oh, it's you. What do you want?"

Dammit, she had known it was him before she opened the door. Another log added to the fire of his anger. "It's personal. I'd like to speak to Miz Walker. I know she's here."

"I don't think she wants to talk to you."

"Ma'am, I know she's your niece, but this doesn't concern you. She's got something of mine and I'd like to have it back. I'd really appreciate it if she'd come to the door and talk to me."

The door closed. He thought he heard low voices on the other side. The door opened again and the skinny one stood in the doorway, blocking entrance. "Okay, you can come in. But only because you work for Harley and he's a friend of ours. But mind you, we don't want any trouble in here. If you start anything, you'll have our local sheriff to deal with. And he's our friend too."

"And you might even have to deal with my husband," the one named Debbie Sue added.

Nick had met the local sheriff, Billy Don Roberts, and he wasn't worried. Getting crossways with Buddy Overstreet was a horse of a different color. "I don't intend to start—"

Woof! Bwoof! Bwoof!

The deep barks came from behind a closed door, followed by staccato high-pitched barking, a humming snarling sound and frantic scratching on the floor and on the door. Dammit, they had Buster locked up. A new anger flew through him. "I know one of those sounds is my dog barking." He looked around. "But I don't see Miz Walker."

"She isn't here," the aunt said.

"Why are we lying?" Debbie Sue said, her arms crossed over her chest. "She's in the back room." She yelled toward the closed door. "Sandi, come in here and take care of this."

It was a good thing she had spoken up because he was out of patience. He just might call the sheriff himself, even if the guy was their friend.

The aunt walked over to the door to the back room and eased it open. Sandi stood there, holding a shivering, growling Chihuahua under one arm and with the other hand, hanging onto the leash of a little dog that yapped with such vehemence all four of his feet came off the floor with each bark. If she thought she was going to pawn some grouchy bald-headed Chihuahua or some yip-yapping thing that looked like a long-haired rat off on him instead of Buster, she had another think coming.

Buster scrambled to follow her, but she scolded them to "stay" and closed the door against him. He continued to scratch and whine and bark.

"You must've forgotten our appointment," Nick said to Sandi.

"Of course I didn't. I deliberately avoided it." She heaved a shoulder-lifting sigh. "Mr. Conway, we might as well stop this nonsense. Your friend's idea about sharing Waffle was dumb."

Nick didn't disagree.

Buster continued to create a commotion at the closed door. "Why don't you open the door?" Nick snapped. "Afraid to let your allies see who Buster wants to be with?"

The Chihuahua bared its teeth and snarled. She ran her hand over his almost hairless head. "Pablo, be a sweet doggie." The other little dog let out several loud barks. She yanked on his leash. "Hush, Adolph." She slid a hand into her pants pocket, pulled out treats and fed one to the jittery Chihuahua, then one to the barker.

From out of the blue, the gentleness she showed to these two ugly dogs touched him. They were dogs with neurotic behavior and would never be claimed as pets. If not for her, no doubt they would have already been put to sleep. The woman was either the nut he had thought she was when he first met her or she had more heart than any one person's body could hold. The thought came to Nick that she would make a great mother. *Whoa!* Where had that notion come from?

Her attention came back to him. "I'm not afraid of anything and I'm not afraid of you. I don't know if Waffle was your dog—past tense, Mr. Conway, past tense. You haven't proved it. If he was, maybe you should've kept a closer watch on him. I found him when he was in terrible condition and nearly starved, eating in alleys and out of dumpsters. He had been living on the streets for weeks. He was lucky to be alive. I nursed him back to health and I've given him a home where he has good food, regular veterinary care and he's safe."

Nick reined in his temper, feeling sheepish and a little guilty. He had no explanation for why Buster had run off from him in the first place, but he knew one thing. In this environment and under these circumstances, venting his anger would get him nowhere. "Ma'am, you said your goal—"

"Please do not call me ma'am. I suspect I'm younger than you are."

"Ma'am, I was taught me the polite thing to do was call women ma'am. It has nothing to do with your age. As I started to say, you said your intent is to find good homes for the animals you rescue. I'm here to tell you Buster did have and will have a good home with me. Always."

"Finding homes for the animals I rescue is my intent, but Waffle's different from the other dogs I've taken in," Sandi replied. "I love him and he loves me. I'm not going to just give him to you. I'm willing to give you one or even both of my other large dogs, Ricky and Fred. I'm looking for homes for them. They're—"

Nick stopped her. "Ma'am," he said as softly as he could manage, given his state of mind. He hadn't expected her to be so honest. "That just won't work. I've had Buster since he was only days old. We're friends. We've relied on each other for several years. Having him around helped me through a rough time. I've trained him to be a cattle dog. You've seen that he knows me. He wants to be with me."

Her eyes began to glisten. "He and I are friends too."

Tears? Shit. His memory flew backward to the evening he had bought her a hamburger after she had delivered the parrot to her aunt and the bawling episode all through the meal and how much difficulty she had seemed to have with placing an order for food. The last thing he wanted was a replay.

Suddenly, she squared her shoulders and looked him in the eye, the tears gone, eyes sparking with anger. "You know what? You should go."

The Chihuahua began to growl and bare his teeth. She muzzled him with her hand. The one named Adolph began to bark again. "Adolph, no!" She squatted and began to pet him and talk to him softly. "Mama said no. Behave now. You have nothing to be upset about."

She got to her feet, still hanging onto the snarling Chihuahua. "This is too much commotion. It's upsetting to Pablo and Adolph. And this is my aunt and her partner's business. They don't want to be a part of this."

"Then you shouldn't have run down here like a coward and involved them."

"Your insults mean nothing to me. I'll be going back to Midland tomorrow. We can talk there. You can come to my store."

Nick had never been so frustrated. He was accomplishing nothing. He didn't know what to do. He lifted his hands and let them drop. "Okay, dammit, I'm gonna go. But I can't be back in Midland tomorrow to talk about this. I still have a job to do here. It'll be the weekend before I get back up there. But don't think I'm gonna forget about it, Miz Walker. And you're gonna be wasting a lot of gasoline if you need to run down here to Salt Lick every time you think I'm anywhere near."

He stalked out the door and slammed it so hard the glass panes in the upper half rattled.

☆☆☆

Sandi waited anxiously for the panes to fall out of the door. She, her Aunt Ed and Debbie Sue all stared after Nick. No one said a word.

Finally, Aunt Ed spoke. "Lordy, Lordy, niece-of-mine. Something tells me there's more going on than you missing ol' Jake the Mouth. What's this about?"

Sandi broke into tears. "Oh, Aunt Ed..."

Her aunt came over and put an arm around her shoulder, drew her against her. "Now, now. You can tell your dear ol' auntie, hon. I'm not a pinch-mouth like your mother. I don't judge. Were you and Nick lovers? Is that why you're both claiming the same dog? Is it one of those custody things?"

Sandi raised her head and stepped back, her eyes suddenly dry. "Aunt Ed! Nick Conway a lover? Not in this lifetime."

Her aunt gave her the goggle-eye. "You could do worse. Hell, you've already done worse."

"He's trying to steal my dog, Aunt Ed!"

"But he says it's his dog," Debbie Sue said. "And he looked and sounded believable to me."

From the corner of her eye, Sandi angled a look toward her aunt's partner. She wasn't one hundred percent sure she could trust Debbie Sue, even if she was Aunt Ed's friend.

Sandi sank into a styling chair. Amidst tears and sniffles, she told Waffle's story.

At the end of it, her aunt said, "So Waffle's just another stray. It seems like this particular dog is real important to Nick."

"Waffle is important to me, too, Aunt Ed."

"Hell, Sandi, you've got access to dozens of dogs. Like he said, why not let him have Waffle and you take the puppy he offered you. I mean, it's just a dog, right?"

"Ed! Bite your tongue!" Debbie Sue said. "What if I felt that way about Jim, Jack and Jose? Or Rocket Man?"

Jimjack and Jose? Rocket Man? "Those are dogs' names?" Sandi asked, incredulous.

"Jim Beam, Jack Daniel's and Jose Cuervo. I got them back in my partying days before I remarried Buddy."

"Rocket Man's a horse," Aunt Edwina put in. "An old horse she used to ride when she was a champion barrel racer in ProRodeo. He's so old, once when he was sick, I knitted an afghan to throw over his rump."

Sandi shook her head, trying to clear away the cobwebs. Her aunt hadn't told her much about her partner. It sounded as if Debbie Sue had lived a busy lifetime in just two sentences.

"All I know, Aunt Ed, is I don't want to lose Waffle. And I'm never going to be bullied by a man again."

Debbie Sue loomed over her. "So is this uproar about the dog? Or is it about you?"

Sandi raised her gaze to Debbie Sue. "What do you mean?"

"I don't see that he's bullying you. He just wants his dog back. I don't understand why it's such an obsession for you."

Sandi could stop the tears that rushed to her eyes. "I can't help it. It's hard to explain. After two husbands left me for other women, I was so lost. My self-esteem was so beaten down. My mother says I have terrible judgement when it comes to men."

Aunt Ed patted Sandi's shoulders with a comforting hand. "That's all right, darlin'. Don't listen to your mother. Her brain cavity has always been a little small."

Sandi looked up at her aunt in shock. "Aunt Ed! Why do you say mean things about my mother? She's your sister!"

Her aunt lifted her shoulders in a shrug. "Can I help it the way she is?"

"So you're projecting," Debbie Sue said.

"What the hell does that mean, Debbie Sue?" Aunt Ed said. "Whose side are you on?"

"I'm just saying, Sandi, that maybe you're projecting your need for some guy to love you onto Waffle. That's why you're afraid to let him go."

"Maybe that's true," Sandi replied. "When Waffle came along, maybe I needed something to love that loved me back."

She plucked a Kleenex out of a box on her aunt's station and blew her nose. "I have so much love to give, but I can't seem to find a human who wants it. Only animals. And most of them only want to be fed and housed. Waffle's different. He has a personality and he gives back."

"I have to believe that you know he really is Nick's dog," Debbie Sue Said.

"There's somebody out there for you, Sandi," Aunt Ed said. "You just haven't found the right one. Sometimes it takes a while." She drew a big sniff. "Just look at your ol' auntie. It took me four tries to get a good one."

Sandy clamped her jaw tight. She had no intention of ever having four husbands. One more time was all she was willing to give to an attempt at marriage. If the third time didn't prove to be a charm, she would give up love and romance with the human male altogether and become a cat lady. She was already well on her way.

She gave her aunt an arch look. "No offense, Aunt Ed, but two ex-husbands are enough. I don't want three. I might never get married again, but if I do, it'll be for good."

Chapter 14

DURING THE LONG, silent drive to the Flying C, Nick's thoughts and emotions churned. Those women were never going to give Buster up. It was time to take control of the situation. He knew where the aunt lived. He would have no trouble coaxing the dog to come to him. He turned his truck around and headed back to Salt Lick.

Driving by Edwina and Vic Martin's mobile home, he concluded no one was at home. He studied the mobile and the yard around it. Neatly kept, large lot, fenced back yard with a gate into an alley and an open fenced pasture beyond. All he had to do was wait for the right opportunity. He parked at the end of the alley behind a large mesquite tree, hoping he was concealed, and waited.

Twilight came and still no one was at home. Those women probably all went to eat supper somewhere or maybe they went out for a night on the town. But what town? Salt Lick had no night life. If they went out, they would have to go to another town. And would they take Sandi's dogs with them or leave them locked up in the beauty shop? Neither scenario sounded logical.

He shifted in his seat, hoping they showed up soon. His back ached, his butt ached and he was starting to feel tingles in his feet. The consequences of old football injuries plagued him every day. He'd had concussions, sprains, broken bones and a back injury. He'd had surgeries on his back and both knees.

Added to that, since those days, he had spent many of his waking hours on horseback in all kinds of weather. That probably hadn't done his body a lot of good either, but he had always been a cowboy and it was the profession he had chosen for his adult life. He couldn't imagine doing anything else.

He stepped out of his truck and walked around it, hung onto the tailgate and did a few squats, then climbed back inside.

Soon after dark, lights came on in the mobile home. The back door opened and Sandi and Buster came out into the back yard. Buster's head turned toward him, his nose in the air. He began to bark. *Shit!* The dog had his scent.

He made sure his truck's automatic headlights were off, then fired the engine, backed out of the alley and made his way to one of the two gas stations in Salt Lick. There, he ate a hot dog and visited the men's room.

He soon returned to his vigil. Sandi Walker sneaked into his mind. She was an interesting woman. Good-looking, great body, obviously smart and loyal. Though they had clashed over Buster, he suspected she was honest to a fault. They had some things in common and she would make a good companion.

He couldn't recall the last time he'd had those thoughts about his female acquaintances. The fact was, for a long time, he hadn't looked for anything in women other than the obvious. But that didn't mean he wouldn't enjoy having the right one to go home to after a long day. He did get lonesome.

The mobile home lights went out, halting his mental meandering. He checked his watch. 11:30 p.m. No Buster. That meant a long night ahead. He stepped down from behind the wheel, climbed into the backseat and was soon asleep.

He awoke to a sky just turning pink with daylight. *Oh, hell.* Had he missed Buster coming outside? Feeling as if he were paralyzed from the waist down, he creaked to a sitting position one limb at a time. His feet longed to be freed from the boots he had been wearing since yesterday morning.

Daylight and a night's sleep, even a fitful sleep, brought clearer thinking. Was he out of his mind, planning to sneak Buster out of somebody's back yard? This was behavior that conflicted with every bit of common sense he had. Last night, when he had conjured up this plan, he had definitely been acting out of anger. He should just go home.

Before he finished thinking the worst about himself and what he was doing, the back door opened and Buster came out of the house alone. Neither Sandi nor her aunt were anywhere in sight. Nick looked around the back yard, saw no sign of a human being. Buster trotted toward the back of the yard, began to sniff around the gate. *Bingo!* Temptation raised its head. In a matter of a second, it overcame Nick's cleared thinking and common sense.

Ten minutes later, he had his dog in the passenger and he was headed for the Flying C.

The drive to the ranch gave him time to get his wits together and regret acting out a juvenile impulse. He had to explain the situation to his boss before anybody else got to him first. Thus, when he arrived at the ranch, his first stop was at Harley's house.

Harley and C.J. were up and C.J. was fixing breakfast and lunches for their kids. He apologized for appearing so early in the morning and interrupting their routine.

Harley, a gracious man who was always a gentleman, invited him into his office and listened attentively. At the end of Nick's story, Harley said, "I'm sympathetic, but I'd just as soon stay out of it. My wife and Debbie Sue Overstreet are good friends. Have been their whole lives. And I consider her husband Buddy a friend."

"I understand, Harley. I'm just giving you a heads up because I expect to hear from one or all three of those women. Fact is, I suspect *you'll* hear from them."

Harley chuckled. "Edwina and Debbie Sue do have a way of getting everyone's attention. But don't worry about it. We'll handle it."

"The whole thing is kinda silly. This woman, Sandi. She collects unwanted animals. It should be a relief for me to take a dog off her hands, especially when he was my dog in the first place."

☆☆☆

"Oh, Sandi, I am so sorry," Aunt Ed whined, looking out over the huge, empty pasture that spread behind her mobile home. "I didn't know he would run off."

Sandi gave her aunt a bug-eyed look. "Aunt Ed, you didn't go outside with Waffle?"

"Lord, no. I've never had a dog I had to hold his paw while he peed. There's a high cyclone fence out there. I thought he would go potty, then come back to the back door."

Sandi had thought so, too, though she hadn't been entirely certain. Waffle hadn't been exposed to the wide open spaces since he had come to live with her. And he had run off from somewhere before, hadn't he? Maybe this was a pattern with him. Not knowing what he had been like before she got him was a disadvantage.

"Let's go on in to the beauty shop," Aunt Ed continued. "Maybe Debbie Sue will have some ideas."

"Are you going to leave Jake home alone today?"

"Oh, no. Wouldn't hear of it. When Vic's not home, he goes to the shop with me."

They dressed and put on makeup hurriedly. When they were ready to leave, Aunt Ed went to Jake's room and came back with him sitting on her arm. Under his feet, she was wearing a glove that looked like a gauntlet.

"What is that, Aunt Ed?"

"It's a hard leather glove. His toe nails cut into my skin."

Jake made a sneezing noise. "Too much spray net."

"Is he talking about your hair?"

"Hell if I know. After all of the years I've been in the beauty shop business, I'm a little psychic, but even I can't read a parrot's mind. I think spray net is something new for him."

Sandi walked over to the parrot. "Good morning, Jake."

"Hello, pretty lady. Wanna fuck?"

Aunt Ed rolled her eyes and Sandy found a laugh. "He hasn't changed. I hate to say it, but it was a huge relief you taking him off my hands."

"I'll just bet it was," Aunt Ed said, placing Jake into his carrying cage.

"Stop! Stop! Call nine-one-one," Jake screeched.

Sandi put Pablo and Adolph in their carrier and they trundled to the Styling Station in Aunt Ed's Mustang with Sandi in the passenger seat of the two-seated car, buried under both Jake's and Pablo and Adolph's carriers.

As Aunt Ed drove, she angled a look at Sandi's position under the carrying cases. "Exactly how many dogs do you have?"

"Just five."

"And you've got other animals besides dogs?"

"A few. They come and go. It's hard for me to say no, knowing they'll likely be euthanized. Right now, besides the dogs, I have six cats, some chickens and a gerbil. I'll probably have them forever. They're animals no one wants. They've all got something wrong with them. The shelter tried to get me to take some goats the other day, but I don't have a place for goats to live."

"Lord, girl, do you have time for a social life?"

"Not much. Fortunately, Richard works all the time, so he doesn't seem to notice how often I'm tied up with something related to the animal shelter or the SPCA. Of course, he complains about the animals I have at home."

"Sounds to me like you'll have to eventually make a choice between him and them."

Sandi had not let herself think that far ahead. It didn't matter anyway because she had never been able to visualize a future with Richard. "As you say, maybe I'll have to make a choice."

"Well, that's a definite maybe. If that's how you feel about him, why on earth are you wasting your time with him?"

The question was a good one, but Sandi simply didn't let herself think about the answer. And she sure couldn't think about it today. At the moment, all she could think about was Waffle and where he could be. They rode in silence as she pondered.

Aunt Ed finally spoke. "If you're looking for a new man, that Nick Conway is sure a good-looking sucker and he's single. I hear he's the salt of the earth. Got those gorgeous blue eyes. Women would kill to have those eyelashes. Hell, I know a few women who would kill to have the rest of him, too."

Sandi hadn't forgotten that her aunt had a penchant for matchmaking. She had to head her off. "Not interested, Aunt Ed."

"Well, you should be. He's got a good job. C. J. told us Harley thinks a lot of him. Knowing Harley like I do, I'm sure he's well paid. It can't be bad having the respect of a multi-millionaire like Harley Carruthers. And he likes animals, too."

"That last fact might be his one redeeming quality. But Nick is not my friend, Aunt Ed. Don't forget that."

"Oh, I know. I'm just saying…"

At the beauty salon, they found Debbie Sue waiting for them. She helped Aunt Ed put Jake in his luxury home in the corner and sort his toys. "Some life, huh?," Debbie Sue said. "Just sit around on your perch all day, play with toys and spout off."

"And crap all over everything," Aunt Ed added.

"He's like a damn celebrity," Debbie Sue said.

They placed Pablo and Adolph in the back room.

"Where's Pablo?" Jake squawked when they returned to the salon.

Without thinking, Sandi fell back into her old routine of explaining her actions to Jake. "He has to stay in the other room. Dogs can't be in the beauty salon."

"Poor Pablo. Poor Pablo. Bad boy. Bad boy."

"Pablo has not been a bad boy, Jake. It's Jake who's a bad boy."

Only after all of them were settled did Debbie Sue ask about the whereabouts of Waffle.

"He's, uh, disappeared," Aunt Ed said. "I let him outside to go potty this morning and we haven't seen him since."

Debbie Sue's jaw dropped. "Edwina-Perkins Martin. You are shitting me."

Aunt Ed shook her head. "I know, I know. It's my fault. I take full responsibility."

"But that doesn't get the dog back," Debbie Sue replied. "As much as I hate it, we're going to have to go see Billy Don and tell him. In case Waffle's been dognapped."

"Pablo's dognapped," Jake said and made a sound like a guffaw. "Poor Pablo." He hopped to a higher perch.

"Who's Billy Don?" Sandi asked.

"Who's Billy Don?" Jake repeated.

"Our sheriff," Debbie Sue answered. "Since we don't have an animal control department in this town, he's in charge of that, too."

"Nine-one-one," Jake squawked. "Call the cops."

Sandi stepped back and raised her palms. "Just hold on, y'all. I'm not sure about getting the sheriff involved. I don't want to make a big issue of this. For one thing, I don't want Nick to know I've let Waffle disappear. He'll think I'm an irresponsible dog owner."

Debbie Sue gave her a pointed look. "Why do you care what he thinks?"

Sandi squared her shoulders and looked directly at Debbie Sue. "I don't."

Debbie Sue planted her fists on her hips. "Hasn't it occurred to you that Nick could have taken Waffle?"

"What is this?" Aunt Ed asked, looking at her partner with a frown. "Yesterday, you were on his side."

"Fuck that. Today I'm not. I don't believe Waffle ran away. I think Nick stole him."

On a gasp, Aunt Ed slapped her forehead with her palm. "Oh. My. God. You're right, Debbie Sue. Waffle just vanished. No noise, no commotion. That was because Nick was somebody he knew. My back yard isn't burglar-proof. Any kid could easily open the gate. So Nick just walked right up, opened the gate and let Waffle out."

Debbie Sue's chest puffed up and she gave a smug grin. "See? That's why we're detectives. Because we know how to figure things out."

Sandi had little interest in why her aunt and partner were detectives. She was more concerned that Aunt Ed had just turned Waffle out into the yard alone. "Damn," she stage whispered.

"Even if I think he's really Nick's dog," Debbie Sue said to Aunt Ed, "for the guy to sneak into your private property and take something you didn't give him is just fuckin' rude. And you know what you always say about rude behavior, Ed."

Aunt Ed pointed a finger at Debbie Due. "You're right. Let's go see Billy Don."

As the three of them trouped into Debbie Sue's red pickup truck, Sandi had an eerie feeling she had completely lost control of events. Her aunt and Debbie Sue were like steamrollers.

The sheriff's office was a low-slung rectangle made of ugly pinkish brick. An obviously hand-painted sign that said JAIL hung on one end. A fence taller than the building and topped by razor wire showed from behind the building. Another sign that said OFFICE hung over a door in the middle of the building. Sandi blinked. She had never seen anything quite like it. "This is the sheriff's office? And the jail is in the same building?"

"Yeah. Also Billy Don's living quarters."

Sandi's gaze swung to the opposite end of the building where tiny flower beds flanked a screen door and a patch of grass grew in front. A skinny cowboy stood out front swinging a lariat loops around a fire hydrant.

"Billy Don's the sheriff, but his dream is to be a calf-roper," Debbie Sue explained.

Sandi was acquainted with people in law enforcement and every single one of them was too busy to rope fire hydrants. Every cell in her brain told her that what she and her new crazy companions were doing was a mistake. She couldn't keep from asking, "He doesn't have anything else to do?"

"Trust me, darlin', we're all better off if he doesn't do anything," Aunt Ed answered.

As Debbie Sue shoved the transmission into park, the cowboy gathered his lariat and sauntered over to the driver's side window with a big grin. "What are you ladies up to so early in the morning?"

"Ed's niece's dog has been dognapped," Debbie Sue answered.

"Uh-oh," Billy Don said. "Well, come on in and give me the details." He ambled toward the door under the OFFICE sign.

Sandi and her aunt and Debbie Sue scooted out and followed him into the tiny office where they told their story and gave Waffle's description.

"Any idea who would just snatch him out of Edwina's back yard?" the sheriff asked. "Must've been a stranger." The sheriff gave a huffy heh-heh-heh. "Everybody knows who Edwina's husband is."

"We think it was the new general manager out at Harley's ranch," Debbie Sue said.

"Nick Conway?" The sheriff's head began to shake. "Oh, I don't know about that, Debbie Sue. Ol' Nick is a square shooter. I doubt he'd steal anything, especially not somebody's dog."

"We want you to investigate," Debbie Sue said.

"Why do you need me? You're an investigator yourself. If you think he's really got the dog, why don't you drive out to the Flying C and tell him to give it back?"

"It's a long story, Billy Don. Can you help us or not?"

"Debbie Sue, I don't go out to Harley's place for much. He takes care of his own problems. He might throttle me if he thought I was out there bothering one of his hands, especially his general manager."

"But if the guy has broken the law —"

Billy Don tilted his head and raised a palm, stopping her. "We don't know that. One thing your husband taught me was never to bother something that ain't bothering me."

Debbie stamped her booted foot. "Billy Don, that applies to rattlesnakes and wild animals. Didn't you hear me? He took a dog out of Ed's back yard."

"We don't know that."

"Listen to me. He had to open the gate. He might have even gone inside her fence. Uninvited. He broke in. If you go to Ed's yard, you'd probably find his footprints."

Aunt Ed tucked back her chin and gave her partner a look. "Footprints? There's nothing in that back yard but sand and rocks. A herd of buffalo could tromp through it and not leave any footprints."

Debbie Sue threw up her hands. "Y'all are making me crazy. Fuck it. I give up. It isn't my dog anyway." She stamped out of the office. Aunt Ed followed and Sandi trailed behind, breathing a sigh of relief. Debbie Sue's personality was a lot to contend with.

"Okay, now what?" Aunt Ed asked as they rode back to the Styling Station.

"We could find out easy enough if Nick's got him," Debbie Sue said. "I can just call up C.J. and ask her. She can see the manager's house from her kitchen window."

"If Nick took him, he wouldn't leave him outside alone," Edwina said. "That wouldn't make sense. Calling C.J. would be a waste of time and you might scare her."

"Nah," Debbie Sue replied. "When we get back to the shop, I'm going to call her."

Only when she looked in a mirror had Sandi seen anyone with more determination than Debbie Sue.

The minute they walked into the beauty salon, the woman picked up the phone and pressed in a number. "Hey, C.J., what are you up to today?... Uh-huh.... Uh-huh.... Sounds like fun. When are you leaving?... Oh, I see.... Listen, C.J., can't you see into the yard of your manager's house?... Does he have a big dog running around over there?"

Debbie Sue gave Aunt Ed a look and pumped a fist. "What does it look like?...Uh-huh.... Uh-huh. That sounds like him all right.... Oh, nothing much. Your manager was in the shop for a haircut and telling Ed he was getting a new dog. He mentioned us picking him up and dropping him off at the vet's to be groomed.... Well, listen, you're so busy, I'll let you go. Drive careful going up to Odessa.... Come to see us, ya hear?" She hung up.

Sandi didn't know who C.J. was, but the conversation sounded like Waffle had been found.

Debbie Sue looked up. "Okay, y'all, Nick's got him. He went by C.J and Harley's house earlier and told Harley about getting his dog back. The dog and a puppy are in his back yard."

"That would be Randy," Sandi said.

"What would be Randy?" Edwina asked.

"That's the puppy's name. Randy."

"Debbie Sue, I'm ashamed of you," Aunt Ed said. "It's not right lying to C.J. like that. And she's a friend of ours. She's gonna find out about this and I wouldn't blame her if she never speaks to you again."

"Ed. Stop and think. Was it right that Nick took Waffle out of your back yard? Just remember, sometimes, when you're handing out justice, you have to make tough choices. I've heard Buddy say it a hundred times and so have you. C.J. will be fine. She knows me. She'll understand."

"Hah," Aunt Ed said, and planted a fist on her hip.

"So here's the plan," Debbie Due went on as if Aunt Ed hadn't scolded her. "Harley sent Nick up to Odessa to do some kind of business and he'll be gone all day. Nick left Waffle behind in the back yard. Harley's already gone to his office in Midland for the day. C.J. is taking one of the kids up to Odessa to the dentist. We'll just drive out to the Flying C in my truck, pick up Waffle and come back to town. Everything all wrapped up an hour." Debbie Sue dusted her palms. "Then Sandi can put him in her SUV and take him back to Midland with her."

"Oh, yeah? And what if one of Harley's hands sees us slinking around?"

"And what if one of them doesn't? They're supposed to be out on the range. Besides, we aren't going to slink. You heard what I told C.J. We'll just say Nick asked us to take Waffle into town to be groomed."

"Harley's hands have all got guns. I've heard Harley say so."

"Of course they do. They use them to shoot varmints when they're out on the range."

"And what if one of them decides we're varmints? What if he shoots first and asks questions later? We could get killed. And we'd be lucky if we did because it'd be quick. If Buddy Overstreet, on the other hand, finds out we've done this, he'll skin us alive and stake us out on a red ant bed."

Euwww! Legends about the Texas Rangers abounded, but did they do that sort of thing these days? Panic began to flutter inside Sandi's stomach. All of the stories she had heard inside her family about her crazy aunt and her partner's zaniness were coming to light right before her eyes. "Ladies, please. I appreciate your help more than you'll ever know, but I don't have time to do this. I've got to go home. I've got two young girls taking care of my store. I've got a business to run and animals to feed."

Aunt Ed spoke to Debbie Sue as if Sandi hadn't said a word. "And if Harley and C.J. get pissed off, I guess you can explain everything, smartypants. They're better friends with you and Buddy than they are with me and Vic."

"It isn't a problem, Ed. I told you, C.J. will understand and she'll make Harley understand. Just like I make Buddy understand things."

"You mean sex."

"Well, of course."

Sandi stood there blinking at both women, trying to sort out the connection between sex and "understanding things." That feeling of being on a carnival ride with no brake had returned. Hoping to avert disaster, she meekly asked, "Wouldn't going into Nick's yard be breaking and entering or something?"

"We won't be breaking or entering anything," Debbie Sue said. "We'll just open the gate and let Waffle come out, just like Nick did in Ed's yard."

Aunt Ed released a great sigh. "Okay, Okay. Looks like we're gonna do this. Let me call and re-set some appointments."

No. No. We can't do this, Sandi wanted to shout, but she could see that Debbie Sue's steadfast resolve would override anything she said. The woman had a rebuttal for everything anyone said. Sandi had never met anyone with such a commanding personality.

Soon, Sandi was belted into the back seat of Debbie Sue's crewcab pickup and they were flying down the highway while Garth Brooks blasted "I've Got Friends in Low Places" from the radio. From where she sat, Sandi couldn't see the speedometer, but Aunt

Ed was hanging on to the dash with one hand and the "oh Jesus bar" with the other. Sandi could feel her heartbeat drumming in her stomach. She didn't know if her case of nerves was from the speed they were traveling or because she was about to break into someone's yard and steal a dog.

"Don't forget that curve up ahead," Aunt Ed cautioned.

At the Flying C, they saw no people. Only a sprawling Spanish-style ranch house of tan stucco with wide verandahs and huge pots of beautiful colorful flowers. Debbie Sue drove past it to a smaller but still nice redbrick house with a chain-link-fenced yard all around it. They and Waffle spotted each other and he began to bark and trot along the fence.

"There he is," Debbie Sue said, catching Sandi's gaze in the rearview mirror.

She drove behind the house, came to a stop at a gate in the fence and shoved the gear shift into park. She turned back to Sandi and said, "Go get him."

You go get him, Sandi wanted to reply. *This is your idea.* Instead, she bit down on her lower lip.

"Do you need any help, hon?" Aunt Ed asked.

"I don't think so." Sandi picked up the leash she had brought with her, eased down from the back seat and tiptoed toward the gate, looking left over one shoulder and right over the other.

"Jesus Christ, Sandi, you don't have to sneak up on him," Debbie Sue hollered out the driver's side window. "There's nobody here but us."

Still, Sandi was cautious. She eased the gate open and Waffle trotted to meet her, a big smile on his face. She bent down to hook the leash on his collar and he licked her face and made happy dog noises. A memory of how he had reacted when he saw Nick came back to her. Waffle was as fickle as most of the other males she knew.

With no trouble, she hooked the leash onto his collar, took the time to re-latch the gate, then easily led Waffle into Debbie Sue's pickup. And just like that, Waffle was hers again.

As soon as they reached Salt Lick, giving no more thought to what they had done, Sandi hurriedly gathered all three dogs, their respective toys and abodes and hit the highway to Midland.

Chapter 15

NICK ARRIVED HOME mid-afternoon, but didn't see Buster in the backyard. He parked and walked through the house and out into the yard. Randy was there, bouncy and happy to see him, but where was Buster? Had he escaped and run off again? If so, how had he gotten out of the yard? Anxiety skittered through Nick's midsection.

He walked the perimeter of the fence, looking for a break or a sign the fence had been cut. He investigated the gate and latch, which appeared to be untouched. He called and whistled to no avail. Just like before, he had no idea where to look. The dog was as elusive as quicksilver.

Scanning the landscape, he saw Harley's wife watering plants on their patio. Heartsick over losing Buster again, he walked over. "Evening, C.J."

"Oh, hi, Nick. Are you looking for Harley? He hasn't come home yet."

"I'm looking for my dog. You know, the big dog I brought home yesterday?"

"Oh. He and your new puppy were in your back yard this morning. I saw them playing. But I left early and was gone all day. I didn't even look when I got home. He's not there now?"

Nick shook his head.

"Aw, I'm sorry. Maybe he hasn't come back from town yet."

Nick's head snapped up. "What town? What do you mean?"

"You know. Salt Lick. The vet's wife sometimes grooms dogs for people she likes. Debbie Sue mentioned that you wanted Buster groomed. She and Ed probably came out here and got him."

Shit. Buster was either back at Sandi's aunt's house in Salt Lick or back with Sandi in Midland. Relief surged inside Nick. At least Buster was safe. Nick felt better, but only slightly. Now he had to figure out how to get his dog back again.

"Oh. Okay, thanks, C.J." He touched his hat brim to her and walked back to his house and his new puppy.

The next morning, he awoke with Buster, the Salt Lick sleuths and the good-looking redhead on his mind. This BS had gone far enough. It was interfering with his job. But before he took further action, he had to be sure that Buster hadn't run off again, that Sandi and her pals had him.

A plan evolved in his mind. After readying for the day, he went into his home office and typed up a flyer on his computer. A beauty shop would be an ideal place to leave handouts. Of course, once he asked Sandi's aunt and her partner to allow him to leave the handouts in the Styling Station, they would know he had removed Buster from the aunt's back yard. Guilt threatened to stop him, but he swallowed it and moved forward.

At the Styling Station, while he sat out front drumming his fingers on the steering wheel and trying to decide the best way to approach the situation, Debbie Sue walked out of the beauty shop and up to his window. He buzzed it down. "Hey."

"Hey yourself. Whatcha doing?"

Nick made a spur-of-the-moment decision to come clean. He truly believed honesty was the best policy and he didn't want to make enemies of Edwina and Debbie Sue. And he especially didn't want to make an enemy of Sandi. If everything got un-screwed up, he would like to know her better.

"My dog is lost again." He lifted the small stack of flyers off the passenger seat and started to hand them to Debbie Sue. "I was hoping you'd—"

"Ever hear that old saying, what goes around comes around?"

Her ire radiated all the way through his truck window. *Uh-oh.* He angled a cautious look at her. "Yeah, I've heard it."

"Then think about it." She paused, looking him in the eye. "You're wasting paper on flyers."

"Wait a minute." He opened the door and stepped down from his seat. "Why do I think you know where Buster is?"

"*Waffle* is at his home in Midland with his *owner,* Sandi Walker. You shouldn't have stolen him out of Ed's yard."

"I know that. It was dumb. I know I owe Edwina an apology."

"You owe Ed and her niece both an apology. And you might as well apologize to me, too. Ed and I stick together. And because she's my friend, so is her niece."

"You said you have dogs."

"I do. Three of them."

"Big dogs or little dogs?"

"What difference does it make? This isn't about me and my dogs."

"The difference is you know what different dogs are like. Buster isn't a frou-frou lap dog. He happens to be a working dog. A cattle dog."

"He isn't a born-and-bred cattle dog. He doesn't even look like a cattle dog. He's a mix."

"That might be, but he has the instincts of a cattle dog. He loves to be busy. He shouldn't be cooped up in a house or a store. He needs to have room to run."

For a fleeting moment, he thought he saw understanding in her eyes, but she turned on her heel, prissed her ass-in-tight jeans into the beauty shop and slammed the door with a *Crash!*

Women!

He sat a few more minutes, absorbing all that he thought he now knew. So those crazy women had come out to his home on his employer's ranch and taken Buster out of his back yard. Nervy. Harley's words from yesterday came to him: *Edwina and Debbie Sue do have a way of getting everyone's attention.*

If he gave in to his instinct for fair play, this was poetic justice in a way. Debbie Sue was right. He shouldn't have taken Buster out of Edwina's yard. Later, after tempers had a chance to cool, he would come back to town and apologize to Edwina.

But at the moment, he was more concerned with getting his dog back and after all that had happened, an apology to a crazy woman wouldn't solve that problem.

He returned to the ranch and dug his Midland phone book out of a desk drawer. He paged through the yellow pages under "Attorneys" and found Aubrey

Hester's name and an office address in downtown Midland. Like Jason Webster, Aubrey was an old high school acquaintance, though Nick hadn't seen him or talked to him in years.

The phone operator in Aubrey's office told him the lawyer was out for the day, but after some cajoling and a little teasing, she said he was probably playing golf. Nick's memory zoomed backward to when he and Aubrey were in high school. The Aubrey Hester he remembered was too blind to follow a golf ball in flight, didn't have an athletic bone in his body or a muscle anywhere.

Nick prowled through his desk until he found the roster listing the names, addresses and home phone numbers of the Midland High School class of 2001. An office number and a cell number were listed for Aubrey. Nick pressed in the cell number.

The lawyer answered right away. After Nick told him who he was, a monotonous who's-died, who-lives-where-now and what's-who doing-now conversation ensued. Minutes later, Nick got an opportunity to explain the situation.

"Hey, no problem, Nick," Aubrey replied. "We'll get that pooch back to you in no time. I just have to talk to the judge. He's a friend of mine."

Wow. Back in their high school days, every person in Midland High School would have said that Aubrey Hester was more likely to be standing in front of a judge than being friends with one.

"Where did you say the dog is?" Aubrey asked.

Nick gave him Sandi's store name and address.

"You can trust me to take care of this, Nick. I'll do it first thing tomorrow. If I need more information, I'll call you."

"Fine."

"Listen, I gotta go, buddy. They're waiting on me to putt out. We need to get together sometime and have a beer.... Oh, and Nick? One more thing. Don't go near her. Or the dog. Just leave things alone and let me take care of it."

Nick hung up, satisfied that something would be done. He didn't know exactly what, but something. He should have called a lawyer in the first place and not fooled with a deputy sheriff. Then an afterthought came to him. Calling up a lawyer on a golf course probably wasn't the greatest idea. Nick had told Aubrey Sandi's address and phone numbers, but he felt sure Aubrey hadn't written them down.

☆☆☆

After so much confusion and stress, Sandi had a calm, uneventful week. The weekend came. Richard took her out to dinner and they saw a movie. He seemed morose. Probably because John Wilson was still in jail. Not wanting to ruin a pleasant evening, Sandi didn't broach that subject.

On Monday, just after finishing up a fresh batch of Atomic Energizer, the front door chimed and a man wearing neatly pressed jeans and a long-sleeve dress shirt stepped into the store. He had "cop" written all over him. "Miss Sandi Walker?"

"Yes, I'm Sandi Walker."

He thrust a folded blue document at her. Reflexively she took it and unfolded it. "What is this?"

"It's a summons to court, ma'am."

Stunned, she looked up at her antagonist.

"Judge Theodore J. Bellamy. It's an informal hearing." He touched the bill of his cap. "You have a good day, ma'am."

He walked out, leaving her with her jaw hanging.

She quickly recovered and began to read. She was ordered to appear in court with Waffle accompanying her at one o'clock exactly one week from today. *Oh. My. God.*

On trembly knees she walked to the back room, sat down at the table and began to read the document again.

"Are you okay?" Betty Ann asked.

"Not quite. Can you bring me a cup of coffee?"

Betty Ann reappeared with a mug of steaming coffee and set it on the table.

"Thank you, Betty Ann."

"Mind if I sit down?" Without waiting for an answer, the employee seated herself opposite Sandi and nodded toward the document. "What is that?"

"It's a summons. I can't believe it. Nick Conway is trying to take Waffle away from me through the court system."

"Can he do that? I mean, I never heard of anybody suing somebody over a dog. And on such short notice. Nick must know the judge. Is it an official paper?"

Sandi turned the document over, but the back was blank. "It looks official." She continued to read, barely hearing Betty Ann. "Oh, my God. He's saying I stole Waffle and that I'm using him as a guinea pig for my weird pet food. What an asshole."

Betty Ann made a dismissive gesture with her hand. "Oh, don't worry about that. Those lawyers make up shit to make you look bad."

She sighed and sat back in her chair. "I know only one thing. I cannot afford to hire a lawyer."

"Can't you represent yourself?"

"I don't know the first thing about doing that, but I guess I'll have to."

That afternoon, a frantic Richard called. "Sandi," he blurted without even saying hello. "I saw your name on Judge Bellamy's court docket. What is going on?"

Sandi walked to the back room and took a seat at the table. "You're overexcited, Richard. Nick Conway is suing me for custody of Waffle."

"This is insane. I know Judge Bellamy. He's a tough judge. Hardline all the way. Just give that guy the damn dog and be done with this."

Richard had never had a pet, not even as a boy. He couldn't relate to her affection for Waffle or any animal. She gasped. "I will not. Not unless I have to. I have rights, too, you know."

"I swear, Sandi, I've never seen this...this intransigent side of you."

"How well I know. Well, you know what? Being some guy's doormat has been one of my shortcomings for years. Good ol' good sport Sandi. Just go along to get along. Well... no more."

"Even if I had the time to help you, frankly, I don't know if I want to be seen defending a dog. That's a moot issue anyway because I'm tied up in court myself. I'll see if I can find someone who'll represent you on short notice."

"No. I can't afford a lawyer."

"Sandi, I'll find someone who'll do it pro bono. As a favor to me."

"You mean for free? No, Richard. I don't want someone you know to represent me for free. I don't want to owe you or your friends. You're embarrassed by my animals. You don't like Waffle. And half the time, I wonder if you like me. I want you to stay out of it and mind your own business."

"Those are some nasty allegations, Sandi. I care about you. I feel obligated to help you. If you'll just do as I tell you—"

"And if I don't follow orders, will you still care about me, Richard?"

"All I've ever wanted you to do is being reasonable about those animals. But no. You've just kept taking on more."

"You're heartless, Richard. At least my animals haven't robbed an elderly woman and cut her throat or carjacked any cars. All they want is a decent place to live out their lives. They have unconditional love for me. Do thieves and murderers do that for you?"

Big sigh on the line. "Okay, so we're back to John Wilson again and what I do for a living. I think we'd better end this conversation. I'll just leave you with this, babydoll. If you go before Judge Bellamy without a good attorney, you'll lose."

"If I do, it'll be because it was meant to be. I have to go. I've got a million things to do. I'm going to hang up. And one more thing, Richard. Do not *ever* call me *babydoll* again."

Sandi disconnected, then sat at the table for a few minutes, thinking. Her relationship with Richard was toxic. He annoyed her more often than he pleased her. They no longer had anything in common. Maybe they never had. Lately, he brought more stress than good times into her life. She should end it.

Six o'clock came. As she prepared to close, though Richard rarely came to her shop, he appeared. "Richard. What are you doing here? I don't want to continue our earlier argument."

"I didn't like the way our phone conversation ended. Let's go to dinner. I want to clear the air." He bent down to kiss her, but she turned her face away. He straightened and stepped back, glaring down at her. "Oh, so it's that way, is it?"

"I've been thinking all afternoon, Richard. I think we should end it. We don't seem to have much going for us as a couple. You don't have the time to put into a relationship and you don't like my animals."

"We've been together a year, Sandi. How can you say that? You just need to meet me halfway."

"By doing what? Surrendering my animals to be euthanized? Giving up my work with WLA? I'll never be able to do that, Richard. Now that I've seen how many unwanted creatures there are and how needy they are, I'm called to do this. I couldn't live with myself if I threw it to the wind. I'd think you'd be relieved to be rid of me."

His eyes glistened. Was he going to cry? "I don't want to be rid of you. I just want... I just want —"

"Oh, Richard, you just want everything to be the way you want it, without regard to the way things are or what *I* want. Why don't we agree to be just friends for a while and see how it works out?"

Chapter 16

A WEEK LATER, Sandy was prepared for her and Waffle's day in court. As much as she could manage, she had researched representing herself in a hearing in front of a judge. On Sunday afternoon, she practiced in front of her vanity mirror.

She prepared for bed Sunday night cautiously confident of tomorrow's outcome. Surely a judge would see that Waffle was better off with a soft life with her than with being out racing around a pasture tending a herd of cattle and possibly encountering God knew what.

Before turning in, she let Waffle outside for his nightly ritual. He had been out only a few minutes when she heard a chorus of loud, hysterical barking—not just from Waffle, but from her other big dogs, Ricky and Fred. Pablo began to pace and growl. Adolph, too, barked and yipped louder than usual. Smelling a skunk odor, she strode to the back door. Adolph trotted along beside her, looking up at her anxiously.

She opened the door and walked out onto the patio.

Waffle had something cornered outside Ricky and Fred's pen and the two dogs were barking and clawing at their wire fence as if they were wild animals. A few seconds later, she was able to see Waffle facing off against a skunk.

"Oh, no! Oh, my God! Waffle! Come here!... Come here, boy!"

When he didn't obey, Sandy dashed across the yard, waded into the fray and grabbed Waffle's collar. The clamor halted for a few seconds. Suddenly skunk odor pierced the air, as indescribably potent as if the small varmint were standing right beside her. The putrid smell threatened to take her breath. "Oh, my God!"

All three dogs began to shrink back and whimper. Waffle was whining and wiping at his face and nose with his front paws. He shrank to the ground and rolled his head and face on the grass. The skunk raced across the back yard and disappeared through the fence.

"Oh, my God, no!" she shrieked. She, too had been sprayed.

Oh, dear God. "No, no, no."

Sandi stood there in the reeking air paralyzed by panic.

With all of the pets she'd had, she had never had one that had been in a confrontation with a skunk. She had never been close to a skunk either. She turned back into her house, seeking to slam the back door against the breathtaking smell, but she carried it with her.

For lack of an immediate solution, she picked up the phone receiver with trembling fingers and pressed in her aunt's number. Aunt Ed and her husband would know what to do. They knew everything.

"Hey, babygirl, what in the world are you doing calling your dear ol' aunt at ten o'clock at night?"

"Oh, Aunt Ed, my dogs and I got sprayed by a skunk and the stench is sickening. Waffle has to go to court with me tomorrow and —"

"What are you going to court for?"

"Nick is suing me for custody of Waffle. We have to be there at one o'clock for a hearing."

"That bastard! Who's your lawyer? I hope you've got a good one."

"Of course, I don't. I can't afford lawyers. I'm representing myself. What am I going to do about this odor? I think I might throw up any minute. I can't go into the courtroom with me and Waffle smelling like a skunk."

"Tomato juice, hon. Tomato juice. That's the only remedy. Get about a gallon of it and wash them down."

"What about me?"

"Wash yourself down, too, I guess. Hell, I don't know. I don't know any humans a skunk got to."

"Oh, dear, Aunt Ed. Gallons of tomato juice are not something I keep around the house."

"Then you'll have to go to the store, darlin'. Listen, I'm sorry, but I need to run. My honey and I are in the middle of something." She hung up.

Sandi glowered at the phone. Her aunt had never hung up on her.

Recovering her wits, she grabbed her keys, dashed outside to her car and headed for Walmart, the only grocery store she knew would have a large quantity of tomato juice on hand. Once there, she cleared one whole shelf of half-gallon cans of tomato juice. Fortunately, with the late hour, few people were in the grocery store, but the ones that were there, backed away and stared at her. She lifted her chin as if she were wearing the world's most expensive perfume and pushed her basket to the cash register.

Back in her driveway, she called her neighbor. "Fiona, what are you doing?"

"Nothing much. Chilling out. Listening to some tunes."

"Is there any way you can come over and help me? I've got to go to court with Waffle tomorrow, you know. He and I and my other two big dogs got sprayed by a skunk and I have to bathe them and me in tomato juice."

"Oh, shit," Fiona said. "I thought I smelled a skunk. How did you get sprayed?"

"It's too long a story to tell right now. I just need your help."

"I'll be right there. Have you got enough juice? I've got some spaghetti sauce."

Mental eyeroll. "I bought ten half-gallons of juice. Surely that will be enough."

Fiona showed up dressed in pink babydoll pajamas and high-heeled house shoes with huge white pom-poms on the toe. Her bleached blond tresses were tipped with hot pink.

Two a.m. came. Sandi and Fiona had drunk a pot of coffee. Waffle, Ricky and Fred had been scrubbed with tomato juice, then washed with doggie shampoo. Sandi had doused herself in the red liquid, then showered with cucumber-melon shower gel. The kitchen and bathroom looked as if she and Fiona had butchered a hog, then taken a hose to both rooms. And the dogs still stunk.

Through it all, Waffle had looked at them with sad eyes and cooperated as best he could. He was sorry for causing so much trouble. Sandi believed that and it made her love him all the more. How could she ever give him up?

Adolph, for the first time since Sandi had owned him, had stopped yapping, retreated to his bed and covered his face with his paws. Pablo looked on from afar, continuing to snarl and growl.

"I give up." Fiona poured herself another cup of coffee and collapsed onto a dining room chair. Her pajamas and white pom-poms were soaking wet and stained red. Her long hair hung in thick wet clumps with pink tips. "I think that's the best we can do without scrubbing their skin off. But they still stink. There must be a better solution, but I don't know what it is."

Sandi sighed. "Maybe it just has to wear off, but at least they don't seem to be suffering anymore. I'll call the vet as soon as his office opens and see what he says."

Sipping her coffee, Fiona nodded.

"Listen, thank you again for helping me," Sandi said. "I owe you some new pajamas and a new pair of house shoes."

Her neighbor waved the offer away. "Forget it. You'd do the same for me."

"I would, but I still owe you. If you hadn't helped me, I would've been at this until daylight."

"Hey, we're neighbors, right? But I'd better get going. It's after two o'clock. I need some sleep so I'll be bright-eyed in court tomorrow."

Sandi walked with her neighbor to the front door. "You don't have to be there. You've done enough."

"Hey, I'll be there to support you, girlfriend."

Prissy, too, had already said she would be there as well as Betty Ann. That her friends might take the time out of their busy days to be present at the hearing that meant nothing to them had touched Sandi's heart.

"Besides," Fiona continued, "it's worth it to me just to get a look at that Nick Conway. Sylvia says he's plumb larruping when he's all dressed up." She giggled wickedly. "I could do larruping, if you know what I mean. I'm probably as good at it as Sylvia." She bobbed her eyebrows.

Good grief! All Fiona thought about was sex. Sandi was too exhausted to be shocked by what her neighbor had said.

As soon as Fiona cleared the front porch, Sandi returned Ricky and Fred to their pen in the back yard. Waffle was already in his bed. She had spent weeks getting rid of the smell Jake had left in her house. Now skunk odor filled the air around her. Tomorrow, when she had a few free seconds, she would think about what to do about it.

Only after she fell into bed did she realize just how much she, too, still smelled like a skunk.

☆☆☆

Dawn came. Sandy barely dragged herself out of bed. The repulsive odor still lingered, but not nearly as potent as it had been a few hours earlier. After scrubbing herself with tomato juice and showering with cucumber-melon gel, Sandi didn't feel a need for another bath, but she had to try to get rid of the smell. She drew herself a bath and loaded it with lavender bubble bath.

Prissy had volunteered to bathe and groom Waffle and have him looking his golden best, but he, too, had already been washed in tomato juice and scrubbed with doggie shampoo. Surely he was clean enough, although skunk odor still hung on and his coat was slightly red-tinted.

She called Prissy early and told her what had happened and that she didn't think taking him into the Pampered Pooch for grooming was necessary.

"Did you trim his hair?" Prissy asked.

"I didn't have time."

"Did you clean his teeth?"

"Well, no—"

"Did you do his nails?"

"Prissy, I don't think he needs a manicure."

"Were you able to get rid of the smell?"

"It's still there a little bit, but it isn't as strong as it was. I have no more energy to give to the problem, Prissy. I guess this is the best I can do."

"Nope. Bring that doggie in here. I'll bathe him with a tried and true formula for getting rid of that skunky odor."

"Okay, I guess. I hope he doesn't get a rash from all the scrubbing and washing."

At the Pampered Pooch, Prissy bathed Waffle in her recipe—peroxide, baking soda and dishwashing soap. Afterward, he did smell better, but the skunk odor still wasn't gone entirely. As promised, Prissy cleaned his teeth and gave him a dog biscuit guaranteed to give him sweet breath. She manicured his nails and Sandi chose a new collar from her store display.

At home again, she donned a dark green business suit she had worn when she worked as a bank vice-president, a pale green silk tank underneath it, a pair of stockings for the first time in months and nude-colored pumps. She wrangled her long, thick hair into a sleek chignon and hung gold hoops in her ears. For someone who had been awake most of the night and burdened with an anvil of stress, she looked reasonably well. "Bring it on," she growled into the vanity mirror.

She spritzed herself with a heavy dose of Juicy Couture perfume and for good measure, she heavily sprayed Waffle with the same potion.

At the courthouse, she saw her dear sweet Aunt Ed and her partner Debbie Sue standing on the sidewalk out front. She was wearing a fire-engine-red sheath and pounds of gold jewelry on her skinny body. Debbie Sue had on a green dress and cowboy boots. Sandi hadn't expected them. Tears misted her eyes as she and Waffle hurried to meet them.

"Aunt Ed. Debbie Sue. What are you two doing here?"

"Why wouldn't we be here?" Debbie Sue asked. "Ed's a witness."

"I wouldn't let my favorite niece go through this without me being here, hon," Aunt Ed said.

"Yeah," Debbie Sue added. "After all, Ed caused the problem. She shouldn't have let Waffle out into the back yard alone."

Sandi had to laugh even though she wasn't in a laughing mood. "Thank you so much. I so appreciate your support."

Her aunt frowned and sniffed the air. "What's that smell?"

"It's Juicy Couture, I think. I sprayed myself and Waffle. Is it too much?"

"Oh, don't worry. It'll probably be okay if you stay downwind."

Just then, Fiona, Betty Ann and Prissy hustled up and joined them. Sandi introduced them, too.

"Oh, my God, I love your shoes," Fiona said to Aunt Ed.

Everyone's attention veered to Aunt Ed's feet. She was indeed wearing the most darling spike-heel pumps. They looked like ice cream sundaes dripping with chocolate syrup, with bright red cherries on the toes.

"Oh, my Lord," Sandi gushed. "Those shoes are so to-die-for, Aunt Ed. Where ever did you get them?"

"My honey bought them for me in L.A. He's got excellent taste when it comes to shoes." She bent and scruffed Waffle's head. "So is this culprit ready for his big day?"

Waffle grinned up at her, his tail whipping.

"I can't believe all of you are here," Sandi said, using her pinky finger to wipe a tear from the corner of her eye. "I've got quite the entourage."

"We are not about to sit still and see you or Waffle treated unfairly," Prissy said firmly.

"I do the bailiff's wife's hair every week," Fiona said. "She and I have been talking about this hearing." She giggled. "She wanted to come with me today to get a look in person at Nick Conway, but her husband wouldn't let her."

"Look, I don't think this is going to be a big deal," Sandi said. "Please don't say anything unless they ask you to, okay?"

"Oh, we won't," Debbie Sue said. "We know how to behave. If I made an ass of myself in a courtroom, my husband would hear about it for sure. He'd lock me in the house and never let me out."

As they passed through the security scan, Sandi held her breath, hoping that her aunt and/or Debbie Sue weren't carrying. She wouldn't put it past either one of them. To her relief, the only thing that set off the alarm was Waffle's new collar.

Outside the courtroom, a man met them and introduced himself as the bailiff. "Are all of you together?" He sniffed a couple of times, then pulled his handkerchief from his back pocket and wiped his nose.

"We are," Sandi's entourage answered in chorus.

He asked for custody of Waffle.

Debbie Sue stepped up. "Hold on. Why? Where are you taking him?"

"He can't go into the courtroom, ma'am, unless Judge Bellamy asks for him. We'll hold him outside here in the hallway."

Sandy reluctantly handed over Waffle's leash and the bailiff gestured her and her group into the courtroom.

Sandi had never been inside a Midland courtroom. She had never been inside a courtroom anywhere. She hadn't even served on a jury. In both of her divorces, the proceedings had been handled by lawyers without her presence. In the cavernous space of rich dark wood walls and formal furnishings, she felt small and ineffectual. Scrolling through her mind like an endless chain was one thought: *I'm going to lose this fight.*

Leaving her group in the public gallery, she summoned her courage and strode forward toward an empty long table across from the judge's tall bench.

She stole a look at Nick seated at a long table to her right. His hair was perfectly styled and combed, his jaw clean shaven. A tan leather blazer stretched across his wide shoulders. Starched and creased denim jeans hugged his long thighs. He looked good enough to eat with a spoon. She felt that little squiggle in her midsection that seeing him always caused.

A balding man with glasses sat beside him and they talked in low tones. His lawyer, no doubt.

Nick turned and looked behind himself as her little group seated themselves on one of the long bench seats. His eyes rolled. *Damn him for judging her and her friends!* A burst of anger replaced the intimidation she had felt on first arriving. He had his nerve stealing Waffle then suing her. Her jaw clenched.

The judge breezed in, his long black robe billowing behind him, half-glasses resting on his nose. As he seated himself in all of his self-importance, Sandi couldn't keep from noticing his ill-fitting toupee. She heard a stifled giggle from behind her. Fiona the Hairdresser, no doubt. Hopefully, it hadn't come from Aunt Ed or Debbie Sue. Sandi almost laughed herself.

The judge could barely be seen behind the tall bench. As he sorted papers on top of the bench, his nose wrinkled. "What's that smell?"

"Uh, must be something in the air, your honor," the bailiff answered.

The judge made an exaggerated sigh, followed by a brief opening statement. He then turned to Sandi. "You were ordered to bring the subject dog to court today. Have you done that?"

"Yessir. I had to give him to your bailiff."

The judge turned to the bailiff. "Bring in the animal."

The bailiff left the huge room and soon returned loosely leading Waffle. The dog trotted along beside him as if he knew he was the center of attention.

"What *is* that smell?" the judge asked again. "It almost smells like a skunk."

"It must be coming from outside, your honor," the bailiff answered.

"Well, make sure the door is closed tightly. Enough two-legged skunks pass through this courtroom. We don't need a four-legged one."

No one dared laugh. One of the cops present hurried to secure the door.

At that same moment, a white cat with big black spots sauntered out of a room behind and to the side of the judge's bench. It suddenly halted. Its back humped into a mound, a *meoooowrrrrr* came from its throat and it threw itself at Waffle.

The dog ripped loose from the bailiff and lunged for the cat, snarling and barking. *Woof! Bwoof! Woof!*

"Waffle! Waffle! No!" Sandi cried.

The cat scrambled up the side of the judge's bench.

The judge sprang to his feet and banged his gavel. "Order! Order!"

On a feline yowl, the cat darted across the top of the bench, scattering papers in a cloud and tipping over a glass filled with water.

"Desiree! Desiree!" the judge shouted, futilely grabbing for the cat. His toupee loosened and slid down over one eye.

Waffle stood on his hind legs, frantically scratched on the side of the bench, trying to climb it.

Sandi clasped her jaws with her palms, looking on in horror. A hooting laugh came from the group sitting behind her.

Waffle darted around the front of the judge's bench upending the court reporter and tipping her backward. Her equipment hit the floor with a loud clatter and crash. Nick rushed forward to aid her.

Sandi lunged for Waffle's leash, but he was too quick. He began pawing and clawing at the opposite side of the judge's bench. The cat met him yowling and hissing. Perched on its haunches, it boxed Waffle's nose. Waffle barked and whined and clawed at the side of the judge's bench.

The judge finally grabbed the cat with both hands, but the short-haired animal, as if it were greased, escaped, leaped to the rail that separated the jury box from the courtroom and dashed across the jury panel chairs. Waffle chased after it, barking and clawing his way over the chairs. The bailiff followed.

"Order! Order! Goddammit, I said order!" The judge banged his gavel so hard the handle broke and his toupee flipped off and onto the bench. He collapsed into his chair and fell back, his bald head shining, his glasses askew.

Two armed policeman rushed in. Fearing for Waffle's safety, Sandi hiked her skirt and climbed over the jury box rail. Stumbling and falling through the chairs, she captured Waffle by flinging both arms around his neck. He continued to bark and strain against her, dragging her through the jury box chairs until he escaped her grip altogether.

All at once, the cat was nowhere to be seen. Calm began to return. Sandi found herself lying prone across two chairs. She sensed a presence and looked up. Nick loomed over her, a tight grip on Waffle's collar. "Are you all right?"

Her heart was pounding so hard she thought it might jump out of her chest. "Do I look like I'm all right? Don't speak to me."

She struggled to a sitting position. Her stockings were torn, she had lost a shoe and a sheaf of her chignon had come loose and hung down the side of her face.

Nick offered a hand. She took it and got to her feet, then yanked up her skirt and climbed over the jury box rail a second time. She looked around. Her aunt and her friends stood in a line behind the gallery rail, anxious looks on their faces. Her knee throbbed and burned like fire and felt as if it had been hit with a hammer. She inspected it and saw a large bleeding scrape.

"Looks like you skinned your knee. Here, let me fix it." Nick pulled a handkerchief out of his back pocket, then knelt on one knee in front of her and tied it around her knee. "There, that oughtta help 'til you can get to some first aid." He bent over the rail, retrieved her shoe and handed it to her.

She shakily clasped his arm as she bent and slipped on her shoe. "I don't know what happened. I don't know what would make Waffle attack a cat."

Nick shrugged nonchalantly, as if bedlam had not just occurred. "He's a dog. Why does he stink? What did you do, spray him with perfume? And why is he so red?"

Nick's lawyer came up behind him, clearing his throat and wiping his nose. "Can we, um, be seated? I think the judge has a statement."

"And I've got a question," Nick snapped. "What the hell is a cat doing in a courtroom?"

Leave it to a man to blame the cat, Sandi thought sourly.

Nick's lawyer shrugged and gave an arch look. "Judge Bellamy is a cat lover. That one, Desiree, is his favorite cat. She usually stays in his chambers with him."

"Shit." Nick said.

Prissy had taken charge of Waffle and she and Betty Ann had removed him from the courtroom. With much grumbling and throat-clearing, Sandi's remaining entourage took their seats. She limped back to the long table, scanning the courtroom and the destruction wrought. A little surge of guilt pinched her. They could have avoided all of this damage and turmoil if she and Nick had just done what his friend, the deputy sheriff, had suggested in the first place.

She squeezed her eyes shut and clamped her jaw tight. *Dear God.* How much was this going to cost her?

The judge cleared his throat. "Mr. Hester. First, I will tell you that this is a frivolous proceeding. It's a waste of the court's time and taxpayers' dollars. I should instruct the county to bill you and your client for the damage done to my courtroom, but I recognize a mitigating factor." He looked lovingly toward Desiree now resting smugly in the bailiff's arms.

Taking his attention back to Nick, the judge continued. "Mr. Conway, I've read your written statement. What is wrong with you? You're an adult. A well-educated, accomplished man. A scientist. You, sir, have a graduate college degree."

"Yessir," Nick said meekly.

The judge swung his gaze to Sandi and she cringed inside. "You, madam, have a college degree and as I understand it, you own your own innovative business. You are not a stupid woman."

How the judge knew such personal things about Nick and her, Sandi didn't know. "Yessir," she said meekly. "I mean nossir."

"I don't know why anyone would want such an obnoxious dog, but I'm convinced his true owner is Mr. Conway."

"But your honor—"

"I'm speaking, Miz Walker. I am ordering custody of the dog known as Buster—"

"It's Waffle, your honor. His name is—"

The judge glared at her over the top of his half glasses. "Do not press your luck, Miz Walker." He cleared his throat. "I am awarding custody of the dog known as Buster to Mr. Nicholas Conway."

Sandi fought back tears. But why was she about to cry? Hadn't she known this was the way this hearing would go?

"However, I am also ordering that Mr. Conway share the dog with you freely, allowing home visits and allowing you to have dog in your custody at least once every two weeks. If this does not occur, you are to report the infraction to this court. Understood?"

"Yessir."

Mollified though not exhilarated at the ruling, Sandi stole a sideways glance at Nick. He stared straight at the judge, his jaw clenched.

Sandi bit down on her lower lip. *Oh, dear. This isn't going to be easy.*

Chapter 17

NICK FOLLOWED SANDI, her aunt, Debbie Sue and the short woman with pink-tipped hair out of the courtroom. Outside on the sidewalk, they met Mrs. Porter and one of Sandi's employees Nick recognized from LaBarkery. Buster, wagging his tail, looked toward him longingly. Nick walked over to the group. Though tightly held in check by Mrs. Porter, Buster barked and danced.

Nick touched his hat brim to the women. "Ladies."

Silence.

Purse-mouthed, the aunt glared at him. Mouth curved in a horseshoe scowl, Mrs. Porter handed him Buster's leash.

"Thank you, ma'am. I know that right now, you ladies think I'm an ogre, but—"

"That would be the kinder of our thoughts," the aunt said.

"No." Sandi shook her head. "We don't. Or at least, I don't. The important thing is that Waffle will have a good, safe place to live and will be loved and—"

Before she could finish, a tall guy wearing a suit and tie strode up, clasped Sandi's shoulders and looked into her face. "Sandi. Is everything okay?"

Who the hell is he? Nick wondered

Scowling, Sandi peeled his hands away from her shoulders. "Richard, I asked you to stay out of this. I told you I didn't want your help."

"I know that. But in case you needed me, I came as soon as I got out of court."

"Even if I had, you're too late. That's the problem we've always had, Richard. You're too preoccupied with your career to worry about what I'm doing except to criticize me and my animals. And by the way, just like you said, I lost Waffle."

"That's a good thing, Sandi. You've got too many critters."

He he turned to Nick with a toothpaste commercial smile and put out his hand. "I'm Richard L. Townsend, Sandi's boyfriend. I'm an attorney. You're the lucky winner, I presume?"

Though Nick had never seen Richard Townsend, he instantly detected arrogance and he felt an immediate dislike for the man and didn't like seeing him. Furthermore, he had put his hands on Sandi when she didn't want them there.

"Uh, yeah, I guess so." Nick shook the guy's hand, but didn't offer his own name.

Townsend made a sheepish titter, possessively looped an arm around Sandi's shoulders and pulled her against his side. She tried to step sideways, but his grip was too tight. "Sandi and I had a little spat over this dog," he said. "Personally, I think it's a good thing she's gotten rid of him. A few weeks ago, she got rid of a parrot. Now if I can only persuade her to relieve herself of her other dogs and cats, the chickens and who knows what else might crop up, everything will be just fine."

The aunt stepped up, her fists jammed against skinny hips. "Who the hell are you to tell her she can or can't have pets?"

Townsend turned to the aunt whose jaw was clenched, her bright red lips pursed. Wearing tall high-heels, she looked Townsend eye-to-eye.

He moved backward a couple of steps. "Madam, may I ask what your interest is in this?"

"You bet, you can ask. And I'll damn sure tell you. I'm Sandi's aunt. And I'll have you know a person who loves unwanted animals has a special place in heaven. Do you believe in heaven?"

"Well, yes. I—"

Debbie Sue stepped toward the newcomer, fire in her eye, her chin thrust out. Towsend backed up a few more steps and Nick didn't blame him.

"I've got three rescue animals myself and an old horse," Debbie Sue said. "We're friends. I'm their whole world. Without me, someone would kill them. *Kill them!* Do you hear me? Have you ever thought about that?"

Townsend opened his palms, obviously nervous. "Madam, please. I just came here to—"

"You should go, Richard," Sandi said. "All of us are already stressed and you're only adding to it. You're no longer my boyfriend. We already settled that."

"But I know you didn't mean it."

"I did mean it. I'm tired of us, Richard. Please. I want you to leave me alone."

This Richard was starting to get on Nick's nerves. How many times did a man have to hear a woman say she didn't want him around? "I think the lady has made a point, Mr. Townsend. She doesn't want your company."

The fucker had the nerve to bristle up. "Butt out, mister. This is none of your business."

"It's damn sure *my* business," the aunt said, her face thrust forward, her fists jammed against her skinny hips. "I'm family, hotshot."

Nick had never seen a more venomous look than the one in the aunt's eye. *Oh, boy!* This could go south in a hurry. These women might pounce on poor Richard and beat the shit out of him. Nick moved between them and Townsend. "Ladies, ladies. Let's calm—"

Before he could finish the sentence, the aunt drew back a fist and with a roundhouse swing, slugged Townsend square on the nose.

His head snapped back. "*Aargh!*" Blood gushed from his nose, staining his tie and spattering the front of his shirt. He looked down at himself and gasped. "Jesus Christ! I'm bleeding!"

Mrs. Porter thrust a tissue toward him. He grabbed it and pressed it to his nose. "Are you nuts?" he said to the aunt through the tissue, his voice a nasally whine. "You *are* nuts. Sandi's told me how batty her family thinks you are."

"Did you say batty? I'll show you batty, you smartass!" The aunt cocked her arm and made another fist.

Before she could slug Townsend again, Debbie Sue stepped between them. "Wait a minute, Ed. Calm down."

"I don't wanna calm down. I'm gonna whip his ass."

"You can't. You'll get us arrested. And the next thing you know, I'll be the one in court. Divorce court."

She turned her attention back to Townsend. "Listen, Richard, Ed's my friend. She's not—"

"Richard, do you need a doctor?" Sandi asked.

"No," he barked.

"Then please go. You're causing trouble. Please."

Just then, the cop who had been hanging around the courthouse steps walked over. "Everything okay here?"

"Yessir," the women chorused.

He gave Townsend an intense look, as if he were assessing his injury. "Do you need medical attention, sir?"

"I'm fine, officer. Just suffering a nosebleed. Happens often. Allergies, you know. But you might want to keep an eye on the one in the red dress."

The cop looked at each of them as if he didn't believe what Richard had said. Finally, he said, "Have a good day then," and walked away.

He might have walked away, but Nick could see he was standing close by, his hands resting on his utility belt. And he was watching them.

"Okay, Sandi, I'll go," Richard said, his voice now both thick and nasally. "But I'm warning you. I won't be back. This was your last chance to come to your senses."

Nick's sense of chivalry kicked in. This Townsend dude was a bully. "Mr. Townsend, I say again, I think the lady has made her point. It'd be wise for you to go. When a woman tells you she doesn't want you around, she means it."

Richard glared above the wadded tissue he held to his nose. "What are you implying?"

Nick was hardly intimidated by a man who didn't have a muscle anywhere and who was already suffering a punch to his nose by a woman. "Just what I said. Leave her alone."

"Yeah," the aunt said.

Townsend straightened his jacket and stalked off.

"Well, that was cute," Aunt Ed said, staring after him and pacing back and forth. "Arrogant fucker. That was Richard, huh? The one who's defending a man who tortures and murders old women?"

"He's a defense lawyer, Aunt Ed," Sandi said. "Someone has to do it."

The aunt was still loaded for bear. "Oh, I don't know. Why does someone have to do it? And what does doing it say about the someone doing it? Personally, I don't think a lynch mob is out of the question for that John Wilson ass. And maybe they oughtta string up his lawyer with him."

Debbie Sue gave an exaggerated gasp. "Good grief, Ed. You've certainly found your violent streak today."

"You know how I am. I refuse to tolerate rude behavior. Especially from a self-centered butthole who's trying to order my niece around like he's smarter than she is."

Debbie Sue turned to the group and explained. "She's seen *Lonesome Dove* two dozen times."

"I'm glad you punched him," the short woman with pink-tipped hair said. "He had it coming. If I wasn't so short, I would've hit him myself."

Mrs. Porter's head was shaking slowly. "My goodness, Sandi. I never dreamed all of this would come to violence. How could you take up with such an awful man?"

"Ladies, Debbie Sue's right," Nick said. "We need to break this up. That cop has got his eye on us." He looked down at Sandi. "I'm gonna go, but can I speak to you in private for a minute?"

She took a few steps away from the group. He followed. "I want you to know I intend to honor what the judge ordered. We won't have any disputes over your coming out to visit Buster or taking him to spend time with you."

Looking down, she nodded. She looked defeated and he hated knowing he had caused her to feel that way. Somehow, he had to compensate for her losing Buster. "I know he means a lot to you. I don't think I've ever seen anybody fight so hard for an animal."

She looked up at him then. Her pretty green eyes held a glister of tears. She lifted a shoulder in a shrug. "It's what I do."

"Like your aunt said, that says something about your character."

"I don't know, maybe. Is that all?"

"Yes, ma'am. I guess it is. Except that I'd like to trade phone numbers with you. So we can get in touch with each other about visits. As you already know, I'm down in Salt Like during the week, but I'm usually up here in Midland on the weekends."

She nodded and gave him her phone number and address. He did likewise.

"I'll be wanting to buy some of your homemade dog food," he said. "I've analyzed it and it's nutritious stuff. I'm sure that by now, it's an integral part of Buster's diet. Probably why he looks so good and has so much energy. It'll be good for the puppy, too."

She shrugged again. "Just come into my store. It's available every day."

With nothing left to be said, he touched his hat to her. "I'll be seeing you." With that, he led Buster away.

☆☆☆

As Edwina maneuvered herself into her Mustang with her spike heels and tight skirt, Debbie Sue agilely scooted into the passenger seat. "Ed, I thought I'd die when you slugged Sandi's boyfriend. And with a cop only a dozen steps away. I could see myself having to call Buddy to get us out of jail."

Edwina turned the key in the ignition and revved the Mustang's big engine to life. "The sonofabitch had it coming. Everybody said so."

"That doesn't mean we wouldn't get arrested."

"Well, we didn't."

"I just hope Buddy doesn't hear about us making a scene in front of the courthouse."

Edwina pulled out of the parking lot and headed for the highway. "You're too uptight about Buddy. No matter what happens, all you worry about is what Buddy is gonna think. You didn't used to be like that."

"He didn't used to have the job he's got now. How would it look if a Texas Ranger captain's wife constantly embarrassed him in public?"

"Yeah, yeah, I get it. So the court thing didn't go very well for my niece, did it?"

"I'm not surprised. Ed, the dog belongs to Nick. It's obvious to everyone. Sandi was fighting an uphill battle."

"I know, I know.

"What will she do now?"

"Hell, I don't know. It's just a dog. She can get another one, although I don't know why she would. It ain't like she needs one. Listen, I just thought of something. Do you realize where we are and what time of day it is?"

"I wonder if I dare answer."

"We are in Midland, Texas, and it's damn near suppertime. I'm thinking we haven't had real good barbecue in a long time. We should stop by Tag Freeman's joint." She laughed impishly. "You never know, girlfriend. We might run into Quint Matthews."

"Hah. That's all I need to wind up an insane day. The last person in the whole wide world I want to run into is Quint."

"I'm hungry. Let's go eat." Edwina made a U-turn in the middle of the street and headed for Tag Freeman's Double-Kicker Barbecue & Beer. "You haven't mentioned that horny little fucker lately. Do you know where he is?"

"Bandera, the last I heard."

"That's good. A helluva long way from here. How long has it been since you've heard from him?"

"Couple of years. An old rodeo friend told me he got married again. The daughter of some super-rich rancher from South Texas. But it only lasted for a little while."

"That's the way it is when a guy can't have the one he wants. He's like a honey bee, flitting from flower to flower. Never settles down. And all the money in Texas wouldn't make a difference."

"Don't start, Ed. It wasn't especially me that Quint wanted. He wanted what he couldn't have."

"Hello, Scarlett. You just keep telling yourself that, but don't try to make me believe it."

"Whatever. I hardly ever think of him anymore and his name hasn't come up between Buddy and me in a long time. That's the best way to keep it."

"Oh, I know. But wasn't it exciting when the little bastard was constantly trying to stick his nose under the tent and Buddy got madder than a peeled rattler every time he heard his name?"

"Ed, no. Those days were hard on Buddy and me both."

"I thought for sure Buddy would end up shooting him. I even hoped for it."

"I swear, Ed, where did this violent streak come from?"

They reached the barbecue restaurant and found a parking slot in front. Debbie Sue hadn't been here in months, but nothing appeared to have changed. People still gathered around to watch and ride the mechanical bull near the front entrance. Food was still served on long picnic tables covered with red and white checked cloths. Loud country music still pounded from the sound system. At the moment, Carrie Underwood was belting out "Two Black Cadillacs."

With the food served cafeteria-style, she and Edwina picked up trays and started through the line. They each ordered a rack of ribs, corn on the cob, mashed potatoes and plenty of pickled jalapeno peppers on the side, topped off by peach cobbler. As they took their seats at one of the long tables, a server met them with little ceramic pots of honey and real butter and a basket of steaming yeast rolls as soft as pillows. They dug in.

"Far as I'm concerned, this is the best barbecue in Texas," Edwina said, chomping on a rib.

"Austin says it has the best barbecue in Texas," Debbie Sue said.

"What does Austin know? There's so many Yankees and West Coasters down there, they wouldn't know good barbecue if a rack of ribs smacked 'em upside the head." She pushed a pile of rib bones to the side of her plate.

"Jesus, Ed. That plate looks like you ate a baby dinosaur."

Just then, the thick hand of a man set a mug of beer on the table in front of the empty space beside Debbie Sue. A large diamond winked from a gold horseshoe on his ring finger. Debbie Sue looked up and nearly swallowed a rib. "Quint! Where did you come from?"

Three-time world champion professional bull rider and multi-millionaire stock contractor Quint Matthews, stepped over the wooden bench seat and sat down, tipped his head toward Edwina. "Edwina. How're you?"

"Why, I'm just fine, Quint. What a shock. I thought you might be dead."

Quint gave a deep huh-huh-huh. "Not yet, darlin'. Not yet."

Debbie Sue sat still as a mouse, but her heartbeat had zoomed into the stratosphere and she was having trouble breathing. She had no explanation for this rush of adrenaline. Her memories of her mercurial relationship with Quint had been filed away long ago.

He turned to her. "I was at the bar when you came in. I couldn't believe it was you. It's been so damn long." He picked up a sheaf of her long hair and pushed it behind her shoulder. "That pretty hair I used to love to bury my nose in gave you away, darlin'."

"Wha—what are you doing in Midland, Quint? I heard you were living down south."

"I was. But I bought a little place up here a couple of months ago and moved back. Tag and I are still partnering on some bulls. Life in the rodeo business is easier when he and I live closer together."

Debbie Sue gave a nervous titter. "Still making money off Double-Trouble, huh?"

"Nah. He's getting old. After he bucked off every cowboy in the business, we put him out to pasture. All he does these days is graze and make new winners. Tag and I've got a couple of real good new ones right now."

Debbie Sue returned to her food, stealing a glance at Edwina who was sitting as if she had turned to stone.

"You're lookin' awful pretty, darlin'. Never did see you in a dress much. You should wear one more often, show off those pretty legs and that perfect body. Looks to me like you haven't changed any in that department. Whatcha been up to?"

Edwina cleared her throat.

Suddenly Debbie Sue's supper roiled in her stomach as if it might come back up. She swallowed a big gulp of iced tea. "Ed's niece had a court hearing today. Ed and I went along for support."

"I'd like to buy you something a little stronger than tea. At some place a little quieter where we could talk. Catch up on the good ol' days."

Hah. Buddy Overstreet would kill you and me both. "I can't take the time, Quint. Got to get back to Salt Lick."

"That busy, huh?" He picked up his mug and sipped his beer, then with a chuckle, set it back on the table. "You know, moving back to Midland has brought back a lot of memories, Debbie Sue. Know what I was thinking about just the other day?"

I'm afraid to guess. Debbie Sue bit into her ear of corn.

"The National Finals. You ever think about that?"

"I have nothing to do with rodeo anymore, especially rodeo in Las Vegas." Debbie Sue dabbed at her mouth with her napkin. "It's almost that time of year though. I suppose, if you've got two good bulls, you should be thinking about a big rodeo."

"It ain't bulls that was on my mind, sugar. I was remembering those three days we spent in that fancy Vegas hotel after I won that little contest the first time."

Quint had the money—and the scars—to show for his wins. The year of his first championship had been momentous for her as well as for Quint. That year had been her debut performance as a professional barrel racer.

He ran his fingers down her arm. Her cheeks warmed. Goosebumps raised on her skin. Why was he affecting her this way? She stole a glance across the table at Edwina. She had never discussed details of her relationship with Quint with Edwina or anyone else.

"Hah," she said. "The National Finals isn't exactly a *little* contest.

"Back in those days, my body was in top shape and yours was, too. No broken bones, no sprains, no bumps and bruises. Plenty of energy. I could go all night. Remember that?"

Oh, Jesus. He was talking as if Edwina weren't sitting across the table two feet away. *Shit! Shut-up, Quint.* Debbie Sue's cheeks flamed.

He grinned like a monkey. "We didn't come up for air or put on a stitch of clothes for three days and nights."

"Quint, stop it." She slashed the air with a flat hand. "That train has left the station."

"Oh, yeah? Then why is your pulse fluttering in your throat? See? I notice those little things, darlin'."

Reflexively, Debbie Sue's hand lifted and her palm flattened on her collar bone.

"Look at me, Debbie Sue."

Everything inside her told her not to turn her head toward him, but she couldn't resist. He was still a beautiful man—chiseled features, sky-blue eyes that constantly showed a twinkle, thick caramel-colored hair. Brad Pitt probably had no idea he had a doppelganger in Texas who was a world champion bull rider. And this evening, he smelled like a men's cologne counter in a fancy department store.

His eyes captured hers. "I've been wanting to say some things for a long time, Debbie Sue, but every time I've thought I had the chance, something always screwed it up."

"Oh, yeah? Probably that parade of buckle bunnies that's always followed you around."

"For me, that week in Vegas was outstanding. I don't think it's ever been as sweet as those three days."

Damn him. He had always been able to skate right past anything that cast him in a bad light.

"How about you?" he said. "You ever think about us? Is it still good with you and that long-legged cop?"

"Sure is. He's doing great, isn't he, Ed?" A comment from Edwina would surely kill this embarrassing conversation.

"He's a captain in the Texas Rangers now, with a sterling reputation," Edwina put in.

Thank God Edwina had caught the cue.

Quint didn't even look at Edwina. His eyes were still locked on Debbie Sue. "Sure he is. But that doesn't mean a damn thing to me. When y'all crawl in bed at night, does he make you scream like a banshee? The way I used to?"

Debbie Sue's cheeks turned to pure fire. Her face must be the color of a fire engine. "Cut it out, Quint. You're wasting your time and embarrassing me in front of my friend."

"It was hot between us, darlin'. Women don't forget that. And I haven't forgotten it either."

Edwina cleared her throat with a loud rumble, climbed over the bench seat without stumbling and falling on her face and stalked away.

"See what you've done?" Debbie Sue snapped. "Now I'm going to have to listen to a raft of shit from her all the way home."

"I want you back, Debbie Sue. I mean it. It was more than sex between us. It was spiritual. When ol' Ace of Spades got the best of me that time, if I hadn't known you were in that surgery waiting room, I might not have come back from that tunnel."

She well remembered that night in Denver. After a wild ride on a dangerous bull that had bucked him off, gored him and left him with a skull fracture and a broken femur, he had been close to death. During a long recovery, he had talked then about "going through the tunnel," but knowing she wouldn't be on the other side had made him come back. But that incident hadn't made him a steady, loyal man. Nor had it cured his roving eye.

"You had no idea I was there, Quint. They hauled you out of that arena unconscious."

"I admit it took me a few years and a few women to figure it out. But I finally did. No woman nowhere does it for me like you did. I know that now."

She lifted a shoulder in a shrug. "Maybe it has nothing to do with me. Maybe you've finally grown up. It doesn't matter anyway. I'm a happily married woman. This conversation is nonsense."

"No, it isn't. Listen to me now. Buddy Overstreet will never make a dime more than the state of Texas pays him. He's not a money man. I made more last year than he'll make in his whole fuckin' life. And look at you. A beautiful woman like you wearing a Walmart dress—"

"My dress did not come from Walmart, for your information. But so what if it did?"

She had bought her dress at Target. But Quint wasn't wrong about her life, she couldn't keep from thinking. She and Buddy would never be rich. They still lived in an old house that had belonged to her grandparents and they didn't even talk about living somewhere else.

Quint continued as if she hadn't interrupted him. "Standing on your feet all day in a chickenshit beauty shop in a shithole of a town. I'm a rich man, Debbie Sue. I'd dress you in beautiful clothes. Shower you with diamonds and rubies. A fine house, fine horses and fine wine. Anything your heart desires."

"You don't get it, Quint. You never did. I wouldn't care if Buddy were dead broke. I love him. And furthermore, he loves me. He'll always fight for me. And he's loyal. You cheated on me too many times."

"I've changed, Debbie Sue. Like you said, maybe I've grown up."

His tone had a ring of sincerity to it, which made this encounter even more frightening. If she could believe him, she didn't know what she might or might not do. Quint had always had an uncanny ability to reach the deepest part of her and talk her into doing things no one else would ever be able to talk her into. She had to stop this. She pushed herself to her feet. "I've got to find Ed and get going. We've got customers tomorrow."

He sighed and stood with her, held her elbow as she stepped over the bench seat. She picked up her purse, hooked it on her shoulder gave him a lingering look. "Take care of yourself, Quint."

She turned away from him and walked toward the front of the restaurant, hoping like hell that Edwina was waiting for her there.

"It's good to see you, pretty girl," he said behind her. "I'll be seeing you again."

Debbie Sue didn't look back. She did not want Quint to think she was affected by his sudden appearance or any of the things he had said. And the absolute, very last thing she wanted was for him to show up in Salt Lick.

She found Edwina almost hidden at one end of the bar near the mechanical bull. "Let's get out of here, Ed."

They rode in silence until they cleared the Midland city limits.

Finally, Edwina said, "Well, are you gonna tell me what that was all about?"

"It wasn't about anything. Just Quint being Quint."

"I always figured you two were hot together. I can see both of you now. Ride 'em, cowgirl. Now, I ask you. Could he really go all night?"

Debbie Sue's whole head heated all the way to her hair follicles. Her hair might fall out completely. "I don't remember."

"Hah. Pardon me if I think you're lying."

"I just hope Buddy doesn't find out he's living in Midland."

"Oh, he'll find out. Quint never was able to stay away from you if he was within shouting distance. If he's been living back here up for two months, I'm surprised he hasn't put in an appearance in Salt Lick already. My crystal ball tells me it's just a matter of time before a whole new chapter will start up with him and you and Buddy."

Debbie Sue clenched her teeth and growled. "Really, Obi Wan?"

"Really, Scarlett. I swear, girl, this is the stuff soap operas are made of. My God, half the women in Texas would crawl from here to Dallas to have the likes of Quint Matthews or Buddy Overstreet in love with them. But to have both of those guys chasing you around? Hm-hm-hm."

"Bite your tongue, Ed."

Edwina had the nerve to chuckle. "Hell, that long-legged cop might end up shooting the cheeky little fart after all. I can see the headlines now. Texas Ranger murders—"

"Shut-up, Ed."

"He's still a pretty bastard, I have to say. Not as pretty as Buddy, but not too many women would kick him outta bed. And he's in great shape. That body of his does a pair of Cinch jeans and those custom-made shirts proud. He must still work out, huh."

"Edwina Perkins-Martin, if you don't shut your mouth, I'm gonna get out of this car."

Chapter 18

A WEEK PASSED. The end of October and cooler weather rolled around. Fall had definitely arrived. Sandi missed Waffle terribly. She missed him coming to wake her every morning with slobbery doggy kisses, missed his happy grin and wagging tail as she prepared his breakfast, missed his presence in LaBarkery. To compound her depressed feelings, almost every regular customer asked about him.

Still, she had stuck to her busy routine. She put out pet sweaters and warm booties for sale, updated the pet Halloween costume display and created Halloween treats for her customers to hand out. She worked with her web designer on her website, made bulk Atomic Energizer and dozens of Barkies, Little Fidos and Mousekins to sell in LaBarkery and in general distracted herself from her favorite dog's absence by showering attention on her other animals.

On Tuesday, Juanita from We Love Animals called. "Betty Ann told me what happened in court. I can't believe they let a cat come in. I'm so sorry, dear."

"Thanks for your thoughts, Juanita. I wasn't surprised at the outcome."

"Got time to come by today? I've got a new little dog for you to look at."

"Oh, Juanita, I don't want another dog right now."

"Oh, I understand. But she's sure a pretty little thing. So white she looks like a snowball. And so much personality. Her name is Betsy. She looks like a Westie."

"Betsy the Westie? That's too cute. I think there was once a doll called Betsy Wetsy."

Ignoring Sandi's sarcasm, Juanita went on. "I'm sure she isn't a purebred. That doesn't matter anyway. The neighbors told me she's been spayed, so she wouldn't be a breeder."

Sandi recognized Juanita's spiel. The woman could wear down a granite wall. Listening to her and eventually weakening against her verbal assault was how Sandi had ended up with the menagerie she presently had. "Does that mean she has to be groomed? I already pay to have Adolph groomed, you know. I can't afford the additional expense."

"I understand, honey. I'm just telling you about her. Poor little thing. Her owners moved to Dallas and just left her roaming the neighborhood. No food, no water, no safe place to sleep. They didn't even try to find her a new home."

"Oh, no! How mean."

"I know. One of the neighbors caught her trying to hide behind his air conditioner, poor little thing. She was filthy and starved and shaking all over. She's too little to survive on her own. Since we're a no-kill shelter, he brought her to us. Otherwise, she probably would've been picked up by the county."

Sandi mentally shook herself. She could not take on another pet at this moment. "Juanita, please. I just can't. A new dog would not only take up more of the time that I don't have and it would remind me that I don't have Waffle anymore."

"Maybe you need a change of pace, darlin'. Or a change of pets, so to speak. We've got this darling little miniature pig that needs a home."

A vision of the huge hogs her grandparents had raised for meat passed through Sandi's mind. "A pig? You're kidding me. How big is it?"

"About thirty pounds. Well, maybe forty or fifty. Bigger than a cat, smaller than Waffle."

"I've heard about those miniature pigs, Juanita. It could get to be a hundred pounds or even more."

"No, no. She won't. She's already four years old. Well, she might get a little bit bigger, but not that much."

Sandy was skeptical. She had read how people were sometimes duped into believing they were taking in a miniature pig that eventually grew to a full-size hog.

"Her name is Bella," Juanita continued, "after some character in a movie. She's the sweetest little thing. She's so pink and so affectionate. Housebroken, too. Uses a litter box. And you should see her in the bathtub. She loooves playing in the water."

Sandi had to admit she was curious, but she didn't want to share her only bathtub with a pig, miniature or otherwise. At least she could bathe her dogs in her second bathroom's walk-in shower. "She has to be bathed in the bathtub?"

"Well, you'd want her to be clean. Pigs like water, you know."

The memory of the smells that accompanied Jake assailed Sandi as well as her more recent experience with skunk odor. A house pig was bound to be a dozen times worse. She took hold of herself and hardened her resolve to be strong. "I can't, Juanita. My house hasn't recovered from Jake yet. I don't want another exotic animal that has to live inside and I don't have a place for it outside."

"Oh, she couldn't live outside anyway."

"Why did the owners get rid of her?"

"They're dumb kids. Thought a pet pig would be cool. They paid a thousand dollars for her. Can you believe that?"

"Let me guess. The novelty wore off and they got tired of taking care of her."

Juanita released a big sigh. "Adopting a pig ain't like adopting your basic dog or cat. A pig takes a commitment."

Anger spread through Sandi. "Typical," she grumbled. "That's behavior that produces unwanted animals and even abused animals, isn't it? I'll tell you something, Juanita. Since I've started fostering unwanted animals, I've lost a lot of respect for my fellow humans. I'm starting to believe that people who want a pet should be thoroughly screened to learn their motives for getting a pet and their qualifications for having one as well as their intentions for the future of the poor animals."

"I couldn't agree with you more. I feel the same way," Juanita replied. "Well, I'll let you get back to work. Just wanted to let you know about our new residents."

Sandi disconnected from the call in a state of aggravation. Now she wouldn't be able to get a sweet little dog and a cute pig that couldn't survive outdoors off her mind.

And being aggravated took her thoughts to her nemesis, Nick Conway. She hadn't heard one word from him about allowing her to visit Waffle or have him for a weekend. Should she call him and tell him it was her turn? Or should she just call the court and report him to the judge?

"What does Juanita want you to adopt now?" Betty Ann asked.

"Oh, she's got a new dog. And a miniature pig. Do you want a pet pig?"

"Hardly. Since I've been working in this store, thanks to you and Juanita, I've adopted two dogs and three cats. I live in a one-bedroom apartment. I absolutely cannot take any more animals."

"Then I guess you wouldn't be interested in adopting a little dog that looks like a Westie."

Betty Ann's interest was immediate. Her brow tented. "Aww, really? I adore those little dogs. They're so cuuute."

"She's a spayed female. Her name is Betsy. Juanita says she has a sweet personality."

"Hm. I should at least look at her, don't you think? I mean, there are just so many unwanted animals and not enough people to take care of them. It's so sad. How much more space would one more little dog take up? I think I'll call Juanita."

"You'd better think about it, Betty Ann, before you commit. One thing I've learned — and you'll have to learn it, too — you just can't take every single animal. Juanita will unload a whole zoo on you if you don't resist her."

Just then, before Sandi could launch a lecture about getting sucked in by Juanita and We Love Animals, her cell phone warbled. She checked the screen and that tremble that had become familiar passed through her midsection. "Oh. My. God. It's Nick Conway."

"He's a god all right," Jessica put in. "A Greek god."

"It's about time he got in touch with you," Betty Ann said. "I was wondering when he was going to."

Instantly, Sandi's mood shifted and she keyed into the call. "This is Sandi."

"Hey, how are you?"

"I'm fine. Funny you should call. I was just thinking about Waffle, wondering when I was going to get to visit him."

"How about the weekend? We're down in Salt Lick now, but we're going up to Midland on Friday night. I'd like to show you around my place, let you see that I've got a good environment for a busy dog like Buster. A section of land is plenty of room for him to run and play."

A section of land. Those were the words that stuck in Sandi's mind. She had no idea he had a whole 640 forty acres. Of course, in Texas, a section wasn't much land, but compared to Sandi's backyard, it was as big as another state. "Well, I—"

"If it works for you, we could do it Saturday afternoon. Then Saturday evening, I could grill a couple of steaks. Harley furnishes me meat out of his private locker. I can bring up some choice ribeyes. It's premium grass-fed beef. I can't think of any restaurants where you'll get better steaks than that."

"You don't have to feed me. I could just come out and play with Waffle for a little while."

"Then who would I share these steaks with? My horses and those llamas would turn up their noses and Buster...that is, *Waffle*, has his own food."

Oh, wow. He had called Waffle by the name she had given their mutual dog. This could only be an effort on his part to get along with her. "Okay, I guess. I can bring a bottle of wine." She grabbed a pen and a notepad. "You'll have to give me directions to your place again. I don't remember the route from when you gave it to me before."

"Nuh-unh. I was planning on picking you up at your house like a gentleman should when he's got a date with a nice lady."

What? What did this mean? Was he attracted to her in *that* way? Even after all that had happened between them? The part of her that didn't dislike him certainly found him physically attractive enough, she had to admit. Her heartbeat picked up a pace and she couldn't stop the stupid grin that spread across her face. "This is a date?"

"'Course it is. Dinner and wine? Sounds like a date to me, even if I'm the one doing the cooking. Or maybe it's a negotiation. I've already got the wine, by the way."

He has the wine? Hah. Cowboys didn't drink wine. They guzzled beer. And what was left to negotiate? He had already whipped her legally and soundly.

"I've got your address," he said. "How do I get to it?"

She paused for a few seconds, vacillating as she thought about dates from hell. It wasn't like they weren't acquainted, was it? After all, they had seen each other at their worst. Things could only be better going forward. An invitation to dinner was a friendly gesture, right? Should she give good will a chance?

After all of her emotional yo-yoing, her biggest concern was being caught at his house miles out of town without her own transportation. What if she wanted to leave in a hurry? "Listen, I do want to visit Waffle and a steak dinner sounds good, but I think I should just drive out to your place in my own car. That's a lot more convenient for both of us."

A pause, then a sigh. "Okay. Suit yourself."

His tone had changed. He was almost snappish, but she stood firm.

"You need to show up before dark so we can take a tour in my Jeep," he said sharply.

Holy cow, was he mad because she had rejected his picking her up at her house?

"Wear jeans and boots," he continued. "You never know when a rattlesnake might be hanging around."

She owned a pair of cowboy boots — what native West Texas female didn't? — but she hadn't worn them in months. "I assure you, rattlers aren't the kind of snakes that worry me. Besides, it's October. Aren't snakes hibernating by now?"

"There might be one that that doesn't have a calendar. You never know."

She gave a little grunt at his attempt at humor. "The directions?"

As he had done before, he quickly rattled off exactly how to reach his house. Scribbling to keep up, she cursed the great state of Texas for having such confusing roads and highways with numbers instead of names. After they disconnected, Sandi noticed her heartbeat had become a tattoo that made her giddy.

She turned to Betty Ann and Jessica who had been standing by eavesdropping and waiting for her to share. "Okay, girls. One of you is going to have to mind the store on Saturday afternoon. I will be leaving early. I have an invitation for a steak dinner."

Betty Ann pumped a fist. "Yes!"

"Yum," Jessica said. "I'm talking about the guy, not the steak."

"You don't have to worry about Sunday," Betty Ann said enthusiastically. "I'll open the store."

Sandi gave her a look. She rarely asked her girls to work on a Sunday. "Why would I need you to do that? I always work on Sundays."

"In case you decide on a sleepover."

"Oh, my Lord, Betty Ann. Where is your head, girl? I barely know this guy. I'm not even sure I like him."

"That doesn't make any difference," twenty-one-year-old college student Jessica said. "He's a hot body. He's got that look. You know, like he'd be a great fu—I mean I'll bet he's a super good lover. You don't have to like him to do it with him."

These two were her *employees!* Sandi tried to maintain separation between them and her personal life, but the three of them worked in such close quarters, these two girls felt more like pals than employees. She gaped and gasped. "Girls!"

They might not be so much younger than she, but their attitudes about men and sex made her feel out of touch. "Listen, all of my meetings with him have been so bizarre I don't think there's a danger I'll be spending the night with him."

☆☆☆

On Saturday, Betty Ann and Jessica pushed Sandi out the door of her store mid-afternoon and she headed home. She still hadn't shaken off the fear that she smelled like a skunk, so she showered and shampooed her hair again and doused herself with Juicy Couture. The temperature was forecast to drop after dark, so with her best pair of jeans, she put on a beige turtleneck sweater. She dug the cowboy boots out of her closet, wondering all the while what, other than a dog, she had in common with a man who had chosen "cowboy" as a career.

After feeding everybody, she drove toward Kroger, the grocery store that she knew had a good selection of wines. He might have said he had wine, but probably, it was packaged in a cardboard box. She didn't want to drink rotgut alcohol with choice steaks.

Again, why am I doing this? she asked herself as she drove. *Do I really need to have dinner with a man who makes me uncomfortable just so I can visit Waffle?*

At the grocery store, she bought the best bottle of Merlot on the shelf, certain it would taste better than what he would supply.

To her surprise, she didn't get lost. She reached a neatly kept older house surrounded and shaded by live oak trees. The trees were huge, which meant they could be a hundred years old. And so could the house from the looks of it. It had a wide gray-painted porch wrapping around two sides.

Nick, Waffle and Randy came out the front door as she parked in the driveway. Randy strained at the end of a leash. Nick was wearing his signature Wranglers and boots, a long-sleeve blue button-down, a bright blue puffy vest and a gimme cap with the Purina red-and-white checkerboard logo. He looked all luscious and coordinated.

She opened her car door and had put only a foot out before Waffle leaped forward, placed his front paws on her shoulders and began to lick her face. "Oh, Waffle, I miss you so much. Everyone misses you."

His weight pushed her back into the car and he continued licking her face and making that keening noise in his throat that he always made when he was happy. She hugged him and rubbed his back and head.

"Buster, get back here." Nick gripped his collar and pulled him back.

Sandi dug into her purse for the Barkies she always kept there and offered them. Waffle wolfed them down, then danced in a circle and wagged his tail furiously. Randy, too, gobbled up a couple of the cookies.

"Looks like he's glad to see you," Nick said. "Randy, too."

She looked up and Nick was smiling down at her, his hand resting on the top of her SUV's door. For the first time she noticed that the ends of his hair touched his collar. And his jaws looked freshly shaved. Close up, he was even better-looking than that day in court.

Crap. Why can't he be ugly?

Though her stomach had flipped and her brain had temporarily disconnected, she managed a smile. "Wish I could have brought the rest of the gang with me. Waffle's like their family. He was their leader."

"He's an alpha dog all right." Nick the Beautiful bent down and scruffed Waffle's ears, a clean-smelling scent of his cologne drifting her way. Waffle leaned into his hand and gently nipped it. Nick rubbed his head. "Good dog, good dog."

He straightened. The two dogs stood there looking up at them as if awaiting the next compliment or order. Or in reality, they were probably waiting for another treat.

Nick looked past her into her car. "Where's your jacket?"

"This sweater will be warm enough."

"You need a jacket. Be right back. Hold this." He handed her the end of Randy's leash, turned and strode back into his house.

"Well, Mr. Randy. Isn't he bossy?" she said to the puppy.

Randy wagged his tail and barked.

Nick soon returned with a red fleece jacket bearing a black Texas Tech logo, bringing back their conversation months back in Hogg's: ...*Went to Texas Tech on a football scholarship. Got a degree in biology. Been through A&M's range management program. Studied grasslands enhancement with Dow Chemical. I've got a Masters in animal nutrition. ...*

She pinched herself mentally. Nick might look and talk like a dumb cowboy, but appearances could be deceiving.

While she shrugged into the jacket that swallowed her, he opened the back gate of an old Jeep Wrangler. Waffle jumped inside, but Randy was still too small to make the leap. Nick picked him up and placed him on the Jeep's deck beside Waffle. "Here ya go, Little Bit. Going for a nice ride. That sound good?"

She was touched by the gentleness with which Nick treated the puppy that obviously would grow up to be smaller than Waffle.

He came around to the passenger side and opened the door for her. "This is my chariot. Climb in."

She did, he scooted behind the wheel and they trundled off toward the pasture behind his house.

"Thanks for the jacket," she said. "But I feel like a traitor wearing it. I went to college at UT Permian in Odessa."

He grinned and winked. "Thirty minutes from now, you won't care. It'll feel good."

He drove over the rough terrain with confidence and competence. *Crap.* She hated seeing him display that masculine self-assurance that appealed to her. She hadn't often seen it. At the bank where she had worked for years, most of her male co-workers were milquetoasts who worked at clerical-type jobs and had no muscles. Richard was the same way.

"Nice day," he said as they bumped and lurched along.

Discussing the weather? Ugh. But then, what had she expected? He was probably like most of the rural people she knew who worried every day about the weather. "Yes, it is."

A river of silence flowed between them as they inched along. Finally, she said, "What are you going to show me?"

"I'm gonna let you see how much fun Buster has working with the cattle."

Waffle sat on the deck behind them, his head and front paws almost between them. Once, he craned his head forward and licked her cheek. She turned around and rubbed his head.

"So did you study some kind of animal science?" Nick asked.

"I majored in business with emphasis on marketing. Why do you ask?"

"Just wondering how you got to be an expert on what animals oughtta eat."

"Research. I'm very good at research. I don't call myself an expert, but I'm friends with a couple of vets who advise me."

"How many animals do you take care of?"

"At the moment, fifteen. Four dogs, six cats, four chickens and a gerbil."

"Chickens?"

"A little old lady's relatives took her to a nursing home and they called the SPCA to pick up her chickens. They all ended up at We Love Animals and almost as soon as they got there, they started dying. Juanita, my friend who runs the place, talked me into taking the four that were left. Three hens and a rooster."

Nick chuckled. "Chickens, eh. She must be persuasive."

"She is, but truthfully, she didn't have to try very hard. I felt sorry for them. At first, I just took two of them. Sophie, one of the white Leghorn hens, had a broken wing and she was losing her feathers because the other three pecked at her all the time. Juanita said they would finally kill her or she would just die, but I wanted to try to save her. I scoured books and the Internet for information about chicken ailments. My favorite vet and I gave her extra special care and she gradually got better. Then Juanita talked me into taking the other two."

They had started following a barbed-wire fence. "Okay," he said, "I'm going to drive you along this fence line so you can look across the pasture and see the place."

What's to see? Flat land, mostly beige grass and sage brush.

"That's quite a story about those chickens. I doubt if many people can say they saved a chicken's life. Or who would even want to. It must have taken a lot of patience."

"Taking care of wounded animals has made me find patience I didn't know I had. They're so grateful."

"What's going on with Sophie now?

"She's snow-white and pretty, as chickens go, but her wing healed funny and it droops. She's odd-looking to her peers. They still mistreat her if I don't pay attention." She sighed. "That's the way chickens are, you know. The stronger ones pick on the weaker ones."

"That's the way it is in most of the animal kingdom. Some will actually kill off their own that are too weak to survive. I saw it happen in the wild horses when I worked over in New Mexico. In some ways, people behave the same."

"You sound like a cynic. You don't like people?"

"Haven't met too many that deserve liking. I get along better with animals."

Had she heard him right? He was an animal lover? She couldn't pass up the opening he had given her. "You wouldn't like to have some chickens, would you? They need a permanent home. My backyard is small and you've got lots of room."

"They wouldn't make it out here. Too many predators. I've got coyotes and foxes both. Even weasels and coons and hogs. All of the above would love a chicken dinner. I couldn't build a pen stout enough that a weasel or a coon couldn't figure out how to get in."

"Too bad. I've always thought chickens should live in the country. My neighbors think so, too. One even complains regularly to the City Council. So far, I've been able to convince them that my home is only a temporary stopover. That's a little white lie, of course. My animals are castoffs that have something wrong with them. No one wants them, so they'll be with me forever."

"You've got a business to run. Why would you take on the care of damaged animals?"

Unexpectedly, tears rushed to her eyes. Thinking about the condition her animals had been in when she acquired them often made her cry. She wiped the corner of her eye with a pinky fingertip. "Without me, they'd have no one. They'd be killed or left to die. I could never abandon them. I remind you, if I hadn't taken in Waffle, you probably wouldn't have him today."

"I get that. And I'm grateful you were the one who found him. So these chickens, do they lay eggs?"

Hah. He doesn't want to discuss my claim to Waffle.

"They sure do and the eggs are really good. I let them forage and I feed them healthy food. I get at least one egg a day. I'd get more if I didn't have a rooster."

He laughed. "You're really down on us males, aren't you?"

She shrugged. "What can I say? I have to throw away quite a few eggs. I guess males are males whether human or chicken."

"Speaking of men, have you heard from that toolbox that was supposed to be your boyfriend?"

She had never heard anyone say such a negative thing about Richard. "I assume you're talking about Richard. No, and I don't expect to."

"Good. If we're gonna be sharing custody of Buster, we'll be seeing more of each other. I don't want to run into him anymore."

And what does that mean? "Richard is a good guy, really. Just not for me. I shouldn't have gotten involved with him. I gave up on men after my second divorce. I should've stuck with that plan."

He looked across his shoulder, his brow arched. "You've been divorced *twice*?"

She didn't miss the emphasis on two times. Her defenses rose. "So?"

"I didn't mean anything. It's just that you seem kinda young to have gotten married and divorced two times."

"I'm thirty-two. What difference does my age make?"

He made no reply, didn't continue the conversation, didn't give her an opportunity to explain. The river of silence widened. Soon, she could stand it no longer. "My mother has always said I have lousy judgement in men."

"Is she right? Do you?"

She heaved a great sigh. "She has that opinion because both of my exes cheated on me."

"That's not good."

"It gets worse. My last husband took up with our neighbor's daughter. She was nineteen. They fooled around for a long time. Hell. For all I know, she was under eighteen when he first started… seeing her."

"How old was he?"

"At the time, thirty-four."

His head shook, one, two, three times. "That's unbelievable."

Not to mention illegal, Sandi thought bitterly.

You're a beautiful woman," he went on. "He should've appreciated what he had."

Beautiful? She hadn't heard a man say he thought her beautiful or even pretty in a long time. She angled her head and looked at him. "Boy, you're really racking up points. What are you up to?"

"Nothing. I'm just saying you've got a lot going on. You're smart and you seem like you'd be good company if you liked somebody."

"I don't know how smart I am. When I told my mom about his girlfriend, she said I should've seen it coming."

"Is that true? Should you have known he was a low-life?"

"You want to know the truth? I didn't see it because I wasn't looking. I was too busy building a career at the bank that laid me off even after I had been there over five years. Mom says Ken was immature from the start. And maybe he was. He needed a lot of attention."

Crap. She was rambling worse than Jake, but she couldn't seem to shut up. "I don't know why I'm giving you so much personal information."

"I'm easy to talk to. I don't judge."

"You probably don't know what it's like, but when someone who's supposed to be loyal to you abandons you for someone else, it does something to your self-esteem. And when it happens twice, well…"

He turned toward her and gave her a smile she could only call tender. "I *do* know."

Holy cow. Had someone cheated on him, too? How was that possible? He was a scholarship athlete, a football hero. And he looked like Chris Hemsworth. In college, he must have had his own harem. Sylvia Armbruster flew into her mind and she became extremely interested in his history with women.

Before she could pursue his comment or say anything about Sylvia, Waffle began to agitate behind them.

Chapter 19

"JUST HOLD ON, BUDDY," Nick said to his excited dog. He gave his companion a look. "He always gets excited when he sees birds. And he knows we're coming up on the cattle. When he lived with you, you must've seen how intuitive he is."

"Of course I did."

He stopped the Jeep, stepped out and walked to the backend. The minute he opened the back gate, Buster leaped out and loped across the pasture barking. Nick loved watching him run. Not only was he fast, he was powerful and in his prime. Randy scrambled and whined to go with him, but Nick sat down on the Jeep's deck and began to pet him and calm him. He would never be the dog Buster was, but that was okay. He was still a good little companion. "You're still a baby, Little Bit. It won't be long before you can go."

Sandi came around to stand beside him, her arms crossed under her breasts as she watched Buster's activities. "What's he chasing?"

"A bird. He likes to chase birds."

"I never knew that about him."

"That's because you tried to make him something he wasn't."

A hot glare from those pretty green eyes came at him and she made a little gasp.

Uh-oh. He had said the wrong thing.

"How could I know he was a bird-chaser? I have a small yard and I had him only a few months."

There it was again, that attitude she took on when it came to Buster. Could anything he said or did ever change her mind? The snappish response brought silence to their conversation. She was still bitter and while he understood that, he couldn't, wouldn't concede that she was right when she wasn't. She was a strong woman with her own ideas. Winning her over was going to be harder than he had anticipated.

Looking up at the late day sky, he continued to rub Randy's head and back. A hawk floated high above them, hunting for his supper. Bird songs from a distant somewhere were the only noise in the air. The quiet sounds of nature seeped into Nick's soul and he inhaled a deep breath of the fresh air. "Peaceful," he mumbled.

"You're right," she said, brushing back a few strands of her long red hair that had blown across her face. "A person could get used to it."

"Yep. Sometimes I drive out here and just sit and watch and listen. This is part of why I hang on to this place. No people. There's always chaos where there's people."

The corners of her mouth tipped up into a hint of a smile. "That's the second time you've said something that makes you sound like a recluse, but I know you can't really be like that. If you were, you couldn't have made so much success of your life. No one would have hired you as a general manager of anything, not even a ranch."

"I'm different when I'm here."

Her head tilted to the right and she appeared to be studying him. "You do seem less edgy. Which person is the real you?"

He lifted a shoulder in a shrug. "Most people have two faces. Even two personalities. A person almost has to these days. If how you feel about something isn't politically correct, you're better off keeping your mouth shut."

"That might be true, but you don't seem like the kind of person who worries about political correctness."

"Depends on the circumstances."

He couldn't think of what to say next, so they stood there until the silence started to become uncomfortable.

"I'm distantly acquainted with your girlfriend," she blurted all at once.

Whoa, whoa, whoa. Where had that come from? He crossed his arms over his chest and gave her a look. "I don't know who you're acquainted with, but I don't have a girlfriend."

"Yes, you do. Sylvia Armbruster? I've seen you at her house."

"You know Sylvia?"

"We went to college together. I didn't know her well, but we had a couple of classes together. And my neighbor, the one with the pink-tipped hair, who was at court with me—"

"Sylvia and I have been friends for years, but she's not my girlfriend."

Nick considered Sylvia a friend-friend, but he would never call a woman who slept around the way Sylvia did a girlfriend.

Sandi made a gasp. "You sleep with her."

"How do you know?"

"Because, as I started to say, she told my neighbor who does her hair. She has a huge crush on you."

He shook his head and looked out over the pasture. Sometimes the world was just too damn small. What could he say that wouldn't dig a deeper hole? "I haven't seen Sylvia in a long time."

"Look, I'm just trying to make conversation. You asked me about Richard, so it seemed fair for me to bring up who you're seeing."

"Nobody. I'm not seeing anybody."

All at once, a different bird call floated through the air and saved the day. A full-blown smile lit up her face. She was a beautiful woman and when she smiled, even the sun brightened.

"Oh, listen. Is that a mourning dove?"

"Yep. They're always out here."

"Oh, wow. I love hearing them. I never hear them at my house in town."

"What you probably hear at your house is birds coughing." He chuckled at his own joke.

"Listen to you. Midland doesn't have air pollution."

Just then, Buster raced back to them, barking, dancing and panting, his tongue hanging out. She bent down and rubbed his head, patted his side. "Having fun out there, are you?"

"Hey, boy. Want some water?" Nick leaned back and grabbed a bottle of water and a stainless steel pet dish out of a box. He poured the dish full of water. Buster lapped up every drop. Nick scruffed his head and petted and patted him. "You'd better rest. We'll be coming up on the cows pretty soon."

He put Buster back into the Jeep. As he closed the back gate, he looked at her. "Ready to go?"

She made a little huff. "Do I have a choice? I think I'm too far from the house to walk back."

He moved to the passenger door and opened it for her again. She climbed in, he closed her inside and they set out again.

"Looks like he had a good time," she said. "Is that how he got lost in the first place, running off like that?"

Luke geared down to cross over a rough patch. "I don't know. Maybe."

"Then maybe you shouldn't let him do it."

He sensed her eyes drilling into him, but he coached himself to control his tongue. She might have visiting rights, but Buster was *his* dog. "He's penned up a good part of the time. He's an energetic dog and he's curious. He likes to explore and run and play."

"I suppose you know he'll probably get lost again someday."

"No, I don't know that."

"Well, you should."

More silence. Was she pissed off? Maybe having her come out for a visit wasn't such a good idea. The situation seemed to be going downhill.

Then, "You've never said where you got Waffle in the first place," she said.

"From my neighbor a few miles down the road. He had a bitch that was always having puppies he didn't want, but he was too stingy to have her spayed. She had another litter and he was gonna shoot all of them, including the mama. So I took them off his hands. Buster was one of the pups."

Her big-eyed stare came at him. "Why didn't you tell me that?"

"Tell you what?"

"That you had rescued a whole litter of puppies and their mama."

"You didn't ask. And it didn't seem important to tell you."

"How many puppies were there?"

"Four."

"What did you do with them?"

"I found homes for three of the pups down in Salt Lick. The mama was old, but she was still a good dog. You know how it is. Nobody wants an old dog, so I kept her."

"So you used an old dog as a working dog."

"I did not. She'd been abused and was a little bit crippled up. I figured she deserved for some part of her life to be easier. I got her some veterinary care and put her on a good diet. I took good care of her and she had a good life 'til she died last year."

Sandi looked at him blinking, her eyes glistening. She quickly wiped her eye with a finger. Was she gonna cry? He hoped not. He had already experienced a supper with her in tears at Hogg's. To his relief, she didn't break down.

"Humph," she said. "You are such a phony. You have a soft heart and you never hinted at it. Every time I turn around, I learn something new about you."

He gave her a grin that he hoped charmed her. "I'm a pretty simple guy. Meat and potatoes. I try to respect all living things. I try to remember God put 'em here for a reason."

She cocked her head and looked at him for a few beats. "I don't think you're simple at all. I wonder if you're going to step into some phone booth and come out as Superman."

He grinned. "Don't have phone booths these days."

She smiled, but said nothing. She seemed to be in better spirits.

They began to see a few cattle scattered across the pasture. "Ready to see Buster work the cattle?"

"I can't imagine Waffle doing that, but why not?"

Nick stopped and let him out of the Jeep, again. "Go get 'em, boy."

Buster loped across the pasture again. As he had done countless times, he began to bark and move the individual cows, eventually collecting them into a close group.

"See how much fun he's having?" Nick said.

"I'm fascinated. I had no idea he could do this."

"Watching a good dog work cattle is a pleasure. This is his element. He loves it. He might not look like most cattle dogs, but he's got the instincts. Didn't it make you feel a little bit guilty keeping him in the house or in your store all the time?"

She looked away. "What's the point of having him gather all these cows like this? So he can play? Or work?"

"Both. It gives him something to do, which he needs and it gives me a chance to look over my little herd. Make sure none of them are sick or injured. If I didn't have a good dog and my old Jeep, I'd be out here horseback all day."

"So Waffle is nothing more than a tool for you."

"I've told you, he's a working dog. My helper. My partner. But he's more than that. He's my friend. I don't have that many friends."

"Somehow, that doesn't surprise me."

He couldn't let her keep arguing a point that had been settled. "Ma'am, I'm not gonna let this conversation turn into a fight between us. We disagree over "working dogs" versus "pets" and I know you're still smarting after being beaten in court for Buster's custody. I think it's time to change the subject."

They stood in silence a long time, watching Waffle keep his little herd in a tight circle.

"Seems like a lot for one poor dog to do," she said. "How many cattle does he have to take care of?"

"Right now, about eighty bred cows. And he isn't hurting. I told you. He likes it."

"A bred cow is one that's carrying a calf, right?"

Surprise, surprise. She knew something about ranching. Few people outside the industry knew the terminology that well. He turned to face her and gave her a smile. "Hey, that's right. I just sold all the calves, so pregnant mamas are all I've got left."

"You probably thought I knew nothing about ranching, right?"

"Have you lived on a ranch?"

"No, but I used to lend ranchers money and I heard the jargon all the time. I was a V.P. in the loan department at Community Bank before USA Bank took them over."

"Ah. A big shot."

"Hardly. USA Bank didn't blink twice when it came to laying me off. That's why I started LaBarkery. Besides being unemployed, I was disillusioned with big business. I decided that if I'm going down, I'd rather sink on my own."

"Good for you. If you can do it, being your own boss is always better than being a hired hand."

"In your job down in Salt Lick, do you consider yourself your own boss?"

"Most of the time. I just don't own the ranch. Harley doesn't have much interest in the nuts and bolts of ranching. He likes ranch life and owning all that land. He thinks it's a good environment for his kids. And it is. But what he likes the most are those seesawing pump jacks sucking up oil all over the place and the tax breaks he gets from being in agriculture."

"All I know about Harley Carruthers is that he's rich and owns an oil company. And my aunt likes him. But you sound like you don't like him."

"But I do. He's a good man and a great guy to work for. He leaves me alone and trusts my judgement. And I trust him. I think we're friends."

"In a job like yours, I suppose trust is important."

"Trust is important in any job. Between people, it might be the most important thing there is."

"Maybe so, but it needs to go both ways. I trusted the people I worked with at that bank, but it was wasted energy on my part."

"And you trusted two men with your heart. Sounds like that, too, was wasted."

She stared at him. Finally, she ducked her chin. "I shouldn't have mentioned my past like that. And I shouldn't have questioned you about Sylvia. We hardly know each other."

"Ma'am, you probably know me better than most of the women I'm acquainted with. As for Sylvia, we've had a mutually satisfying arrangement for a long time. Neither one of us would have a broken heart if we never saw each other again."

"From what my neighbor said, I don't think that's true of Sylvia."

"I meant it when I said I haven't seen her in a long time."

Across the pasture, Waffle sat a few feet away from the tight herd of cattle. "Oh, look," she said brightly. "Poor Waffle has gathered every cow. Now what?"

Time to change the subject again. This wasn't going the way he planned at all. He had hoped that by now, she would have moved on from what happened in court. He hadn't counted on the conversation about Sylvia. "We'll drive over there and take a look."

☆☆☆

Soon, Nick had satisfied himself that his little herd was okay. Buster was back in the Jeep worn out and they were creeping back toward the house. With the waning day, the temperature had dropped and Sandi pulled the jacket he had lent her around herself. "It's nice to have so much elbow room," she said. "How long have you had this place?"

"Lived here my whole life 'til I left home for college."

"You inherited it then."

"Partly. When my dad died, he left it to me and my two sisters. They've got their own families and don't live around here anymore. They wanted to sell it, so I hocked my soul and bought them out of their shares."

What he didn't tell her was that life in the Conway home had been miserable, especially for his two sisters. They had found husbands as soon as possible and run for the hills. He had been more capable of tolerating his dad's drunken belligerence and crude behavior. Football and an understanding high school coach had been his salvation. That and the fact that he was male and out of necessity, he had become a man long before the legal age of consent.

"I see. You've never been married?"

"Was. A long time ago."

"Kids?"

"Nope."

"So now you're a bachelor. You give all of *your* love to your llamas or maybe your old horse or an unwanted dog?"

He turned to her, unable to stop a smirky grin. "Touché. I want you to know I was sorry as soon as I said that. I was a little uptight that day. Guess anxiety overloaded my brain. As for my animals, they don't need much from me. Food, water, a clean, safe place to be. And I give them attention if they're sick or hurt. That's about all most animals need from us humans."

"A few years ago, I might've agreed with you, but I have a different attitude now and I can't help it. After the experiences I've had with SPCA and We Love Animals, the day will never come that I don't think of animals — all animals — with affection.

"I even love those dumb chickens and they love me back. I've been able to teach Anastasia to count to three using a wooden block with spots on it. Sophie comes when I call her. She lets me hug her and she nudges my cheek with her beak. They have beating hearts and personalities and on some primitive level, we communicate, which is more than I can say about a lot of people I know."

He grinned. "Whoa. You're not soured just on men. You're pissed off at the whole human race. What would a mere man have to do to sweeten you up?"

She laughed, shocking him. "Oh, I don't know. Maybe feed me a good steak and glass of wine."

At least she was trying. As long as he didn't give up, he might be able to make something come of meeting her.

When they reached the barn, the llamas stood by the fence, watching them and waiting to be fed. "There's Harry and Albert, waiting for supper," he said.

"Other than shear them, what do you do with them?"

"When I've got young calves, I put them out with the cows to fend off predators."

"Really? They do that?"

"That's what my neighbor used them for. They've done it for thousands of years in South America. Down there, the people even use them for meat."

"Ugh. I can't imagine that. They look so sweet."

"It's all in what you're used to. Llama meat has been tried in a few grocery stores in the western states. They say the taste is somewhere between lamb and beef. The meat is lower in cholesterol than beef. It's also considerably cheaper than beef these days."

"Your neighbor who abandoned them, was it the same neighbor who was going to shoot a litter of puppies and a helpless old dog?"

Nick couldn't keep from smiling. "The same one."

"People," she grumbled and shook her head. "What happened to him?"

"The neighbor? He's an old guy. He sold his cattle and moved into town. Left the llamas to get along by themselves until somebody called the sheriff."

"I'm glad he's gone. I wouldn't like Waffle living next door to someone like that. He might decide to shoot him."

Nick chuckled. "If that happened, he'd have to shoot me, too. His place is for sale. I'm trying to put together the financing to buy it. Look, I'm gonna feed the horses real quick, then I'll feed the llamas. Want to go with me?"

"Can I pet Harry and Albert? I've never been close to a llama."

"Sure. They're gentle-natured. That's Harry by the fence."

Chapter 20

NICK DISAPPEARED INTO the barn, leaving Sandi to her own thoughts. He hadn't copped to sleeping with Sylvia, but he hadn't denied it.

...I meant it when I said I haven't seen her in a long time....

In his world, how long was a long time?

Mental sigh. What more could she expect from him? He was, after all, just a man with feet of clay like all the others. Well...*not quite* like all the others.

This visit wasn't going well and it was her own fault. Why hadn't she left her attitude back in her store? Waffle was no longer hers to be bitter over and she had no right to feel jealousy over Sylvia.

Harry stood watching her and blinking at her. She walked closer to the fence. "Hi, Harry. Are you friendly?"

The llama didn't move, only continued to blink at her and chew on something with his weird protruding lower teeth. He had one hellacious underbite.

"Love your color," she said to him. "And those eyelashes." Sandi carefully put out a hand, intending to pet his head. All at once, a shower of something stinking and repulsive hit her face and front. "*Aieee!*"

Harry startled and trotted to the other side of his pen.

Paralyzed in place by a god-awful smell that filled the air around her, she raised her hand and wiped away oozy green liquid. "Oh, my God! What is this…this crap?" She broke into a wail.

Nick rushed over, a bucket of something in each hand. "What happened?"

She blurted out a sob. "He's—he's sick or something. He threw—threw up on me." She flung her hand, trying to rid it of the mess on it.

"It's spit. They spit when they're annoyed or hungry." He set his buckets on the ground, yanked his handkerchief out of his back pocket. "What did you do to him?" He clasped her chin and began wiping her face. "Close your eyes."

"I didn't do anything to him," she sobbed, her eyes squeezed shut. "You said he was friendly."

"He is…usually." He stepped back. "You can open your eyes. I think I got it all."

"It still stinks," she whimpered. "It's worse than a skunk."

"They've got three stomachs. That stuff was green, so it must come from his third stomach."

"Oh, my God. I think I'm going to throw up myself."

"Swallow. Take some deep breaths." He made a few swipes at the jacket she wore. "If they spit from their first or second stomach, it's mostly just spit and it's not too bad. But what comes out of their third stomach is gross." He looked over his shoulder at the llama. "You pissed off about something, Harry?"

Harry stood calmly watching them from the other side of his pen.

Nick moved on down with his handkerchief, still wiping the front of the jacket. "Good thing you've got this jacket on. He might've ruined your sweater."

Sniffling, Sandi snatched the handkerchief away from Nick and continued to wipe at the foul-smelling spittle. "Animals love me. I—I don't know why he would be mad at me."

"I'm later than usual feeding them and Harry might think he's got competition. I'll put out some hay for them. Go on inside. Soon as I finish, I'll be in. Feel free to use the shower if you want to. It's off my bedroom. Just go up the hall leading out of the living room and you'll see it."

She wasn't eager to go into a strange house alone, but she couldn't wait to get to some soap and water.

She entered through a back door into a utility room and walked on into a kitchen. The house might be old, but the kitchen had obviously been remodeled. Beneath its high ceilings was a hardwood floor, modern cabinetry, a cooking island and tan granite countertops. The whole area was large and open into a dining-living area.

An open wine bottle sat on the cooking island. *Curious.*

She walked into the living room that had also been remodeled. It was spotlessly clean—much cleaner than her own house and decorated in typical Western style with leather furniture, more hardwood floors and cowhide rugs. The smell of leather permeated the air and she didn't find it unpleasant. If she had to think of a single word that described Nick's home, that word would be "welcoming."

She spotted the hallway he had mentioned and passed three empty rooms before she reached a bedroom that was fully furnished and glaringly masculine. Bunkhouse décor — tan walls, rustic Western-style furniture. No trace of a feminine touch. "Cowboy country," she mumbled, moving on into a bathroom. There, she found a large walk-in shower made of tan tile.

After showering and shampooing her hair, she felt better. Unlike the skunk odor, no smell of Harry's stomach contents remained. She found a hairbrush and a hair dryer in one of the vanity drawers and used them. Afterward, she hung Nick's soiled jacket on the back of a wooden rocking chair in the bedroom and followed noises back into the kitchen.

He was busy at the cooking island, seasoning two thick steaks and he was wearing a bright red bib apron. He looked cute. He looked up, wiping his hands on the front of the apron. "Hey, there you are. Better now?"

She was nervous. Using a guy's shower and his personal items like shampoo and a hair dryer implied an intimacy. "That's my third shower today." She drew a deep breath, trying to settle her nerves. "I used your shower gel and your shampoo and your brush and dryer. I had to get that...stuff off of me. I hope you don't mind."

He smiled. "Not a bit. The shower's new. No one but me has ever used it."

A female had never been in his bathroom? She tilted her head and frowned. "Never?"

"Well, not since I moved back here and started remodeling this place. I live here alone. Why would anyone else use it?"

Sandi felt guilty for her thoughts. "What I meant is, no one has ever...I mean you haven't had—"

"What are you trying to ask me? If any women have spent the night here?"

"No! I mean, why would I care? I was making conversation."

He smiled. "You're right. Why would you care? But I don't mind telling you, I don't bring women here. This is my private place and I don't want to mess that up. That's why I don't have a phone here. If I need to have a phone conversation, I use my cell phone."

Should I get a ribbon for being invited? she wondered. "Wow. Maybe you're a recluse after all. I, uh, left your jacket on the rocking chair. You probably want to have it cleaned or something."

"Thanks."

She made a turn, gesturing around the comfortable room. "This place is really neat and clean. You're a good housekeeper."

"Not really. I hire somebody to come in and swamp it out every couple of weeks or so. I'm not here that much, but I like things to be in order."

"Everything looks to be remodeled. Did you do it yourself?"

"Some of it. I'm still working on it."

"So you're a carpenter as well as a cowboy."

"Cowboy, yes. Carpenter, no. But I know how to hammer a nail."

He picked up the two potatoes that were lying on the island counter and slid them into the oven. He returned to the island, leaned on his hand and jammed the other hand against his hip. "You still don't think much of cowboys, do you? I hear the same derision in your voice I heard that day in Hogg's down in Salt Lick."

She winced inside, not liking that she appeared rude. "I don't think anything at all of cowboys. I'm not criticizing. I've just never been around any. I was a town kid growing up, so..." She shrugged, seeing no point in discussing the issue.

"You couldn't live in West Texas and not be around cowboys. You must not've grown up around here."

"I certainly did. I grew up in Big Spring."

"Big Spring's got cowboys, too."

"I still was never around cowboys."

"You did business with ranchers in the bank. Unless you run into some of those investor types from back East, most ranchers are cowboys."

She huffed, closed her eyes and lifted her palms in a peacemaking gesture. "All right already. I've run into a few cowboys."

He grinned. "Point for me."

"Are we having a contest?"

Grinning, he shrugged. "Arguing with you is fun."

"For you maybe. You seem to enjoy picking on me."

"You're so sure you're right."

If you only knew. I'm not sure of anything I do nowadays.

"I should tell you, Harry spitting nasty stuff on me at this particular point in time is really weird. It's like the gods of smells have a vendetta against me. I haven't told you about the skunk. Waffle and I and my two big dogs got sprayed by a skunk the night before we went to court. That's why we smelled so funny that day."

"I wondered what the odd smells on him were. They didn't last long."

"My neighbor and I washed him and me both with everything—tomato juice, cucumber-melon shower gel, dog shampoo. And Prissy bathed him in her special formula. It's a wonder he had any skin left. Then at the last minute before court, I sprayed him with perfume."

"All's well that ends well, right?"

She angled a serious look up at him. "Depends on how you look at it. It didn't end that well for me. I lost my dog."

"You haven't lost him. He's ours together. The judge said so."

"And you don't mind that?"

"It's not a perfect arrangement, but do I mind it? Now that I've had time to consider it, I don't think so. But I can see that you do."

Her mouth slid into an involuntary smirk. "I'll survive. Look, I'm trying here. I don't mean to be a bitch. I hope you believe me."

Nodding, he smiled. "I do."

Then, as if he wanted to end the talk about Waffle, he said, "I don't know what came over Harry. I've never seen him spit at anything other than his partner, Albert. Sometimes they get into a contest over hay and spit at each other. You don't want to get caught in that crossfire." He smiled again. "Maybe a glass of wine will make you feel better."

"Oh, wine. I brought a bottle. Let me get it." She quickstepped out the front door and returned in minutes with the two small bags of Barkies she had brought for the dogs and a plastic grocery sack holding the wine. "I brought some cookies for Waffle and Randy." She set the two bags of Barkies on the counter.

She cleared the bottle of wine of its sack and stood it on the counter beside the bottle that was already opened.

He looked at the two bottles, then looked at her. She couldn't read his expression, but gleeful wasn't a word she would use to describe it. "Lemme see if I've got this right. You didn't believe me when I said I had the wine, you didn't think I had enough sense to make a good choice or one bottle isn't enough. Which is it?"

Wadding the plastic sack into a ball, she frowned and gave a little grunt. "I don't know what you mean."

He picked up the open bottle and proceeded to pour. "A college buddy's dad is a winemaker at Llano Estacado. He keeps me supplied with the good stuff."

If he had said that to impress her, he had succeeded. "Wow. That's the winery in Lubbock, isn't it? I've always wanted to go on one of their tours."

He handed her a glass half filled with red wine. "Try it. You don't have to worry. It won't kill you."

"I'm not worried." She accepted the wine and sipped. "It's good. I haven't had it before."

"My friend and his dad have tried to educate my palate. He says that with red wine, you should open the bottle and let it breathe a while before you drink it. I figure he oughtta know, so I opened it before you got here."

A cowboy as macho as Nick hardly seemed like a wine drinker who used phrases like "educate my palate," but she bit her tongue and didn't say so. He walked over to what looked to be a new stainless steel refrigerator and opened the door. Out came a large bowl of salad.

"You made salad?"

"Who can't make salad? I buy a bag of lettuce and dump it into a bowl. Then I add stuff to make it a more interesting."

She stared down at the salad any cook would be proud to claim. Something red and crinkled showed. *Dried cranberries?* "And what did you add to this one?"

"Some tomatoes and a cucumber. When I told C.J.—that's Harley's wife—I was cooking supper for somebody special, she gave me a jar of her homemade salad dressing. She told me to put some dried cranberries in it, so I went to the store and got some."

Somebody special? What the hell did that mean? He kept saying these puzzling things. Sandi ducked her chin, shaking her head. "Somebody special? You are such a BSer."

He walked over, bent his head and kissed her. On the lips. It wasn't one of those hot, tongue-tangling joinings. Just a nice, sweet kiss. And she didn't stop him, mostly because they seemed to have been headed in this direction ever since her arrival.

"I meant that," he said softly. "To me, you're somebody special."

Before she could recover herself and say a word, he picked up the plate holding the steaks. "I'm gonna cook these outside. Go out with me?"

Now she was more than nervous. She was downright rattled. "Sh—sure."

"Bring the wine."

She picked up their wine glasses and the bottle and followed him outside.

Chapter 21

WARM AND COZY, Sandi came awake reluctantly. She stretched, the sheets soft and silky against her skin.

What?

She moved her hand down her body. She was wearing…panties. And nothing else! *Oh, dear God!*

How had she gotten to this bed with no clothes on? *Oh, dear God!*

The previous evening rushed at her in hazy vignettes. She had drunk sooo much wine. Even with Nick telling her not to, she had argued and drunk more.

And what else had she done? Had she or hadn't she?

Shouldn't she know, even if she had drunk way too much wine and only vaguely remembered the evening, shouldn't she know?

This was terrifying.

At the very worst, she was a moderate drinker. Maybe half a dozen times in her entire life, she had been buzzed, tipsy, maybe even drunk, but never had she lost a night. She shifted in the bed checking for tender places where she normally didn't feel them, but drew no conclusions.

Her tongue felt like sandpaper. Crashing cymbals echoed through her brain in a rhythmic clangs. She dared to open her eyes, turn her head and glance at the opposite side of the king-size bed. A distinct impression showed on the pillow encased in pale blue on the other side of the bed. *Oh, dear God!* She had!

She popped up to a sitting position, hiding her bare breasts with the puffy comforter that covered her. Her head spun and a wave of nausea passed through her. She sat for a minute, letting her stomach settle and seeking her bearings.

He had kissed her. And she had kissed him. They had slow-danced to George Strait on the patio. She strained her brain trying to remember how she got into this bed.

Slowly, she perused her surroundings. She recognized Nick's bedroom. Her clothing was folded and neatly stacked on the seat of the wooden rocking chair across the room from the bed. Nick's soiled jacket no longer hung there. Further evidence that he had been in this room while she was naked.

A glass of milk, three chocolate chip cookies on a saucer and a bottle of Advil sat on the small bedside table, along with a note printed boldly in all caps: DON'T TAKE THESE PILLS ON AN EMPTY STOMACH. EAT THE COOKIES FIRST.

"He is sooo bossy," she mumbled.

She munched on the cookies and washed down two of the Advil tablets with half the glass of milk. How long had he been in this room while she was naked? How had he moved around the room without waking her? How had he undressed her without waking her?

Hunkered behind the Advil bottle was a digital clock showing the time to be 8:30 a.m. and the day to be

Sunday. *Oh, hell.* She had animals at home waiting to be fed. She had a store that needed to be opened. Unfortunately, she had declined Betty Ann's offer to open it today.

She eased out of bed and gathered her clothing. An odor of stale alcohol assaulted her nose.

She fastened on her bra, stepped into her panties, then her jeans and fastened them, then picked up her sweater, the source of the sour alcohol smell. She spread it to look at it. A purple stain the size of a basketball showed on the front. She pressed it to her nose and sniffed. Her stomached lurched.

Skunk spray, llama spit and now stale alcohol. She shuddered.

Across the room was the door to the bathroom. She tiptoed toward it. Once inside, she vaguely remembered being in it last night and washing the front of her sweater with hand soap.

Peeking into the shower, she saw that it was still humid from use and still felt warm. He had showered and she hadn't even known it? She berated herself again.

A nice steamy shower was sooo tempting, but she couldn't take the time.

Her hair looked as if she had been in a windstorm. She used Nick's hairbrush, then opened drawers looking for toothpaste. She helped herself and rubbed her teeth and tongue with her finger.

She crossed the room and eased the bedroom door open. The sound of a TV broadcasting led her to the kitchen where Nick sat at the table reading the newspaper. An ugly mix of embarrassment, confusion, anxiety and anger skirmished within her.

He looked up and smiled his killer smile. "Heey," he said softly. "How you feeling?" He put down the paper and got to his feet. "Come have some breakfast."

She cautiously stepped into the kitchen, too aware that he had seen her naked.

He stood there looking at her, his hands propped on his slim hips. "I fried up some bacon." He gestured toward the cookstove where several slices of cooked bacon lay on a plate. "I'll scramble some eggs."

"I need to get home. I ate those cookies, all three of them"

"You need to eat something with protein." He hurried to open a bread loaf lying on the counter and popped two slices into a toaster. "Take a seat at the table and I'll get it together. Eggs will just take a minute."

With no strength or will to argue, she sank to a chair at the table and set the bottle of Advil beside a salt shaker. She barely remembered eating at this table last night. "Thanks for the Advil. It was thoughtful of you. Although I probably deserve it if you hit me with a hammer. Have you eaten?"

"Earlier."

He dropped a chunk of butter into a cast-iron skillet. It sizzled at once, filling the air with the soothing aroma of melting butter. She watched as he broke an egg into a bowl, than picked up another. "One's enough. I don't —"

But he had already broken the second one. He whipped them madly with a fork, then deftly poured them into the sizzling butter and seasoned them with salt and pepper.

In no time, the eggs were done and the toast had popped up. He put together a plate of the eggs, several slices of bacon and the toast and brought it to her at the table. He even added a jar of strawberry jam. "There you go. Eat up. Nothing like greasy food for a hangover."

He sat down opposite her and picked up the newspaper again.

The thought that he had seen her naked continued to batter her. If he had undressed her, he had touched her bare skin in places. Gluing her eyes on her plate, she swallowed a bite of the soft scrambled eggs. "I need to ask you something."

"Shoot."

Unsmiling, she looked up at him. "What happened last night?"

He sat back, giving her a piercing look. An odd emotion showed in his eyes. "What do you *think* happened?"

The soft scrambled eggs began to feel like lead in her stomach. She drew a shuddery breath. "Did you undress me?"

"Had to. You poured a glass of wine down your front, then soaked yourself with soapy water."

She closed her eyes, arched her brow and shook her head. "You took off my bra?"

"It was dripping wet." His eyes held hers for a few seconds, then broke away. He picked up the newspaper again. "Don't worry about it, babe. I practically raised my two little sisters and I've got an ex-wife. You haven't got anything I haven't seen before." He opened the newspaper.

"Is that so?"

"Yes, ma'am. I might not always be a gentleman, but I don't take advantage of drunk women. Ever. Although, several times, you did extend an invitation."

Inside, she winced. *Oh, dear God.* Had she really done that? If only the floor would open so she could sink through it. She closed her eyes. "I did not."

"Would I lie? You did."

She opened her eyes to see him looking at her across his shoulder, his brow arched.

"And where did *you* sleep?" she asked.

"Beside you. I've only got one bed. And my couch is way too short. I didn't see any point in sacrificing a night's sleep. You were passed out. You never knew I was there."

This situation kept getting worse. She had to escape. She had eaten only half the food on her plate, but she rose on shaky knees. "I have to go."

He closed the newspaper, folded it and dropped in on the table. "Did you want to say 'bye to Buster? I mean, that's why you came out here, right?"

"Where is he?"

"In the backyard."

"I'll stop by and see him on my way out." She looked around and spotted her purse in the living room on a glass-topped coffee table that looked to be made of a well-used wagon wheel. Last night, she hadn't noticed it. She walked over, picked up the purse and hung it on her shoulder, then started for the back door. He followed her.

She stopped, turned around and looked up at him. "I feel like hell and I know I look like it, too. Why don't you look as bad as I do?"

"I dunno. Probably because I stopped after three glasses."

She gave him a squint-eyed glare. "And you let me drink too much?"

He planted his fists on his hips. "What, you think I forced you to drink a bottle and a half of wine? I tried to tell you we didn't need to open that second bottle, but you insisted. I think you said something like, 'I bought it, I brought it and I'm gonna to drink it.'" His brow arched, he stepped back and pointed his finger at her. "Another thing I don't do is argue with drunk women."

A picture of herself turning up a wine bottle came to her. *Dear God. Drinking straight from the bottle. Will I ever live this down?*

Her jaw clenched, her mouth pursed. Without a word, she opened the door and walked out onto the porch.

He followed. "Sandi, stop."

She stopped, turned and looked up into his sky blue eyes and a serious expression on his ruggedly handsome face. "I'm yanking your chain. Seriously, you were so uptight. It seemed like you needed to let your hair down a little. I tried to be a friend and listen. Your virtue or your safety weren't at risk."

She hesitated a few seconds. His eyes were beautiful. And he had thick lashes, like a girl's. *Be a friend and listen? Oh, dear God. What secrets had she told him?* "I was not uptight."

"You were uptight."

"You tried to listen? What did I say?"

He tilted his head and looked at her from beneath his brow.

"Okay. Don't tell me then."

She gave him her back and scanned her surroundings. The day was cloudy and dreary, but still too bright. She dug her sunglasses out of her purse and shoved them on. "Is it going to rain?"

She hoped so. Maybe she would drown. Or at the very least, maybe it would wash away this humiliation.

"Better than a fifty-fifty chance," he said. "We need it. We had a dry summer."

"Where's Waffle?"

He led her to the fenced backyard where Waffle and Randy were play-wrestling. When Waffle saw her, he bounded to the fence. She opened the gate and stepped inside, sank to her knees. He put his front paws on her shoulders and gave her slobbery kisses. "Oh, Waffle, I miss you so much. I wish I could take you home with me." She couldn't hold back the tears that sneaked into her eyes. The sweet dog whined and let her hug him. She had read somewhere that dogs didn't really like to be hugged, but Waffle had always been a hugger.

She soon gave up and started for her car, now sniffling. Nick followed her to her car door and opened it for her. Before she could slide in, he said, "I know you're not feeling great right now and maybe this isn't a good time to ask, but next weekend, I wonder if you'd do me a favor."

"What?"

"I was hoping you might go with me down to Salt Lick. I want to apologize to your aunt and her partner. That might go a little smoother if you're with me. If you'd go with me, I'd drive up here and pick you up."

"Aren't you going to be at work at the Flying C?"

"I'm going back down there later today."

"It's sixty-five miles from here. You're going to drive up here from Salt Lick just to pick me up, then turn around and drive back down there, then turn around again and bring me back here? That's two hundred miles of driving. That makes no sense."

He shrugged. "I don't care if it doesn't make sense. It's important to me. I don't want those two women thinking I'm an asshole."

She shook her head. Pain darted between her temples. She gritted her teeth and closed her eyes for a few seconds.

"Hey, you okay?" he asked, his voice soft and filled with concern.

She drew a deep breath. "I'm fine, I'm fine. Look, I'll let you know. My day off is usually Thursday. If I decide to do it, I'll drive down there and meet you."

She pulled on her door, but he held it and didn't let her close it. "Sandi. I don't want *you* thinking I'm an asshole either."

...I practically raised my two sisters...Ol' Nick is a square shooter.... She didn't know what she thought of him. But she didn't think he was an asshole.

"I believe you when you say you didn't take advantage of me while I was...*incapacitated.* I admit I was awful. Good enough?"

He straightened and smiled. "Good enough. I'll call you in a day or two."

She chastised herself all the way home. He might be right in that she had been under a lot of stress lately, but did that justify drinking herself into oblivion at a virtual stranger's house and winding up undressed in his bed? She might never be able to face him again. And she certainly would never tell anyone what had happened. *Hell.* She didn't even *know* what had happened.

She arrived back at her house in time to feed everyone and shower and shampoo, which made her feel slightly better physically, but she didn't know what would make her feel better emotionally and mentally. She was so confused. She didn't want to like Nick, didn't want to be lured by him, but she couldn't help herself.

She would love to stay at home and nurse her embarrassment, but she started for LaBarkery, satisfied she would get there early enough to open it on time. She found her sweet, loyal employee Betty Ann already there. With her was a cute little white fluffy dog with a pink ribbon tied around a topknot. Betsy the Westie. Sandi knew it immediately. It bounced around and made cute barks that sounded like a puppy. How could anyone who called himself a human being be mean to such a sweet little dog? "What are you doing here?" she asked Betty Ann.

"I was afraid you might not want to come in. Like, you know, if you spent the night. I'm waiting for a full report."

Sandi ducked her chin. "Nothing to report."

"Did you have a good time? Was it great?"

Sandi couldn't keep from laughing. Her two employees were determined for her to have a romance. "It was fine. I see you have a new dog."

"I know I'm not supposed to have her here, but Juanita dropped her off and I haven't had a chance to take her home. I fed her a couple of Barkies. I put the money for them in the cash register."

Sandi walked over to her showcase and removed half a dozen of the Barkies and a couple of Little Fidos. "Here. After what Betsy has been through, she deserves some more. On the house."

Betty Ann gave her a huge grin. "Thank you so much." She picked Betsy up and fed her a Little Fido.

"Say thank you to your ga'ma," she baby-talked to the dog.

Sandi bit down on her lower lip. She was too young to be a grandma. "So Juanita captured you, huh?"

"She brought her by so I could look at her. Look how trusting she is. I couldn't believe the little thing had been left to run the streets alone. What mean person could leave something so sweet and cute, knowing that in the end something bad would probably happen to her?"

"Happens every day, Betty Ann. It's sad, but that's the way it is. I keep warning you about Juanita. Pretty soon you'll be as tied down as I am."

☆☆☆

On Tuesday, before Nick had started his day, Harley called and asked him to drive up to Midland to look at a couple of bulls. Saturday night had nagged at him for two days. He wanted to get better acquainted with Sandi. Saturday night's behavior notwithstanding, he believed her to be a loving, caring person who'd had some bad luck. He pressed in her cell number. Several burrs passed before she came on the line. "This is Sandi."

"How are you?"

"I'm fine. How's Waffle?"

He heard no enthusiasm and no interest in his call. She only cared about Buster. This wasn't going as he had hoped. Still, he pressed on. "He's good. We've been busy. Listen, I'm on my way up to Midland. Got a business errand to do for Harley and I'm gonna stay tonight out at my place. I was thinking about the past weekend and I was thinking...well, hoping we could try it again."

"Supper, you mean? Or another visit to Waffle?"

"Either or both. You like barbecue?"

"Oh...I guess so."

"Well, do you or don't you?"

"Okay. I like barbecue."

"Me, too. Maybe we could go to Tag Freeman's place for some ribs or something. And this time, I'd like to come to your house and pick you up."

A pause. Finally, she said, "This is Tuesday. Thursday is usually the day I take off. I was planning to drive down to Salt Lick to meet you at the Styling Station. My aunt and her partner both are always in their shop on Thursdays."

"That's good. That works for me. Does that preclude us going out for some barbecue tonight? I can pick you up about six."

She sighed. "Okay."

Chapter 22

AFTER CLOSING THE store, Sandi rushed home and pulled her most feminine dress out of the closet. Lavender with clear crystals adorning the sweetheart neckline. The last time she had worn it was to a friend's wedding.

Nick the Beautiful did come and pick her up. He was dressed in starched and pressed Wranglers and a blue-and-white tiny check shirt with a red Cinch logo below the pocket. The blue checks matched his eye color.

He looked her up and down and told her she was beautiful, which left her giddy as a teenager. He drove them to Tag Freeman's Double Kicker Barbecue & Beer restaurant. "I don't get to Tag Freeman's very often," she said.

"You don't like ribs?"

She laughed. "I love ribs, but I'd never eat them on a date. Too messy. I get barbecue sauce all over my face."

He laughed, too. "Well, lady, I've seen you with worse than barbecue sauce all over your face."

Going through the buffet line, they both ordered something safe—sliced brisket and French fries. He found them seats at the end of one of the long tables.

"Holy cow. A whole table to ourselves. Wonder where the customers are."

"Slow weeknight maybe. I'm glad. We can talk."

Without Waffle, what would they talk about? She unwrapped the cloth napkin holding her silverware and spread the napkin on her lap. "An evening of conversation, huh?"

He, too, spread his napkin, then looked her in the eye. "I want you to know I feel bad about all that's happened. I want us to be able to be friends."

Oh. Phooey. That was all he wanted? She felt a letdown. "Don't worry about it. I'm getting over it. I believe Waffle really is Buster and he really is your dog. You were right all along. That judge's ruling was silly. We don't have to stick to it."

"But what if I'd like to stick to it?"

"Why would you?"

"I don't know about you, but I've crossed some thresholds in this whole thing. I've experienced several firsts."

"What firsts?"

"Well, I've never sued anybody before. And if I'd ever thought about it, I wouldn't have thought it'd be over a dog. I know a lawsuit is a hostile thing, but I didn't mean it that way. I got too far into it to back out."

She shrugged, picked up her knife and fork and sliced bites of brisket. "We all survived. What was it Nietzsche said? What doesn't kill you makes you stronger? That's probably true."

"I confess, I didn't read a lot of Nietzsche in school." He tucked into his food.

"Probably wasn't part of the football playbook, huh? You were itemizing your firsts. I'm listening."

"You're the first woman I've ever seen Harry attack."

"Huh. I should probably get a medal of some kind for that one. He never spit on your neighbor's wife?"

"The neighbor didn't have a wife. He was too hard to get along with. No wife would put up with him."

"Ah, I see."

"You're the first and only one I've had out to my house before and for sure, the first one to spend the night. You're the first and only one besides me to sleep in my bed. I've never wanted any of the women I know getting that close."

Her interest piqued. "Really? Why is that?"

"I have trust issues. It goes back a long way. I don't mean this to be a feel-sorry-for-me-story, but my mom split when I was about ten and to this day, I don't know why."

...I practically raised my two little sisters...

Sandi frowned, trying to picture a young boy taking care of two small girls. "Oh, no."

"No, no. Don't say 'oh no.' I know you've got a soft heart, but I honestly don't want you to feel sorry. I'm just trying to explain something to you and make a point. I've always had trust issues with women and I think my mom leaving is why. All through high school, I never had a steady girlfriend. Didn't have one in college either. Even if I liked some girl and she liked me back, I feared the day she would leave me. So I dealt with it by keeping my distance.

"Until I met my ex-wife. We married after I graduated. I was sappy-in-love. Or at least I thought I was. I thought she was, too, but not too long after we got married, she took off to California with my best friend, a guy I'd known all my life."

Oh, my God. No wonder he has trust issues. "Oh, Nick, I'm so sorry."

He stopped eating and looked at her. "The point I'm trying to make is this. After she left, there was no chance I was ever again going to find myself in a position to be left. So since then, I haven't had a close attachment to any woman."

Sandi, too, stopped eating. "But you sleep with Sylvia. Isn't that close?"

"No. Being a woman, I know you don't understand, but Sylvia and I don't share anything. We just…" He sighed.

"Have sex. In my book, that's pretty close."

"But it really isn't. Not in the way *I* think about being close. And I told you. I haven't been with her in a while."

"So what's the point of this heart-to-heart between you and me?"

"After two divorces, I know you've got trust issues, too. I'm wondering if two scared people like us could take a risk and make a go of it."

Sandi's head began to spin. This was the last thing she expected to hear him say. She couldn't deny the part about trust issues. Dare she take a risk? "Well, I don't know. I have a lot to overcome."

"No more than I do, I betcha. I'll tell you something about me that maybe you haven't had a chance to figure out. If I say I'm gonna do something, I always do it. No matter what, I always do it. If I say I'm gonna be somewhere, I'm always there and on time. I always help a friend if I can. And this might be important to you. If I see somebody abusing one of God's helpless creatures, I always fly to the rescue."

She doubted none of what he had just said. Besides that, he made her whole system tingle. "Well, I, uh, I suppose we could try. But I warn you, I won't give up my animals."

Chapter 23

ON THURSDAY, ALL showered and shampooed, Debbie Sue leisurely poured herself a cup of coffee, leaned a hip against the kitchen counter and sipped. Buddy had been gone since Monday and she missed him. Several months back, the governor had appointed him to a special team investigating drug and human trafficking out of Mexico, so he was spending even more time at the Mexican border.

While she thought about a plan for the day, she switched on the TV to *NewsWest* out of Midland.

"...The police will hold a press conference at eleven o'clock this morning. So far, they haven't said how Wilson escaped...."

Stunned, Debbie Sue turned up the volume and stared at the TV screen as a mug shot of the accused murderer came up and the newswoman continued:

"...They're searching the area immediately around the jail from the air and on foot with dogs, but they fear he could already be headed to Mexico...."

Debbie Sue's brain cells began to churn. Salt Lick was located between Midland and the Mexican border. True, it was off the commonly used highways, but wouldn't a fugitive from the law avoid the beaten path? Salt Lick could lie on Wilson's route to the border. She set her mug on the counter with a clack and speed-dialed Buddy's cell.

He came on the line immediately. "Hey, Flash."

"Buddy," she said breathlessly, "have you heard the news?"

"Something tells me you're talking about John Wilson."

"What are you hearing about his escape?"

"Not much. I'm a long way from there. Listen, Debbie Sue, I want you to stay out of Midland. I don't want you and Edwina anywhere near this, you hear? The guy's already got two murders on his sheet. He's proved he's capable of killing. And he's armed and dangerous."

"Buddy Overstreet! I cannot believe you are talking to me like I'm ten years old. Why would Ed and I go near it?"

He chuckled, the devil. "Exactly my point. Why would you?"

"The newswoman says they can't find him, but you've got inside information. Do you know where they think he might be hiding out?"

"It's not something you need to concern yourself with. The cops in Midland or the Rangers up there will take care of it. What's your plan for the day?"

He had changed the subject entirely too quickly. "I'm still thinking about it. Where are you?"

"Laredo. I'm waiting for some information. Soon as it shows up, I'll be leaving for home. I should be back up there this afternoon if nothing happens to keep me here."

"Great. Vic's supposed to get home today, too. Ed and I'll plan something."

He gave a wicked laugh. "Don't make it too complicated. I've got a plan of my own."

She lowered her voice. "Oh, yeah? It wouldn't involve you stripping me naked, would it?"

"It might."

"Hah. I thought so. You are naughty, Buddy Overstreet."

"You do look a lot better without all those clothes."

Instantly, her mind darted toward the sexy red corset and matching panties she had bought from a mail order catalog and hidden in her dresser drawer. "If that's your plan, I just might have a surprise."

"Hmm. I like surprises.... Oops, got another call coming in, babe. Listen, take care of yourself and keep an eye on my pal, Jake. Don't let him get the best of you and Ed."

"Oh, believe me, he'll be busy. Vic's still teaching him. He asks him questions and the silly parrot answers them correctly. You take care of yourself, too. Love you, sugarfoot."

"Love you, too....And stay out of Midland."

Debbie Sue disconnected and shot a look at the digital clock on the oven. Not quite seven o'clock. She rarely called Edwina at home before seven, but talking to her ASAP was necessary.

By the time she finished another mug of coffee, the clock showed 7:02 a.m. She pressed in Edwina's number.

Edwina came on the line. "Mmph."

"Hi. Did I wake you up?"

"What time is it?"

"Have you seen the news?

"I'm asleep. Did a bomb go off?"

"You could say that. John Wilson broke out of jail. They have no idea where he is."

"Debbie Sue, I'm asleep. Why is that important to me?"

"I'm just telling you, they might need some extra help."

"Uh-huh. To do what? Does Buddy know he broke out of jail?"

"Yeah. I just talked to him."

"And what did he say about us offering our services?"

"You know what he said."

"Sounds like good advice to me. I'm going back to sleep."

"Ed, you can't. Get up. Let's drive up to Midland and see what's going on."

"Nope, not doing it, Debbie Sue. I'm not gonna let you drag me into something that might get me killed. Besides, Sandi showed up last night to visit Jake. And she's expecting Nick to meet her at the shop."

"You're shitting me. After all that bullshit in court?"

"I told you they had the hots for each other. You never believe me. Besides that, I've got a light day. Since she's here and it's her fault I've got this loudmouthed pest on my hands, she's gonna help me clean his homes."

Damn! Jake again. Debbie Sue bit down on her bottom lip. She had heard about a person sucking all of the oxygen out of a room, but she had never heard of a parrot doing it. "You know what, Ed? Since you got that parrot, you're no fun at all. It's hard to be an effective detective when your partner spends all of her time poop scooping."

"Effective detective? Poop scooping? Ain't that cute. I think I like it."

Trying to maneuver Edwina in a direction she didn't want to go was an unwinnable battle. Debbie Sue closed her eyes, heaved a sigh and gave up.

She arrived at the Styling Station at 8:00 a.m. as usual. She put a pot of coffee on to brew and checked the appointment book. Edwina did indeed have a light day and so did she. No customers until late morning. She dug the cash for the day out of her purse and put it in the cash drawer.

She had stopped at Hogg's and picked up breakfast, so she sat down in her styling chair with a cup of coffee and a sausage-and-egg burrito. The front door opened and she came to attention. Quint Matthews stepped into the salon. She choked on a bite of sausage and at the same time, her thoughts flew to her conversation with Buddy just minutes ago: ... *then I'll be leaving for home. I should be back up there this afternoon if nothing happens to keep me here....*

"Quint! Forgodsake! What are you doing here?"

"Mornin', darlin'. I figured this was a good time to finish that conversation we started at Tag's place. Hell, Debbie Sue, I left home before daylight."

Panic began to dance in Debbie Sue's stomach. No telling what Buddy would do if he walked in and found Quint here. "We finished it. And Buddy will be back today."

"But not 'til late. And he might not be back 'til tomorrow." He lifted off his hat and set it on Edwina's station.

"How do you know anything about Buddy's schedule?"

"A friend in the Rangers told me, darlin'. He said Buddy is way down south."

The Texas Rangers was one of the most elite and professional law enforcement agencies in the world, its members bound by brotherhood. A Ranger wouldn't reveal the whereabouts of one of its own to someone outside the organization. "I don't believe you."

Quint gave her a smirk. "I guess you don't have to. You got an extra cup of that coffee?"

"You know where the pot is. We haven't moved it."

He walked into the back room and a minute later, returned carrying a mug of steaming coffee. He took a seat beside her in Edwina's styling chair. "Where's your partner in crime-fighting this morning?"

"She'll be here any minute. You'd better go before she gets here."

"Why? She and I always got along fine." He looked around. "Place looks good, darlin'. You and Ed are still busy making a fortune, huh? The experts on beauty in Salt Lick, Texas."

"Don't be a smart-alec. We do okay."

His gaze landed on the corner of the room and Jake's cage. "What the hell is that?"

"It's an aviary. Ed's adopted a parrot."

"And it lives in that?"

"Part of the time when he's here at the shop. He isn't an it, by the way. He's a he. He doesn't like being called an it."

Quint laughed and shook his head. "One of the reasons I always liked hanging out with you, Debbie Sue, is it was always entertaining. A man never knew what might happen next."

A commotion came from the back room, along with the sound of the back door slamming. "Ed's here now. And her niece is with her, so don't say anything stupid."

Quint's mouth tipped up in a mischievous grin. "Darlin', I *never* say anything stupid."

"Humph. That's a matter of opinion. You were pretty stupid at Tag's place the other day."

Debbie Sue rose from her seat as Edwina and Sandi came into the salon. Quint, too, got to his feet.

Sandi carted a box of cleaning supplies. Edwina staggered under the weight and awkwardness of Jake's travel cage.

"*Aarwrk,*" Jake screeched. Lemme outta here!...Toast!...Jake wants toast."

Edwina ignored Jake and set his cage on a footstool in front of a hairdryer. "Quint! What the hell are you doing here?"

"Quint. What the hell are you doing here?" Jake repeated, cocking his head. "Hello," he added and twisted his head 180 degrees.

Quint chuckled, "You got an echo in here. Debbie Sue just asked me the same question and now some damn bird wants to know why I'm here?"

Like a laser, his focus landed on Sandi. "And who might you be, pretty lady?"

Debbie Sue sighed inwardly. He hadn't changed one bit.

He took hold of the box Sandi carried. "Here, darlin', let me take care of that load for you. Pretty little thing like you shouldn't be carrying a heavy box." He set the box of cleaning supplies on the seat of Debbie Sue's styling chair.

Empty-armed, Sandi opened her palms. "Well, I—" She gave a silly titter. She sounded like a teenager.

Quint had that effect on women. He was so damn good-looking and he had a way of making you think you were the only one in the world who was important. Still, Debbie Sue looked on in horror. If he harassed Edwina's niece, Vic might tear him limb from limb.

"Uh..." Sandi stood there blinking. Finally, she stuck out her right hand. "Sandi Walker. I'm Edwina's niece."

"What the fuck!" Jake screeched and turned all the way around on his swing. "What!...The!...Fuck!"

Quint stared at Jake, obviously more than curious. "Did he say what I think I heard?"

Sandi rushed to Jake's cage. "Jake! Stop that. Bad word. Bad word." She turned to Quint. "Seeing someone new, he thinks he's performing. I think he might have been part of the entertainment in a sports bar."

The parrot paced back and forth on his swing, hung a foot on the side of the cage and turned upside down. He squawked a loud jungle call, followed by, "Dickhead. Dickhead."

Quint's expression turned from fascination to wide-eyed amazement. "Did he just say dickhead? Is he calling me a dickhead?"

"Well, if the shoe fits," Edwina said and blew a large gum bubble.

"What the hell? He doesn't even know me."

A hooting laugh burst from Debbie Sue. She couldn't hold it back. Quint's ego was so fragile he couldn't stand hearing even a parrot criticize him.

Quint walked over to Jake's travel cage, bent down and looked inside.

"I repeat my earlier question," Edwina said. "What are you doing here, Quint?"

Quint straightened and planted his fists on his hips. "Jesus Christ. You women act like I'm Satan or something. You've known me a long time, Ed. Now stop and think. Why would I be here?"

"Honey-chile, it's not for me to stop and think. If you're thinking what I think you're thinking, and Buddy Overstreet walks through that door, which could be any minute, he'll toss your ass all the way back to the Alamo. A ride on one of your mad bulls will feel like a cake walk."

"I'm not afraid of Buddy. Besides, I know exactly where he is and I know what he's doing. He won't be here for hours."

Debbie Sue thought about that. Even she didn't know *exactly* where her husband was. But before she could thoroughly analyze that fact, Jake began to squawk and flap his wings. "What the fuck? Lemme outta here! Lemme outta here!"

Rummaging through the box of cleaning supplies, Edwina shook her head. "He's on a tear this morning. He called me Q-Tip again and he upset Gus, howling like a coyote. Poor cat was so terrified he clawed his way to the top of the refrigerator and broke all my magnets." She glared at the parrot. "Then, naughty Jake refused to go into the travel cage, didn't you, Jake?"

"Toast! Jake wants toast!" he screeched.

"You can't have toast," Edwina yelled at him. "You can have a muffin."

"Fuck off!" Jake paced back and forth on his perch making garbled noises that sounded like mumbling.

Laughing, Quint bent down and looked at Jake again. "Ed, did he just tell you to 'fuck off'?"

Jake landed on the bottom of the cage and jumped up and down. "Fuck off, dickhead! Fuck! Off!"

Quint shook his head. "Well, I never..."

"Quint, if you're not gonna leave," Edwina said, "just sit there quietly while we try to figure out what this bird wants. Vic's trying to teach him not to say fuck and you're bringing out the worst in him."

Sandi bent over, eye level with the parrot. "You stop saying bad words. Aunt Ed and I are going to clean your house. Sit here and be a good boy. Take a nap."

"That's such a small cage," Debbie Sue said. "I suppose we could let him out."

"Oooh, no," Edwina said. "Cleaning this aviary thing is bad enough. I don't want to clean bird shit off all the walls, too."

Jake hopped up and down. "Bird shit! Bird shit! What the fuck!"

"Let's get this done so we can put him in it," Sandi muttered. She and Aunt Ed immediately donned rubber gloves and set out to take the plants out of Jake's aviary in the corner of the room.

Debbie Sue picked up one of Jake's toys and shook it at him. "Here, Jake. Play with this."

"Jake's mad!" he screeched. "Lemme out!" He threw his head back and screamed a string of what sounded like an assortment of invectives at the ceiling.

"All right, all right. Just shut up." Debbie Sue opened the travel cage's door and invited Jake out. He hopped out onto the floor, spread his wings and bobbed his head. He began to squawk loudly. He paced back and forth, squawking and bobbing his head.

"What is it, Jake? Why are you upset?" Debbie Sue offered him a handful of hair rollers to play with, but he batted them away with his beak. "Why are you mad, Jake?"

He continued to pace and squawk unintelligibly. All at once, he ran to where Edwina and Sandi were cleaning his aviary and hopped up and down. "Jake's mad! Jake's mad!"

Edwina and Sandi looked at each other, then at Debbie Sue. "Unless it's because I didn't cook toast for him, we don't know why he's mad," Edwina said.

"That sonofabitch is pigeon-toed," Quint said.

Jake made a loud screech and hopped up and down. "Dickhead!"

"Did he call me a dickhead again?"

Jake ran across the floor and bit the toe of Quint's boot.

Quint jerked back his foot. "What the hell?" He stared down at his boot. "He scarred my damn boot. These are custom-made boots."

Jake paced back and forth in front of Quint, volleying between squawking and screeching and making loud unidentifiable noises.

"My God. I think the little bastard is having a tantrum," Edwina said and looked at Sandi. "Does he know he's pigeon-toed?"

"I don't know," Sandi answered, shaking her head.

Edwina gave Quint a pointed glare. "Maybe he doesn't like being compared to a pigeon. Or maybe he just doesn't like Quint."

Quint opened his palms. "What the hell did I do?"

"While you're standing there doing nothing, feed him a muffin," Edwina said. "They're in that bag on the floor by my station."

Quint picked up the bag and began to dig inside. Jake continued to pace and screech and squawk.

Quint pulled out a baggie filled with miniature muffins. "Since when do birds eat muffins?"

On a squawk, Jake attacked Quint's boot again.

Just then a sound came from the back room and Debbie Sue shot a look toward the door to the back room. "Was that the back door?"

"Nah," Edwina answered. "Nobody comes through the back door.

Everyone but Jake stopped what they were doing and listened. Jake continued to squawk and ramble.

Chapter 24

THE DOOR INTO leading into the salon opened. A scruffy unshaven man stepped through and in his hand was a very large pistol. "Okay, folks. Stay right where you are and nobody gets hurt."

Oh, my God! John Wilson!

Debbie Sue had recognized the intruder instantly. He looked just like his mugshot. Her eyes bugged.

He gestured with the pistol barrel toward Quint, who had thrust his arms straight up and turned pale even under his phony tan.

"Dickhead!" Jake took flight and sailed to the top of his aviary in the corner.

Wilson's eyes darted between Jake and Quint. "You," Wilson said to Quint. "Gimme the keys to that truck out back."

"Whoa, buddy. It's not my truck."

Debbie Sue's thoughts raced. *Oh, no. Not my pickup.*

"Gimme them clothes," Wilson said to Quint.

"No way. I can't undress in front of these women."

"Fuck that!" Wilson pointed the pistol at Quint's face. "I don't like wearing bloody clothes, cowboy, but it beats what I got on. Do it!"

"Fuck that!" Jack squawked a noise that sounded like a pistol cocking. "Fuck that! Jake's mad!"

Wilson's attention swerved to Jake. "What the hell is that?"

In a quick move, Quint karate chopped Wilson's wrist with the side of his hand. The gun hit the floor with a deafening blast. *Blam!* The smell of cordite filled the room.

Debbie Sue's heart took off racing even faster. Everyone in the room dropped to the floor, scrambling for the gun. Through the scramble of hands, Wilson grasped it and got to his feet shouting. "I'll kill every one o' you sonsabitches!" He gestured with the gun barrel again. "Get on your feet. All of you."

"*Aaawrk!* Call the cops!" Jake flew to the opposite corner of the cage and began to screech and squawk. "Fight! Fight! Call the cops! Call the cops!

Slowly, they all stood.

He pointed the gun at Quint again. "Gimme them goddamn clothes and don't gimme no shit."

"Okay, okay. Just don't let your finger get itchy."

Slowly, Quint began to undress. Hopping on one foot, he pried off a boot, then moved to the other. Next came his socks.

"Hurry up, goddammit. I woulda already shot your ass if it wasn't for bloodying them clothes."

"I'm hurrying," Quint said, unbuttoning his shirt.

Debbie Sue swallowed a lump in her throat. She had seen Quint without clothes, but not for many years. Finally, all he had left was black boxer briefs that clung to every muscle, sinew and body part. His body hadn't changed much. He was still a fine specimen of a man.

From the corner of her eye, she saw Edwina and Sandi staring at him as he folded his pants and shirt neatly and laid them on Edwina's station, the muscles in his arms and across his shoulders rippling with each movement.

Wilson's voice brought her back to reality. He was pointing the gun at Edwina. "Tie him up."

"With what?" Edwina said.

Wilson strode to Edwina and yanked the long orange, yellow and black scarf she was wearing from around her neck. She caught her breath and jumped back.

"Be quick about it, you skinny bitch. I ain't got that much time." He shoved Quint down into Edwina's styling chair. "Stick out your wrists, asshole."

Quint complied. Edwina took her time and ended with a big brightly colored bow binding Quint's wrists together in front of him.

Wilson stared slack-jawed at Edwina's handiwork. "Goddammit! What the hell is that? I said tie him up."

Along with her heart, Debbie Sue's mind was racing faster than she could keep up with it. If one of them could distract him again, maybe someone could get the gun again. She stepped forward. "Don't you know a bow knot when you see it?"

Wilson stomped over to Quint, yanked one end of the scarf and the knot easily came undone. He pressed the end of the gun barrel against Edwina's temple. Grimacing, Edwina squeezed her eyes shut.

"You crazy bitch, I oughtta blow your ass from here to El Paso. You tie that sonofabitch up so he don't get loose."

"A bow knot if all I know how to tie," she whined and began to sniffle.

"Shut up! Quit bawling!"

Edwina's voice hitched. "I never was...a Gir— Girl Scout...or anything."

"Goddammit," Wilson mumbled, reached across all of them, grabbed Sandi by the wrist and dragged her forward. "You. Tie him up."

Sandi, too, was in tears. "I can't tie either," she whimpered.

"Jesus Christ! What the hell is wrong with you people? You can't tie somebody up?"

Hands shaking, Sandi began to wrap one of Quint's wrists with the scarf.

Wilson pointed his gun at Edwina's chair. "Tie him to that chair arm." He yanked an electrical cord attached to a curling iron out of the wall and threw the appliance at Sandi. "Tie up his other wrist."

Debbie Sue winced. *Shit! My best curling iron.*

He turned his attention to Debbie Sue. "You. Who runs this place?"

"I do."

"You got cash. Where is it?"

"It's over at our payout counter."

"Get it."

Debbie Sue sidled gingerly to the payout counter.

"Move your ass or I'll blow a hole in this skinny bawling bitch."

The payout counter was chest high on most women and hid the desk. Under the desk top was a panic button that sent a radio signal and set off an alarm in the sheriff's office. Buddy had had it installed years back when he was the town's sheriff. They had never used it. Debbie Sue had no idea if it still worked. She could only guess the hysterics in Billy Don's office if and when it ever went off. Before she opened the drawer and pulled out the cash, she pushed that button.

At the same time, she handed over the money. "A hundred dollars. That's all we've got. It's what we start the day with."

Wilson tilted his head toward Quint. "Get his wallet."

Debbie Sue left the payout desk, walked over to Edwina's station where Quint had put his clothing, pulled Quint's wallet out of the back pocket of his jeans and opened it. *Payday!* As he always had, Quint carried a thick sheaf of bills in his wallet. Debbie Sue had known him to have more than a thousand dollars in cash on his person. She pulled the bills out and handed them to Wilson.

Quint closed his eyes and shook his head.

"Nice." Wilson stuffed the wad of folded money into his own pocket. "Who does that red truck belong to?"

"Me," Debbie Sue said.

"Gimme the fuckin' keys."

Debbie Sue started to slide her hand into her jeans pocket. "Wait a minute. Slow. I'm watching you. Come over here."

Just then, the front door opened and Nick Conway strolled in. All eyes swung to him.

"What the hell is this, a fuckin' convention?" John Wilson shouted.

Nick's gaze darted from Quint to Debbie Sue, then Sandi. "Sandi!"

Wilson pointed the gun at Nick. "You! Get your hands up. Get over here!"

Nick raised his hands and sauntered over to where everyone stood in a group. "What's going on?" His eyes homed in on Sandi who was still trying to tie Quint's wrist to the chair arm with the curling iron cord. "You okay?"

She nodded. "Yes, but—"

"She isn't the only one here who might not be okay, you know," Debbie Sue snapped.

"You, mister," Wilson said to Nick. "Nice and easy, pull out your wallet. Gimme the cash."

Nick reached back and pulled his wallet out of his back pocket, thumbed through a small sheaf of bills and handed them over. Wilson grabbed them and shoved them into his pocket.

Just then, with a loud squawk, Jake glided toward Edwina's station and on his way, dropped a huge, messy package onto the front of Wilson's head.

"*Aargh!*" He slapped his palm against his head, brought it back and saw an icky splat of gray and white bird poop covering his palm.

"Thank God for greens," Edwina mumbled.

The parrot landed atop the coat tree that stood beside Edwina's station.

"You sonofabitch!" Wilson fired at Jake. *Blam!*

Jake leaped into the air. "*Aawrrk! Murder! Murder!*" He swooped into the storeroom.

Debbie Sue darted to her own station, grabbed a can of hair spray and blasted it directly into Wilson's eyes.

"*Aaarrgh!*" Blinded, he fired again, barely missing Quint's head. The mirror at Edwina's station shattered. Sandi ducked.

Quint's shoulders scrunched up to his ear lobes. "Jesus Christ!"

All at once, like a football player, Nick plowed into Wilson with his shoulder, taking him to the floor with a *whump!* The gun flew from Wilson's hand. Nick and he wrestled, hurling blows and cusswords. Debbie Sue scrabbled for the loose gun. When she couldn't get a grip on it, she kicked it across the floor, all the way to the payout counter. Sandi grabbed it up and carried it behind the counter.

Debbie Sue dashed back to her station, grabbed a hair dryer and jumped into the fight between Wilson and Nick. She pounded Wilson's head with the hair dryer. *Whack! Whack!* After the two hard blows, he was out, blood spilling over the floor from his head wounds.

Nick got to his feet. Puffing for breath, he dragged Wilson's limp body over to Debbie Sue's chair and plopped him into it. A mouse had already swelled under his eye. "Who the hell is this anyway?"

"Jake! I gotta find Jake," Edwina cried. "He might be shot." She dashed into the back room.

"Oh, no!" Sandi followed Edwina.

The front door flew open. Billy Don charged in, gun in hand. He gave the room a quick once-over, stopped at a near-naked Quint tied to Edwina's styling chair. His eyes bugged. "Whoa! What's going on here?"

"Sheriff!" Quint cried, straining against his bindings. "Cut me loose from here."

"Never mind him," Debbie Sue said. "There's the bad guy over there in my chair. Put some handcuffs on him before he wakes up."

"Who is he?"

"John Wilson. From Midland."

"You don't mean—"

"Billy Don! Shut your mouth and just handcuff him, okay? And put him in a cell. Then call the Midland cops.... Oh, and after you handcuff him, before you take him outta here, dig into his pocket and get our money and give it back to us. He took everybody's money."

"Is this a robbery?"

"At the very least." Debbie Sue answered.

Billy Don's head began to shake. "If this is a robbery, I can't give the money back. It's evidence."

"Nick, his gun is over at the payout desk," Debbie Sue said. "I saw Sandi put it there."

Nick walked over and picked it up, took the time to unload it. "Here, sheriff. Here's his gun."

"This is an *armed* robbery?" Billy Don asked, his eyes bigger yet. He took the gun and stuffed it into his waist band.

"At the very least," Debbie Sue repeated.

Billy Don busied himself handcuffing Wilson with cable ties. "I called our ambulance, Mr. Wilson. They're probably not as fast as folks in the city, but they'll be here pretty quick. They'll have to take you to the hospital up in Odessa. If you think you can't wait, I can ask the vet to come to town and sew you up."

Wilson's eyes had crossed. He mumbled something.

"Goddammit, will somebody cut me loose," Quint shouted, on his feet and straining against the scarf and the cord that bound him to Edwina's styling chair.

Debbie Sue stamped over to Edwina's chair. "You are such a big baby." She opened a drawer, pulled out a pair of scissors and cut the scarf.

"I want to know what the hell is going on here," Quint said. "This is a damn madhouse."

"I'll tell you one thing, mister," Billy Don said, pointing his finger at Quint's nose. "I don't know who you are, but you need to get some clothes on. I doubt these ladies want to look at you half naked."

Debbie Sue gripped the curling iron and started to cut the cord. "Damn, I hate doing this. This is my best curling iron."

Freed, Quint clapped his hat on his head, picked up his pants and shirt and stalked to the back room.

"Oh, my God," Sandi's voice   from the back room.

"Quint! Put your clothes on," Edwina yelled.

"Dickhead! Dickhead!" Jake squawked.

"Sandi?" Nick marched to the back room and disappeared inside.

"Oh, Nick. Thank God you're here."

Nick's deep voice. "You, buddy, get your clothes on."

Debbie Sue rolled her eyes.

Soon, Sandi and Nick walked out of the back room arm in arm. Jake was perched on Sandi's shoulder. Nick glanced down at Wilson. "That's the dude from Midland. What's he doing here?"

"It's a really long story," Debbie Sue answered. "An easier question is what are *you* doing here?"

"I came to meet Sandi. The idea was for me to apologize to Edwina, for breaking into her backyard and taking Buster."

Quint came out of the back room, stomped to Edwina's styling chair and began to pull on a sock. "Debbie Sue, you've got more loony goddamn friends than any woman I ever saw."

He pulled on his other sock. "I don't know what ever made me think I wanted to hook up with you again."

He pulled on a boot. "I can see it was a mistake to drive all the way down here. My God. It's sixty-five miles."

He pulled on his second boot, stood to seat one heel, then the other and stomped toward the front door.

"You can't leave," Billie Don said. "This is a crime scene. You've got to give a statement."

"Bullshit," Quint said, hanging on to the doorknob. "Everybody in this town is crazy. How's that for a statement?"

"He's right, Quint," Debbie Sue said. "You're a witness. If you leave before you give a statement, Billy Don can put out a warrant for your arrest."

"*Aargh!*" Quint growled and plopped down into Edwina's chair again. Jake glided over and landed on his knee. Quint glared at him, but didn't move. "Don't you dare shit on me, you little bastard.

A soft garble came from Jake's throat.

"That sounded like a threat to me," Debbie Sue said.

Billy Don dug a small notebook out of his shirt pocket and methodically turned the pages until he found a blank one.

A new anxiety pricked Debbie Sue. Knowing Billy Don, this could take hours and Buddy might be back before it was over. "We've got appointments coming in for hairdos," she said to Billy Don. "Why don't you take all of these people over to your office to take statements?"

"That's a good idea, Debbie Sue." He urged everyone into a group.

Before getting to his feet, Quint carefully lifted Jake off his knee and set him on Edwina's station. He carefully touched Jake's beak and gently tapped it. "I'm not a dickhead, little buddy."

"Ed and I'll be over there soon as we sort out everything here," Debbie Sue said to Billy Don as he herded his little group out the front door. Debbie Sue slammed the door behind him.

Suddenly, quiet prevailed.

"Jesus Christ, are we okay?" Edwina asked. "I nearly shit myself."

"Jesus Christ, are we okay?" Jake repeated. "I nearly shit myself."

"Does he have to repeat every damn thing we say?" Edwina asked.

"That's what parrots do. They mimic," Debbie Sue answered.

Edwina went to her station where Jake perched, and put out her arm for him to climb on. "I hate to think what might have happened if you hadn't had an urge to poop," she told him. "Did you hear that, poopy bird? You saved the day."

"*Aarrrwk*. Jake's a poopy bird. Jake's a poopy bird."

Debbie Sue bent down and placed a tiny kiss on Jake's beak. "We love you, Jake. You aren't a poopy bird. You're a hero."

Jake touched his beak to her cheek. "Jake's a hero. Jake's a hero."

Debbie Sue straightened. "I shouldn't have told him that. Now he's going to be stuck up." She turned to Edwina. "Are Sandi and Nick a couple now?"

"I think so," Edwina answered. "Next thing we hear, they'll be getting married. Edwina does it again."

"Did you say something to her? Or to him?

"Not much. I just dropped a hint. They already liked each other. They just didn't know it."

"Honest to God, Ed, you should charge for your matchmaking services.

"Nah. I do it for love. There's not enough love in this world."

Debbie Sue pointed at her shattered mirror. "Looks like we're going to be getting you a new mirror."

"See what I've been trying to tell you about chasing criminals? It's a wonder we aren't all dead."

"There you go again, Ed. Thinking the worst. Just remember. We didn't find him. He found us."

"Call nine-one-one," Jake squawked.

Epilogue

A year later …

"I'M GONNA KILL that damn rooster." Nick buried his head under his pillow.

Sandi giggled and snuggled closer to his side "You'll hurt his feelings if he hears you say that."

"I'm the only rooster in this house that's got feelings." His arm came around her and pulled her closer.

She lay there in total comfort against Nick's big body and listened to the birds tweeting, the hens clucking and the braying of two mules Nick had succumbed to taking from someone he knew. The two mules always brayed to Christian Grey's crowing.

After a delicious courtship, she and Nick had gotten married six months ago. In an informal ceremony, Buster had been his best man. Betty Ann had been her maid of honor.

She had sold her house in town and moved all fifteen of her animals to his ranch. She had used the money from the sale of her house to buy the section of land adjacent to what Nick already owned. Now, she was a landowner. Together, they had more cattle.

Her business in town was going like gangbusters. Betty Ann was now the manager. The LaBarkery website was up and running and orders were coming in. She had leased a larger kitchen and hired three more women. LaBarkery had been featured in the local magazine.

Nick still drove down to Salt Lick every Monday morning and came back to Midland every Friday night. He was thinking about going back to school to get a PhD and starting his own consulting business.

Jake continued to live with Aunt Edwina and Vic. Lately, he was telling fortunes in the Styling Station.

Sandi continued to work with We Love Animals, rescuing unwanted creatures and finding new homes for them. Along with Betty Ann, she fought every day not to bring every one of them home with her.

Life was better than it had ever been. Living day to day with Nick's affection and gentle nature, she was discovering that she didn't hate men after all.

About the Author

USA Today Bestselling Author Dixie Cash is sister team, Anna Jeffrey and Pam Cumbie. They have co-written 7 zany romance/mystery novels.

Jeffrey also writes steamy romance novels with a mainstream flavor. Her books have won the Write Touch Readers' Award, the Aspen Gold, and the More Than Magic awards. They have placed in the Ancient City Heart of Excellence and the NEC Readers Choice Awards and have been in the finals in the Colorado Romance Writers award, the Golden Quill and Southern Magic as well as the Write Touch Readers' Award, the Aspen Gold, and the More than Magic awards

She is a member of Romance Writers of America and NINC.